solar nation

Eri

Also by Erica Blaney

Cybernation

Erica Blaney

*Hodder
Children's
Books*

A division of Hachette Children's Books

A Catalogue record for this book is available
from the British Library

ISBN 978 0 340 95033 3

Typeset in Bembo by Avon DataSet Ltd,
Bidford on Avon, Warwickshire

Printed and bound by CPI Bookmarque, Croydon, Surrey

The paper and board used in this paperback by Hodder Children's
Books are natural recyclable products made from wood grown in
sustainable forests. The manufacturing processes conform to the
environmental regulations of the country of origin.

Hodder Children's Books
a division of Hachette Children's Books
338 Euston Road, London NW1 3BH
An Hachette Livre UK company

To Lydia, Phillip, John and Tim,
who are as wonderful as children can be

Acknowledgements

Thank you once again to the many people who helped me in the making of this book. The team at Hodder: you have worked so hard on my behalf: thank you. Emily, especial thanks to you for ringing me up when things are tough, and for doing a superb job with the editing.

Thank you, Lindsey, my agent; you're always there, and always ready to give me what I need, whether it's a bed for the night, or an ear to listen.

So many friends bought *Cybernation* as an act of charity, and ended up enjoying it. At least you said you did. Thank you for your many encouraging words. I hope you enjoy this one as well.

I am most grateful, and very touched, by the help of Heather Pickering in promoting me as an author. Also to Lauren and Ben, enthusiastic proof-readers.

And finally, thank you to my family, who still haven't complained about the housework.

1

'Ruined!' bellowed the cook, hurling a pan of scalded soup out of the door.

Missing Seachrân's head by a whisper, it rolled to the dusty feet of a woman who had just arrived in the kitchen yard. Her skin was as black as night, but her hair, long enough to reach her knees, was white.

The cook hadn't noticed her yet.

Nor had Seachrân. He was too busy making sure that anything else the cook threw missed him too.

'Din't I tell yer to watch it? Din't I, yer sacry half-skin?'

A rack of knives was next to fly, slicing up the sunlight and scattering it over the yard.

'Knew yer'd be trouble, a diably half-skin like yer. I'll skin yer, see if I don't, peg yer ugly skin on the doorpost. C'mere . . .'

Seachrân didn't. He knew from experience what would happen if he was caught. He side-stepped the cook's fist and tried to run for the gate; but his weak legs let him down, and he stumbled.

'Oh no yer don't, yer damny swag-stinkin' mongrel . . .'

The cook aimed a pointy-toed sandal at Seachrân's backside and sent him sprawling into the yard.

'Stop!'

The cook stopped. He had no choice: the woman was pointing her staff at the copper bowl he was holding in the air ready to launch, and he was suddenly unable to move it. His face turned mauve.

'Halig!' Seachrân wheezed in relief. He staggered to her and held her so tight that she could barely breathe.

'Halig,' whined the cook. 'Beggin' yer benefaction. Yer should've let me know yer was comin'.'

'Should I?' said Halig, looking at Seachrân tenderly. He wore his pale hair in short dreadlocks to keep it under some sort of control, but at the moment it stood up in a wild tangle. His legs always had been thin, but now they looked as fragile as sticks dried by the desert wind.

Suddenly self-conscious, he tried to hide them under his short tunic. They had marks all over: bruises old and new. And he wasn't wearing the hated metal braces, designed to support them. They were uncomfortable, and the other servants had sneered, just as they had at his muddy, indeterminate skin and his non-Appaloosian eyes.

'Ah, Halig, this boy of yours, he's a good boy, but a dreamer. Yer know I would never lay a hand on him, but three times this week – three times, I tell yer – he's forgotten to watch my poor sick master's dinner. Burned it like blackstone. Ruined.'

'You beat him,' said Halig, lowering her staff. The bowl clanged to the ground, making the cook curse.

'He's clumsy, Halig,' he blustered. 'I says to him, "Carry this," an' he drops it. I says, "Chop the wood," an' he near takes off his own arm . . .'

Halig prised Seachrân off and regarded the cook coldly.

2

'He was sent because of his skill at mathematics, Ninurtus Worldweb, not because of his muscles. That is what was requested. Sybilla Geenpool was your accountant, not your drudge.'

'Mathematics!' spat Worldweb. 'Pah! No half-sk— no *child* could have the skill to keep a household this size afloat.'

'Seachrân is sixteen,' Halig said. 'Hardly a child. And . . . Seachrân, how many souls work here in the Palace?'

He knew, of course. Numbers were the solace that had kept him going every night, when he had ached so badly that all he could do was lie down and wish he were back at Kloster Hallow.

'T . . . t . . . two h . . . hundred and forty-n . . . nine.'

His voice, barely used since last time he saw Halig, was dry and hoarse.

'And how many actually live in the Palace?'

'N . . . ninety-three.'

'How many meals is that each day, if none of those who live outside the Palace eat breakfast here but half of them need supper?'

The numbers danced their magic for him.

'Six h . . . h . . . hundred a . . . and seventy-f . . . five, not including th . . . the Imperator.'

'He must of read it somewhere!' said Worldweb, but he licked his lips nervously.

'Or perhaps you were covering for Sybilla Geenpool: she cooked the Imperator's accounts, while you cooked his dinner,' said Halig. 'Perhaps there is still something in your ledger you are not prepared to let anybody see, even a "damny swag-stinkin' mongrel" like Seachrân.'

The cook flushed until his face was almost indigo. 'I needed a *kitchen* help, Wise One . . .'

'Mmm. Not Seachrân, I think. There are other youngsters. Ones with bodies more suited to manual work. Just as cheap, but with tongues that tell more easily how it is they got to be so clumsy all of a sudden.' Halig gave a severe bow. 'I am indebted by your clemency. Come, Seachrân.'

Seachrân owned nothing worth delaying his escape to fetch, and ran out of the gate before the cook could think of any reason to keep him.

2

'I thought it was s'posed to be summer,' yelled Etolantie, clutching her blankets around her.

'It is,' Solly shouted back. 'I've never seen it like this before.'

They were in a staticky void in the middle of nowhere. The weather had worsened almost immediately after Sunguide had fetched them from Aube's cave. A fierce gale had brought with it the most enormous snowflakes Solly had ever seen, and the skyboat was being tossed about like a feather.

'Is not rrright,' muttered Sunguide, who was completely white down one side with snow. 'Prpr. Is something wrrrong with weather.'

Only Solly was near enough to hear him. Etolantie and Lalune were strapped in at the other end, hugging each other for warmth, and looking as terrified as Solly felt.

Solly tapped Sunguide's rubbery flaps, shielding his mouth and trying to shout quietly so that the girls didn't hear.

'Where are we?'

'Don't know. Prpr. Too busy keeping skyboat in air,' panted the fungus. 'Tear is rrripping open again.'

Solly looked up, alarmed. The strain of their combined

weight was pulling apart the stitches in the skyboat's wound. They didn't look like they could hold much longer.

'I can't feel my feet,' complained Etolantie, her voice muffled by three blankets.

'Wiggle your toes,' he heard Lalune shout back.

'I trrry to get furrrther up,' Sunguide shouted. 'Get above the storm.'

'No, not higher,' moaned Lalune.

Solly agreed with her. They needed to land. As soon as they could. He glanced again at the gash in the skyboat's balloon. Greenish goo was starting to ooze out. He opened his mouth to tell Sunguide.

But he didn't have time.

A stitch snapped. There was a screech of escaping air, the skyboat dropped, and his stomach rushed upwards.

Etolantie and Lalune squealed and clutched their edge of the skyboat as the whole bowl tilted over.

But Solly wasn't strapped in. He felt himself sliding over the edge, and scrabbled for something to hold on to. He managed to grab a rope just as his hips slipped over.

Before he could wriggle back in, his pack fell out on top of him. It caught on his bandoleer, tugging him even further down. As it bounced in the air below he felt the skyboat tip even more.

'Solly!' screamed Lalune.

'Hold on!' called Sunguide. 'I trrry land.'

Solly felt a sharp wrench as the pack snared on something. The skyboat jerked, and his hands dragged on the rope.

Another pack tumbled over him, and suddenly he was dangling in mid-air. It was all he could do to hang on.

He peered down. His pack was caught in the top of a tree. He tried to kick it free, but only made it worse.

Something became briefly visible through the blizzard. A farmhouse, perhaps. If the skyboat could land they could shelter there.

But first they had to clear these trees.

He looked at the two pale faces above him.

There was only one thing he could do.

Solly let go.

3

Halig caught up with Seachrân at the end of the long drive. A WASP examined their pendant passes, and then they were out, plunging into the noisy, dusty, squabbling capital city. Steel and glass flashed and blazed in the hot sun. Huissiers strutted about minding other people's business. Beggars whined. Kaufers – traders with no permanent pitches – urged them from every side to look at their wares.

'Best fluttery silk robes, all colours . . .'

'Personal WASPs for your children! Peace of mind for you . . .'

'Gen-yew-in Wayfarer gems, Halig! Latest fashion . . .'

Halig laughed, and stopped to inspect the flimsy jewellery stall.

Though she appeared quite austere in her plain white robe, Halig was secretly a little vain, Seachrân thought. She was always buying ornaments to braid into her hair, and lotions to make her skin soft: at least, she always did from kaufers who had come from Kloster Hallow, like this girl, Ébha.

A blue and yellow WASP no bigger than his hand hovered nearby, and the kaufer swatted at it.

'Damny WASPs. Can't get away from 'em.'

'There do seem to be more than ever,' agreed Halig.

'Everything we do is watched,' said Ébha. 'There's even WASPs spyin' on WASPs!'

'Indeed!' said Halig, choosing a hair slide. 'Business is good?'

'So-so,' said the girl with a shrug. 'More Edicts every day. More kaufers jostling for a pitch. More coin for less food. I get by.'

Seachrân wasn't interested in hair slides, and followed the WASP to a nearby kaufer who was selling spray-on bubblescreen. Unlike the other kaufers this man seemed delighted at the attention. He stripped his shabby tunic off so that he was naked from the waist up, and squirted a spray can at his chest.

'Automatically picks up the nearest signal,' the kaufer announced to the crowds. In the filmy sheen of the spray on the man's chest his stall could be seen: the spray-on screen was picking up the signal from the WASP. 'Sell your body as advertising space!'

'Would it work on me 'ead?' enquired a bald man jovially, and the kaufer gave it a generous misting. When the bald man showed them the second face grinning from his head the crowd roared with laughter.

'Well, if you find yourself in difficulty you know you are always welcome at Kloster Hallow,' Halig said, putting the hair slide into her wicker basket. 'The Being's blessings on you, Ébha. Come, Seachrân.'

The white stones of the streets reflected the sun back in his face. It was good to be out in the sun again, but so hot here in the city, where the trees refused to grow.

As they approached the river the throng thinned out a

little so that they could walk side-by-side.

'I am sorry, Seachrân,' Halig said. 'I should have visited you sooner. I have been a little unwell. Si-Sef made me rest for two weeks! Imagine! And there are just so many people wanting my attention these days. Not enough food; not enough water to grow the crops; accidents and ailments; and of course this tree sickness. They say the Imperator has it now.'

Seachrân nodded.

'He is t . . . too sick to leave his b . . . bed. N . . . N . . . Ninurtus W . . . Worldweb says there is a great reward for whoever c . . . can find a c . . . cure.'

Not that Seachrân cared much. He hadn't seen the Imperator in all the time he'd been employed by him.

A woman nearby wearing a huge violet poncho that covered her from shoulder to toe glanced at him, and he saw the familiar look of distaste as she saw his skin: too mottled to be Pelegian, too indistinct to be properly Appaloosian. He gave her a beaming smile in return, mainly so that she got a good look at the round pupils in his eyes. She clutched her poncho to her body in abhorrence as he deliberately walked a little too close for her comfort.

'It is not like you not to pay attention, Seachrân,' said Halig, who was rummaging in her pouch for coin to pay the ferryman, and hadn't noticed what he was doing. 'Letting your master's food spoil like that.'

Seachrân turned two shades of pink, and forgot about the woman. His hand unconsciously slipped inside his drab grey tunic to clutch his dead mother's broken necklace, to feel the comfort of its voice resonating inside him.

'I've b-been d-dreaming again.'

'The same girl?'

Halig paid for their tickets and handed Seachrân a water bottle from her basket.

Seachrân nodded and drank thirstily as they joined the queue for the river ferry. He licked his lips nervously and tried to make the words come out right.

'Sh . . . she is in d-danger, I d . . . don't know why. There's b . . . big white . . . something . . .' Seachrân had never seen snow, and his fingers flickered in the air to describe the blizzard he'd witnessed.

'And you still have no idea who she is?' Halig asked. 'Or where? It is good that you are returning to Kloster. I want you close to me so that you can tell me straight away next time.'

Seachrân nodded unhappily and stared down into the yellow water. The girl had been haunting him for months now. Part of him desperately wanted her to leave him alone: part of him wanted to help her. But he didn't know who she was, or where she was. He knew nothing about her at all.

4

'Solly!' cried Lalune.

The skyboat landed clumsily. Sunguide immediately flew to the gaping wound in its side. Lalune fumbled at the straps that held her in. Etolantie was free first; while Lalune was still tearing at her straps she started undoing one of the ropes that attached the skyboat's balloon to the bowl.

Lalune's strap came undone at last. She scrambled out of the bowl, the wind whipping her viciously.

'Wait for me,' yelled Etolantie.

'I have to get to Solly,' Lalune shouted, and tried to run towards him. But her toes were solid ice and she had no snowskates, and she fell over.

'Wait,' Etolantie called again.

Lalune struggled to her feet, disorientated by her new vision. When she'd been a prisoner in the cyberclinic her eyes had been removed and given to somebody else. She'd thought that was it: she'd be blind for ever. But an angel had appeared to her, sent by the Being, she thought, and had given her a new way of seeing, directly into the world of spirits. It was hard to get used to; everything appeared in negative. Black snow caked her coat: dark snowflakes stung her face.

She scraped the snow off her coat and set off again quickly.

It was Solly's coat, and had his scent, and the smell of outdoors.

'Lalune!' cried Etolantie, running after her.

Lalune didn't want to wait. She liked Etolantie; but Solly had disappeared into the darkness. Even a second could make a difference.

'I got a rope,' panted Etolantie, tugging her arm. 'Pa always made us be tied together in snowstorms.'

Lalune glanced back at the skyboat. It was already a dark smudge in the darker flurries of snow.

I could have been lost in seconds, she thought, aghast and ashamed.

Etolantie tied them together and slipped her hand into Lalune's. The snowflakes were like huge feathers: they could barely see five paces ahead. The deep snow made them frustratingly slow, but at last they reached the trees.

Lalune was colder than she'd ever been. The snow was worse than she'd ever seen.

And Solly was slowly being buried in it.

Her stomach knotted. She held the rope tight.

'Solly!' shouted Etolantie.

The wind whisked her words back towards the skyboat. Lalune doubted that Solly could have heard. But she joined in anyway.

'Solly!'

Nothing appeared to be moving.

'See anything?' she shouted to Etolantie, who shook her head.

'I can go an' get another rope, if you like.'

'What's that?' said Lalune.

'What?' said Etolantie.

'A light. A sort of orange glow...' No, she must remember that she saw colours in reverse now: the light was a patch of intense orange. What was the opposite of orange? 'No, not orange. Blue? Purple? There it is again. Did you see?'

'Yes. Yes! Solly? Solly!'

Together they ploughed on towards the light. The snow was falling thicker than ever.

After a few paces they came to the end of the rope. Lalune didn't want to waste time sending Etolantie back for more.

'Wait here. Hold the rope. Keep shouting and waving so I know where you are.'

Lalune ran towards the orange radiance; hampered by the snow; dodging low branches. Once she looked back to make sure she could still see Etolantie, her small white figure gradually being swallowed by the snow.

She could have gone back and waited for more rope. How long would that take? If Solly was hurt, perhaps he needed help quickly.

'Solly!'

The light was close to the ground. Lalune fixed her vision firmly on it.

'Solly!'

'Lalune!'

His voice was faint, muffled by the snow and the wind. Lalune ran faster, and tripped over again.

Solly yelled as she landed nearly on top of him.

He was buried up to his waist in a snowdrift. He'd been trying to dig his way out.

All around him the air was lit up with tiny grains of dust that looked as if they were made of pure light.

'Fire dust!' she shouted.

'I used the Key to radiate it.'

'I thought you were dead.'

'You can't get rid of me that easily.'

Lalune wiped away iced tears, and suddenly hit him hard on the shoulder, smothering a sob.

'What was that for?'

'For letting go. For scaring us silly.'

'I had to,' Solly yelled. 'The skyboat wasn't going to make it. Anyway, I'm all right. You found me. Eventually. Are you going to help me out, or just hit me again?'

They both began to dig. By the time Solly could move his feet enough to climb out, Lalune's legs were numb from the knees down, and he had to put his arms around her to lift her up.

Solly's snowskates were tied to his bandoleer. He put them on quickly; walking without them was difficult, as Lalune had found out.

'What about the packs?' shouted Lalune. One of them was still hanging from a tree, but the other was somewhere under the snow.

'More important that we get inside,' Solly shouted back. 'I hope you know the way back.'

Etolantie was still standing faithfully where Lalune had left her, stamping her feet and waving.

'You was ages,' she grumbled accusingly.

15

'He was buried in a snowdrift,' Lalune explained. 'I had to dig him out.'

'Sunguide came an' said there's a farmhouse. He's left another rope so we can find it. He's tooked the skyboat in already, an' checked to make sure there ain't nobody there.'

Solly tied the rope to a tree, and they clung to it as they staggered back to where Etolantie had tied the other end to her pack. They found the other rope, and followed it the last few paces to the welcoming shelter of the farmhouse.

5

Seachrân and Halig caught the last ferry before the crossing closed for the snarg-spawning season. Snargs, huge fierce fish that could eat you in one gulp, had been sighted downstream, one of the ferrymen told them; soon the river would become unsafe for boats.

The west of the river was a run-down area populated by Appaloosians and mixed-race folk like Seachrân. The houses were rotting and patched with a hotchpotch of reclaimed materials. The further away from the Palace they were, the more squalid they got.

Usually Halig insisted on walking, but she said she was tired, and hired a camel-cart. It was filthy, with windows too small and dirty to see out of. They were dragged very close to the ground behind the sandcamel in a cramped carriage. The streets were crowded, and they went almost as slowly as they would have walking.

When they arrived, Halig frowned as she queried the price of their ride.

'You saying I cheated you?' snarled the carter.

'I am just saying, it did not cost a quarter that on my journey in,' said Halig.

'I expect on your journey *in*, you din't 'ave a 'alf-skin with you,' said the man, smirking at Seachrân unpleasantly.

Seachrân gripped his mother's necklace, and managed to grin back by picturing the sandcamel relieving itself over its owner's feet.

'I thought that one paid per journey, not per passenger,' said Halig. 'Or parentage.'

'If you can't pay, I'm sure the local huissier'd give you both a room for the night.'

The carter's sandcamel lifted its tail and trumpeted loudly.

Halig snorted softly through her nose and gave the man his coin.

'I am indebted by your clemency,' she said, somewhat stiffly. 'And I am quite certain that the Being will reward you for your generosity. And the hygiene of your cart,' she added.

She turned away swiftly, tugging at Seachrân's sleeve. They had only gone a few steps when the carter bellowed with rage, and they turned back to see him cursing and kicking the sandcamel. His trousers and feet were smothered in dung. Seachrân laughed gleefully.

'What have I told you about using your necklace like that?' Halig reproved him, but she didn't look very cross. 'Though he probably deserved it. Still, it is a shame to have lost all that coin. We can sleep, or we can take a basket in the morning, but we cannot afford both. We are in the Being's hands, Seachrân.'

Halig paid for a bed for each of them in a hostel called 'Five-ef's', which contained nothing but beds: sixteen of them, crammed together as tightly as possible.

Five-ef was a tall Appaloosian lady, her skin pretty bronze and coffee stripes. She apologized for the lack of privacy.

'I'd take a couple of beds out if I could afford to. Taxes are so high it's the only way I can make enough coin, by packing in as many as I can. All the overnighters are the same. People come back here because they know I keep it clean. D'you want me to call you in time for the first basket? My son works the nearest one, I can ask him to try and save you a place if you like.'

'That is very kind, thank you,' said Halig.

Five-ef showed them where they could wash and eat. Seachrân fell into bed fully dressed, and went straight to sleep.

6

The farmhouse door was hanging sadly from one hinge, and snow had drifted inside, but as soon as they were out of the wind Lalune felt the contrasting warmth of the house embracing them. Like all Wayfarer houses, there was a porch where they could leave their snowy boots and outer clothing to drip into the slatted floor. There were no windows: most Wayfarer houses didn't have them. They lost too much heat.

They removed their coats and boots, and Solly pushed the inner door.

His breath hissed as he saw the main room.

'Sacry swag-dung! They've wrecked it.'

The room looked as if a couple of snobrellas had been locked in and left to find their own way out. Everywhere was covered in feathers from a burst pillow. Blackstone had been scattered all over the floor, and blackstone dust lay thickly on everything else. Pots were smashed, carpets ripped up, and a food closet had been emptied out and its contents trampled on by someone with muddy feet.

The skyboat was heaped up in a corner, and Sunguide was fluttering over its wounded balloon with a worried air.

'Is it going to be all right?' asked Etolantie, stroking the balloon gently.

'No, prpr,' said Sunguide. 'Bad. Verrry bad. Is not flying anywhere forrr a while.'

'I'm so sorry, Sunguide,' Lalune said.

She nudged a broken bread crock with her toe and shrieked when a small spotted creature darted out. It skidded to a halt at the doorway, and Solly threw a blanket over it. He fell on to the wriggling blanket, pulled a knife from his bandoleer, and after a few moments the blanket went still.

'Dinner!' he said triumphantly, holding the creature up by its tail.

Lalune swallowed and did her best not to shudder. Solly put it down hastily.

'Spotted poley,' he said. 'Small one, but it'll do for tonight. I'll deal with it.'

Lalune nodded queasily.

'Look at this mess,' she said.

'S' like what they did in my house,' said Etolantie.

'Mine too,' said Solly. 'But we'll have to make the most of what's here. We can't go back out into the blizzard. How long will the skyboat need, Sunguide?'

'Prpr. Not know. Not seen wound bad like this beforrre.'

'Poor skyboat,' said Etolantie.

Solly picked up a brass orbal-oil lantern.

'It's still got oil in it,' he said, getting out his flint box. 'I'll clear the snow out and wedge the door back in place. You girls gather up the blackstone and get the oven lit. We'll feel better when we've eaten.'

'Where do you think we are?' Lalune asked.

'I have no idea,' said Solly, lighting the lantern.

The house looked even worse in the harsh light. Lalune tried not to think about it as she forced her unfeeling fingers to pick the scattered blackstone off the floor and pile it in the oven. They would all freeze before long.

'M-maybe Aube c-can tell us,' said Etolantie through chattering teeth. 'On the m-mirror thing.'

'How would he know?' said Solly, searching for something to use as a shovel to clear the snow.

'He's a Seer, ain't he?'

'Etol-lantie, p-perhaps you'd better t-take off your w-wet clothes,' Lalune shivered. 'You've g-g-got clean ones in your p-pack, haven't you?'

'I din't d-do it up right, and they g-got all wet.'

'Then f-find a b-blanket to wrap round you. I'll look for some c-clothes when I've g-got this oven lit.'

She wound the handle on the flint box as she'd seen Solly do, and eventually a spark lit the scrap of oiled rag inside. She held it to the blackstone in the oven.

'I think you g-got to light some dry moss or summink first,' Etolantie said helpfully, picking up a muddy blanket.

'Oh. C-can you see any?'

Etolantie pointed out a basketful, and eventually, after a lot of puffing and blowing, the oven was lit. While Etolantie took off her clothes and draped them near the oven to dry, Lalune looked for something to wear.

She drew back a leather curtain that covered a large recess. There was a big bed behind it.

'What about me?' said Etolantie.

'What about you?' said Solly, pulling the inner door shut and blowing on his fingers.

'What can I do?'

'Get a broom and sweep up a bit,' he said, picking up the spotted poley.

'Why can't *I* cook and *you* sweep up?'

Lalune pulled back another curtain, and found another, smaller bed.

'Because you'll burn it like last time.'

'No I won't. Lalune, tell him I won't.'

'Let him do it this time,' said Lalune coaxingly. She opened another curtain and found cleaning equipment and a bag of leather and silk scraps. 'You can show me how to cook the next meal. Look, here's a broom. It'll be a lot more comfortable when the place is clean.'

Etolantie pouted, but she took the broom anyway and began to trail it over the floor.

'Oh,' Lalune said, moving back the next curtain, which was already half off its hooks. 'A bubblescreen.'

The room with the bubblescreen was tiny, and held a single chair and a table with a little dip in the middle. Lalune's hand automatically went to the pendant she had worn since a small girl. It was more than an adornment: it was a key to open doors, it held her identity, and it could open up bubblescreens.

Lalune forgot how cold she felt. She could almost hear the Bubblenet calling to her. She slipped her pendant over her head and dropped it into the dip in the table. A bubble sprang out of the table and inflated rapidly, purplish black to her eyes. Lalune leaned towards it, waiting for the blurred picture to resolve itself.

'Welcome to the Bubblenet,' said a bland voice, and the familiar cartoon-like figure of Kenet the Bubblenet helper surfaced.

But only for a second. She wasn't real, but Lalune thought that she saw a gleam of malice in Kenet's eyes before the picture changed, and a different woman appeared. She looked just as shocked as Lalune, her jaw dropping open and her eyes bulging. It took a moment for Lalune to recognize her in negative, but when she did she scraped back her chair in horror.

It was Administrator Forcyef.

For a moment they stared at each other.

Then the Administrator screeched, 'It's that damny girl! She's still alive!'

7

Seachrân and Halig were woken before dawn by a squeal.

'Get it out! Get it out!'

Seachrân scrambled out of bed, and laughed delightedly. A queggel had somehow found its way into the room, and was bounding about trying to find a way out. It looked like a blue caterpillar the length of Seachrân's forearm, with four pairs of legs. A couple of skinny women had spotted it, and were cowering on their beds, clutching their night-clothes to them in terror.

'Don't laugh!' one cried. 'Catch it! Get rid of it!'

'It'll eat our clothes!' cried the other.

Halig suppressed a smile. Queggels were harmless, but they loved to eat cloth, and could munch through a wardrobe of clothes in a night.

'Here,' she said, putting the last of their food into her pocket, and throwing Seachrân the wicker basket.

Seachrân crept towards the queggel and cornered it. Before it could leap away again he slammed the box down on it and quickly shut the lid.

'Thank you, thank you,' sobbed one of the ladies. 'I hate those things, they always make me scream.'

'C . . . can I k . . . keep it, Halig?' asked Seachrân, peering at the queggel through the holes in the wicker box.

'Only until the first time it escapes and eats my clothes,' Halig said, beginning the long process of combing her hair. She looked tired: she must have slept badly.

When they got outside they found that a queue had already formed for the baskets.

'You'll be in the ninth one,' Five-ef said apologetically as Seachrân widened a hole in the wicker box to make sure his new pet was able to breathe. 'It's the chirrel-herders. They're changing shifts. They always beat everybody else to it.'

Halig thanked her, and sat on an iron bench wearily. She didn't seem bothered by their lack of coin.

Peleg City had been built inside a canyon. The walls were red rock, and so high that sometimes rain clouds formed inside them.

Most of the vegetation was here on the south wall, and it grew profusely. Thick green leaves covered the wall almost completely; the only places where the rocky walls could be seen were where lifts had been erected. These were simple see-saws with baskets capable of holding two or three people on either side. They swung up to platforms, some natural, some steel constructions, where the passengers would have to get out and climb into a second basket to take them up another level.

The herder in front of them was holding a new-born chirrel in his arms, and it stared at Seachrân mournfully with its huge golden eyes as it clung on to its foster parent. Herds of chirrels lived their entire lives vertically on the walls, and their legs were on the sides of their bodies instead of underneath. They had mouths in their stomachs, and their eyes were on their backs. A small hard umbrella shielded them from rockfalls, and several woolly white tails hung down from underneath. These tails grew rapidly, and were trimmed regularly and made into a cheap cotton-like cloth.

Seachrân strained upwards, but it was still too dark to see the top of the canyon. He wondered how many baskets they would have to take up there. Some basket systems had forty changes. When he'd first come to the city he'd come by boat, but the snargs made that impossible now.

It was a long wait. Halig got into conversation with the herder. The chirrel mewed, and chewed the herder's long hair. Seachrân jiggled up and down impatiently, and chewed one of his own dreadlocks. A nearby child stared at him and picked his nose. Seachrân crossed his eyes and touched his own nose with the tip of his tongue. The child tried to copy, and his mother clipped him round the ear.

Halig cleared her throat and gave Seachrân a warning look.

At last they were at the front of the queue watching the herder and his chirrel rising into the air.

Suddenly there was a loud *snap*, and the basket opposite, carrying heavy weights, shuddered.

'Watch out!' cried several people, as the beam above the basket cracked again. People screamed, and the chirrel shrieked, clawing the herder frantically as the beam groaned and broke in two.

8

Lalune gasped and plucked her pendant out of the bubblescreen table. The bubble deflated.

'What happened?' said Solly. 'Who shouted?'

'I'm sorry,' said Lalune. 'I'm so sorry. I was stupid, now they'll be able to find us . . .'

'What?' said Solly. 'What did you do?'

'I . . .'

But her voice wouldn't work. Solly grabbed her arms, and she flinched as if he was going to slap her. He didn't, of course, but he did shake her a little.

'Tell me,' said Solly firmly. 'It can't be that bad, can it?'

She nodded numbly.

'It is. I . . . I opened up the bubblescreen.'

'That's not a *really* bad thing,' Etolantie said, yawning. 'I done *much* worse things than that before.'

But Solly understood.

'Somebody saw you,' he said.

'Administrator Forcyef,' Lalune whispered.

Solly went pale and let go of her arms. They fell to her sides.

'As soon as I opened it up Kenet was there,' Lalune said. 'She didn't even wait for me to speak, she just sent me to Forcyef's screen . . . I'm so sorry, Solly.' She paused. 'What are we going to do?'

'Prpr,' said Sunguide. 'This Forcyef. She is powerrrful?'

'She likes to think she is,' Solly said shortly.

'She's got the power to send huissier after us,' said Lalune.

'Huissier?' squeaked Etolantie, dropping the broom with a clatter and gaping at the door as if expecting them to burst in that minute.

'We have to leave,' said Lalune. 'As soon as possible.'

'Prpr. Don't think huissier will rrride in this weather,' Sunguide said anxiously. 'Can rrrest for night and leave in morrrning.'

'You don't know Forcyef,' said Solly. Lalune saw him glance at her face before quickly adding, 'But you're right: even she couldn't send them out in this blizzard. And they've got to come all the way from Twilight. I think we should leave our pendant passes here, though, so it doesn't happen again.'

'I ain't got one,' said Etolantie.

'It was creepy, Solly,' Lalune said in a very small voice, handing him her pendant. 'I sort of felt it calling me, like it *wanted* me to turn on the bubblescreen. It was a dumb thing to do, I know. I'm sorry.'

Sunguide nodded sagely.

'Cyberclinic used much orbal oil to keep you in,' he said.

'It's what was in the pods we slept in,' said Lalune. 'Instead of air. It's full of oxygen. But why would that mean anything?'

'It come from orbal trrrees,' said Sunguide. 'Pods are linked into Bubblenet; now orbal oil is physical part of

Bubblenet. Prpr. Pruppras never deal with orbal trrrees. Verrry strrrange storrries about orbal trrrees.'

'What stories?' said Etolantie.

'Are supposed to be able to take away memorrries, and frrreeze time,' said Sunguide solemnly, making his way over to the skyboat. 'Are also verrry territorrrial. Will kill fungus that trrry to feed on them.'

'Remember the snowcamel that was stuck in the Edge of the World?' said Etolantie. 'Was that frozen in time? It was really yucky, Lalune. Its head an' front legs were alive, but its back legs were all rotting away an' full of maggots an' stingwings an' things, an' you could see all its insides . . .'

Lalune shuddered, and was glad when Solly interrupted Etolantie.

'Well, we've still got to eat, we need to find out exactly where we are, and we need more supplies. We may as well take what we can from here. I don't think we're going to find the stuff we dropped in the snow. If I cook the poley, you two pile up everything you think might be useful. We'll leave first thing in the morning.'

9

The two baskets flew together. Despair filled the herder's eyes.

Halig was quick to act. She pointed her staff at the herder's basket, immobilizing it in mid-air. The other basket continued to swing towards it, but only clipped it.

Five-ef, hearing the noise, came running, her hands over her mouth.

'That's my son's basket. Wundyem! Are you all right?'

A striped face looked down on them from above and nodded shakily.

'Seachrân,' said Halig calmly, though sweat was beading on her face, 'go and take the chirrel.'

She began to lower the basket slowly until Seachrân was able to reach up and take the animal. The herder climbed down.

'The basket!' said Five-ef, distraught. 'However will we mend it? Oh, we're going to lose so much coin, and the tax official comes tomorrow!'

'I can mend it in a jiffy, Mother,' her son called down. 'So long as you can find me a beam.'

'A beam, he says!' said Five-ef, making a superstitious warding gesture. 'D' you want to give us all the tree sickness? As if the trees leave wood lying around for the taking!'

31

Seachrân handed the chirrel back to its relieved owner, who went with most of the queue to other baskets.

An old drainpipe was lying under the bench Halig was sitting on. Seachrân touched Five-ef's hand and pointed at it.

'S . . . s . . . strong enough?' he said.

'Strong enough, I dare say, but how will we get it up there?' asked Five-ef, wringing her hands.

'And how will we tie the rope on safely?' said Wundyem from above them. 'Nothing to hold a rope on it, and we don't have the tools to drill a hole. Not through iron.'

In an instant Seachrân saw how it could be done.

He loved it when that happened: it was like a diagram flowing into his mind, all the details complete.

'P . . . put string through,' he said.

'String won't be strong enough, love, though it's nice of you to try,' said Five-ef.

Seachrân shook his head.

'Put s . . . string through the p . . . pipe, p . . . pull a long r . . . r . . . rope after it, Halig c . . . can lift it w . . . w . . . w . . . with her s . . . s . . . staff.'

He trailed off as Five-ef stared at him.

'Something wrong with his head?' she asked Halig in a loud whisper as if he couldn't hear.

'There is nothing wrong with his *mind*,' said Halig. Her hands were trembling with the effort of holding the basket. 'Difficult birth, that's all: he has weak limbs, and speaking is hard for him. But his mind is very sharp, thank the Being. Seachrân, can it be done?'

Seachrân nodded, pleased by her faith in him.

'What do you need? String?'

He nodded again.

'And r . . . rope.'

Five-ef fetched some of both, looking doubtful. Seachrân made a loop in the string and tied it firmly on to the rope. He took out the wicker box containing the queggel, slipped the loop over the queggel's front end, and pulled it tight enough to stop it from slipping over the creature's middle legs. The queggel squirmed angrily. Seachrân kept one hand over its eyes so that it couldn't see, and took it to the end of the pipe. He pushed it in as far as he could get both hands, then let go. The queggel shot down the pipe, taking the string with it. When the string was through it pulled the rope through after it.

Five-ef clapped her hands.

'He *is* sharp, isn't he!'

'Catch the queggel, Seachrân,' said Halig, putting her foot on the rope so that it didn't all get pulled through.

Seachrân ran to the queggel, now dancing in rage at the foot of the wall. He freed it from the string and popped it back in its box, where it chittered at him angrily. Seachrân brought back the string and tied it to the other end of the rope so that it wouldn't slip out again.

'Now, how do we lift it?' asked Five-ef.

'Halig, c . . . c . . . can you l . . . lift it with your s . . . staff?' said Seachrân. 'A . . . a . . . and Wundyem c . . . catch it?'

'If you two can carry it over to the foot of the cliff, I can try,' said Halig. 'Though it is a little on the heavy side. You might have to help me, Seachrân.'

They carried the pipe over and Halig pointed at it with her staff. She managed to get one end off the ground, but the other stayed stubbornly down.

'Seachrân, could you get the other end?' panted Halig. 'It should be easy for you here. These faluna stones work best at a distance from the Ne'Lethe.'

Seachrân grasped his mother's necklace and pictured the other end lifting. It was hard work, but in the end it started to rise from the ground and up the wall until Wundyem was able to reach it and pull it up.

'That'll do,' he called. 'Brilliant, in fact. Give me a while, and I'll fix it on, then I'll give you a free ride.'

Five-ef was staring at Seachrân.

'He's a *Seer*?'

'He inherited a Seer's necklace,' said Halig, beaming at Seachrân. 'They have their uses. I am glad to see that he has not forgotten how to use it. And who knows what he may be one day.'

'Thank you, thank you so much,' said Five-ef. 'Come back inside, I'll make you some tea while you're waiting. My, my, the coin you've saved us today.'

The sky above them was already pink, and by the time Wundyem had fixed the pipe on, it was blazing blue. Five-ef escorted them to the front of the new queue that had appeared from nowhere, telling everybody how they had surely saved her from the debtor's prison.

10

Only Etolantie ate much. Solly had skinned the poley and fried it with some grain he'd found.

The food tasted fine – he'd been taught to cook by Revas – but Lalune looked as if it were turning to blackstone in her mouth.

Sunguide left the skyboat's side and attached himself to a beam above their heads.

'That's *wood,*' said Etolantie accusingly. 'In a *house.*'

'This is an old house,' said Solly. 'Pa said that a very long time ago they still used wood for building with, if they had to.'

'*My* Pa would've let us freeze to *death*, an' not build at all.'

'I think the trees weren't as dangerous then, or as scarce.'

'Prpr. Don't mind me,' Sunguide said from above their heads.

Lalune raised her blank eyes up to him miserably. It still shocked Solly to see her empty sockets.

I should find her a scarf, he thought.

'Don't mind him,' he said, trying to lighten the atmosphere a little. 'I mean *really* don't mind him. He can go for days without food.'

'What *do* you eat?' Lalune asked him, curious enough to

think about something other than Forcyef for a moment.

'Mould and mildew,' said Solly, and Sunguide blew a raspberry at him.

'Pruppras exchange vital nutrrrients with trrrees,' he said with dignity. 'Can hang here all night to rrreplenish energy. Though living trrrees better,' he added, rather wistfully.

But it was difficult keep up the banter, and they soon lapsed into a depressed silence again. Solly was glad when the Janus mirror, which he'd placed on top of his pack, started to buzz.

Etolantie snatched it up.

'Hello, Aube.'

'Etolantie, m'dear,' Aube beamed at her. 'And Lalune, too, and Solly, and Sunguide. How are you all, hmm?'

Lalune gave a dejected sigh.

'We got caught in a blizzard and we don't know where we are,' Solly said. There was no need to tell him what Lalune had done. Not yet, anyway.

'Ah, well I can tell you that,' said Aube. A large grey shape behind him moved. Solly thought he recognized it as the largest Pruppras of Sunguide's colony.

'See, I *told* you he'd know,' Etolantie said smugly, and Solly scowled at her. 'I bet he Saw us. Did you See us, Aube?'

'Sadly, Seeing doesn't happen to order,' Aube told her solemnly. 'Handy if it did. Wouldn't have to make any decisions again. Though I should imagine life would be a touch dull.'

'Then how . . . ?'

'Just tell us where we are, Aube,' Solly said impatiently.

36

'Children who are encouraged to ask questions grow up to be adults who find answers,' Aube said severely, wriggling his long eyebrows at Solly.

Solly felt both annoyed and ashamed, which only made him more annoyed.

'It was the Pruppras, m'dear,' Aube continued, as if Solly hadn't spoken. 'Spores, you know. Now, there's the thing. The, ah, chief Pruppras here was concerned when the storm began. You were in the worst of it, and the spores couldn't get to you, but at least they found out where you are. And it seems that the storm, violent as it was, could have been fortuitous. It carried you a long way: you are not terribly far from Etolantie's farmhouse, and Latrium. That is where this, ah, Dr Dollysheep told you to go, is it not, hmm? Not more than a day's flying, I should think.'

'But we *can't* fly,' said Lalune in a despairing voice. 'The skyboat's hurt. And we need to get away from here. Forcyef will send huissier . . . I was so stupid, Aube, I opened up a bubblescreen, and now she'll trace us here . . .'

She had tears rolling from the corners of her sewn-up eyes. Etolantie put her arms around her.

'Don't cry, Lalune. Aube'll know what to do.'

'Hmm,' Aube said ponderingly. 'The skyboat is hurt, you say. And huissier on their way?'

The grey shape behind him spoke in its rubbery language, and Sunguide answered it. After a few minutes' discussion Sunguide said, 'They will send pr-help to heal skyboat when storm is over. I stay with him until they arrrive. Prpr. Huissier will not be searching for fungi. But hrumans must go to Latrrrium as soon as can. Not safe here for you.'

37

'If we walk we'll leave tracks,' Solly said. 'And we'll be slow. They'll be in snow skimmers.'

Aube was consulting the Pruppras now. He had picked up some of their language, and was using a mixture of the two, which sounded very odd.

'If you start walking, I shall come and pick you up as soon as I can in another skyboat,' he said. 'Leg's much better now. Can hobble about with a stick. Go to Etolantie's farm. Fetch your snowcamel. What's his name? Star? He is in good shape, the Pruppras tell me. I shall meet you there and take you along to Latrium. Sunguide can join us there when he can. And once we're there, well, perhaps your next move will become clear, hmm?'

11

Seachrân and Halig began their ascent at last, rising slowly from platform to platform. The night hadn't been cool, and now that it was daytime the temperature was soaring. Halig was quite breathless with the heat, and the effort of lifting the pipe.

It took them nearly two hours to reach the top. They could feel the wind, known as the Sandblaster, from five platforms down, shaking everything and howling through the thick branches. Seachrân gingerly tested the strength of the platform struts, and Wundyem, who'd come up with them, laughed.

'Don't worry, these platforms have been here years. Strong as my breath in the morning!'

'The wind will be even worse when we reach the top,' Halig said, handing Seachrân a large square scarf made of green chirrel wool. 'I was hoping to be a lot earlier. Wrap this round you.'

She had a pale blue one, which she wound around her head and bare arms. Her legs were covered already, but Seachrân's tunic was short, and the scarf only came to his knees. He regretted not bringing his baggy trousers from the Palace now.

The wind yanked at Seachrân's dreadlocks, and whipped

Halig's braid into her face before she gathered it and stuffed it into her robe.

It was nothing, however, to what hit them at the top of the canyon wall. Halig, who wasn't exactly light, was nearly lifted right off her feet, and Wundyem and Seachrân had to hold on to her until she got her balance back.

Several people were waiting to descend; all were carrying empty bottles. Wundyem gave them both a gallon of water. Halig shouted something to him, but all Seachrân could hear was the shrieking wind. Wundyem smiled and nodded, and escaped thankfully back into his basket with his passengers. Halig shouted again, this time to Seachrân, and gestured at something almost obscured by the sand the wind was throwing up into the air. It was hard to make out, but four or five hundred steps away stood two upended red boulders. On the other side was a small rocky incline with a low cliff. Between the standing stones was a small cave: the start of the sandcamel trail linking canyons all around the planet.

Clutching their wraps and each other, they staggered towards the boulder, leaning backwards against the wind, their feet skidding on the slippery sand.

The heat sucked the air from Seachrân's lungs. After three steps he felt as if somebody had scoured the skin off his legs. Despite the wrap, red sand managed to get into his mouth and ears, and his eyes stung so badly that he shut them, opening them only occasionally to see where they were going.

Every time he opened them they were slightly off course, but fortunately somebody had carved hundreds of arrows on the naked red rock, so that unless you were blown right into the desert, you would eventually find yourself at the start of the Sandcamel trail.

When they reached the cave, friendly hands pulled them inside, unwrapped them, brushed the sand off them, and swept it back out into the wind. They handed over the water thankfully.

The cave smelled comfortingly of sandcamel and frumenty. A small group of carters were sitting drinking tea. The only other passenger was a cheese merchant waiting for the next basket down.

'Kloster Hallow, Wise One?' one of the carters enquired, noticing Halig's staff with its faluna stone, which she was clinging to while her breathing returned to normal.

The carter was an immensely fat Appaloosian with dark brown skin covered in irregular splashes of red, the same colour as the rocks. Seachrân imagined that he would be well camouflaged if he stripped off his white tunic and trousers. *Camouflaged but bloody,* he thought, glancing at his own legs, which were now speckled with gore.

'I am afraid that this is as far as our coin will take us,' said Halig regretfully. 'We had a bad deal with a carter down in the city.'

'They're all the same, those city carters,' said the carter contemptuously, spitting out a gob of brown liquid.

'Think they're harddone by,' agreed another; and a third said, 'Whiners, all of 'em. Send 'em up here to work in the Sandblaster, they wouldn't last five seconds. And neither will you, if you try to walk in it,' he added. 'The sandcamel trail's sheltered, but not that sheltered, and like as not, you'll be run down by some carter with his eyes shut against the wind.'

Seachrân wandered over to the sandcamels and

scratched one of them behind the ears.

'We have no choice,' said Halig, sinking down on to a narrow bench. 'The river is closed.'

'Wise One, the water you brought is payment enough,' said the fat carter. 'And if you would wait but two hours I am to fetch a wealthy customer from the next canyon, to bring him back this evening, I could detour slightly, and drop you off at the foot of the mountain.'

The sandcamel yawned and closed its long-lashed eyes with pleasure. Seachrân stroked its head.

'That is very kind of you,' said Halig. 'The Being be praised! But will it not leave you out of pocket? There are at least five tolls extra.'

The carter winked.

'Wuneem is a good friend of mine, and news travels up the baskets faster than the wind blows sand. That was a kind deed you did for him and his mother. As I say, a very wealthy customer, and very concerned about the welfare of sandcamels. If I told him I was forced to go out of my way to find them a drink, what will he know? Everybody knows the Sandblaster's especially wicked this year. He'll be glad to pay up.'

'Next time you are anywhere near Kloster, find me,' said Halig. 'My name is Halig Greenpeace. We shall hold a feast in honour of your kindness.'

'Aytem Sixty-Nine,' said the carter, shaking her hand.

Halig brought out what little she did have to give him: a few dry biscuits and some herbs for tea. The carters produced vegetable soup and bread, the merchant cut into a block of cheese that smelt like old socks, and they shared lunch together.

42

12

Lalune didn't sleep at all well. Every strange noise was the huissier breaking in: Etolantie breathing next to her was wild animals. When she did finally doze off she was met in her dreams by Administrator Forcyef shouting, 'Now she's ruined everything, *everything*!' while her mother held up a white trouser suit and said, 'Just look at the grease stain on this, you naughty girl!' When she looked, it wasn't grease, but blood.

She thought that she had woken with a scream, but Etolantie, tucked up beside her, didn't stir.

Lalune was drenched in sweat, and frozen to the bone. She got up and went into the main room to light the oven. Everything was covered in a glistening black substance, and it took a few minutes to work out that it was frost.

I shall never get used to seeing in negative, she thought.

She lit the oven and squatted next to it to warm up.

Solly had left his coat next to the oven to dry. Lalune could see the corner of the Book of the Key peeping out of it. He had showed her how it sang when he held the stone, and had warned her about its ability to control his will. But that was the Key, not the Book.

Curious about the strange language Solly said it was

written in, she slid it out of his pocket. The golden Key on the front winked violet in the firelight.

I wonder how it works.

She pressed the stone, expecting a bubblescreen or something similar to pop up, but nothing happened. She tried turning it, sliding it, and taking it out and replacing it, but she couldn't get it to switch on and reveal its information.

Maybe only the Holder can access it, she thought, disappointed, and leant forward to put it back into Solly's pocket.

But because the vision the angel had given her wasn't at all easy to see with, she misjudged the distance, and the Book fell to the floor. As it landed it broke in half, slicing through the narrowest side like a piece of slate.

Great, Lalune thought. *Another thing I've ruined.*

But when she went to pick it up she saw that it wasn't broken at all. It had simply unfolded as if it had a hinge, exposing slices of a thin organic stuff that felt like fluttery wings. Each slice was attached down one side, she saw, and the segments were crammed with writing that somebody had painstakingly done by hand, not etched on to acetate. There were also drawings, and occasionally some narrow printed columns that had been cut from something else and stuck in.

Lalune chuckled softly.

'So that's how it works!'

She began to leaf through the slices.

'Strange,' she murmured. 'It's as if I *almost* understand it.'

The segments looked black to her, with white writing. But not simply white, she saw now: silver sparkles were shimmering up and down the book.

And there was no doubt that some of the words were familiar.

Was it possible that she had mind knowledge of this code?

When she had been incarcerated in the cyberclinic, she had been attached to the Bubblenet, the cyber network that linked all computers everywhere. The information stored in the Bubblenet – mind knowledge – had been gradually downloading into her brain while she slept. Most of it was locked away somewhere in her mind: she wasn't aware of it unless she needed it.

'But how do I use it when I want to?' she murmured, flipping over another page.

One of the glistening words caught her attention, and she realized that she recognized it.

'Appaloosians,' she said in an excited whisper. 'It says Appaloosians!'

The word occurred quite often on the printed pieces of paper stuck into the Book.

'. . .Appaloosians be . . . be . . . cause . . .'

The meaning was there, only just out of reach, as if a thin veil was covering it. Lalune pulled Solly's coat around her shoulders and stared at the words, willing them to make their meaning clear.

'. . . th . . . their . . . their . . . skin . . .'

Suddenly it was as if a chain reaction began in her mind. With a thrill she began reading from the beginning of the sentence.

'We call them Appaloosians because their skin condition, vitiligo, makes them resemble the horses known as Appaloosas: blotchy, irregular black and white skins . . .' she read slowly.

Blotchy and irregular?

She frowned at her hand. She'd always been rather proud of the symmetry of her markings, and the way the milky-whiteness freckled into the chocolate brown.

It was also one of the few things about her that her mother had been proud of.

Lalune turned back to the Book and found another sentence with the word Appaloosians.

'*The Appaloosians, so-called because we are so appalled at the sight and thought of them . . .* Appalled?' she said to herself, her forehead wrinkled in confusion. 'Why at the thought of us?'

She read on, growing increasingly unsettled.

'*. . . everything about the Appaloosians, from their repugnant skin to their alien eyes, is unnatural and abhorrent . . .*'

'*. . . serious doubt that that those abnormal clones, Appaloosians, could have a soul . . .*'

'*. . . the horrific monsters, known as Appaloosians, will also be on board . . .*'

'"*. . . we could never get the eyes or the skin right," the older Peleg brother, creator of the freakish monstrosities known as Appaloosians, confessed . . .*'

'*. . . all major religions (any official group claiming to worship a Supreme Being) have denounced the Appaloosians as aberrations, soulless monsters . . .*'

'*. . . my opinion that these Appaloosians cannot be said to be human . . .*'

Lalune felt dazed. This was her people they were talking about: her family. They were monsters. Monsters from the very beginning of their existence.

She was a monster.

How could a monster ever be acceptable to the Being?

13

The sandcamel trail was a continuation of the cave: a natural fault-line in the rock. In some places they would have the full force of the Sandblaster on them, so the cart was close to the ground, like the city cart. The windows had been ground nearly opaque by the wind. It was a lot cleaner than the city cart, however, and Aytem Sixty-Nine travelled inside with them after weighing it down with several gallon bottles of water.

At first Seachrân stared out of the window on the left, mesmerized by the shimmering desert that stretched as far as he could see, moving and heaving in the wind like a great red ocean. It went all the way from here to the South Pole, and then on and on until it reached the canyons on the opposite side of the planet.

It was always daytime at the South Pole. Seachrân tried to imagine what that was like, to be awake every hour of every day.

After a while he dozed, waking at the first toll with pins and needles in his leg. He swapped places with Halig and stared out of the other window instead.

This side was a little less uniform. The indent occasionally was high enough to shelter them from the wind completely, and it whistled over their heads hardly disturbing small patches of dry-looking herbs. Where it was low down, he could see sandstorms raging over the barren rock, but sometimes the great mountains could be seen in the distance.

There were more caves along the trail: sometimes man-made, sometimes with tolls. At each one they stopped for Aytem to swap his water bottles for others stored in the caves. They would all have a drink of the lukewarm water, and chat with the toll keepers, who heard all the news. The tree sickness was spreading, they said; harvests had failed, and taxes were up. Nothing new.

Then Aytem would check the sandcamel's eyes for scratches, and they would move on.

'Why d . . . do you s . . . swap the water?' Seachrân asked, the second time they did this.

Aytem showed him the stoppers in the bottles.

'See, we all carry water for ballast, but we all need to drink it too. There's no streams up here in the desert, so we've made our own, sort of: we all drink the stored water, and leave our fresh water here for the next carter along. Otherwise it'd go stale, see. Now, these stoppers are blue. That means they're travelling in the same direction as us. Red ones go back the other way. And these that we're drinking were left by a carter earlier on, so they were fresh this morning. The ones we're leaving are fresher: you brought them. Creates a flow, see.'

Now and then they would pass a cart going the other way, and the carters would yodel greetings to each other. The next time this happened Seachrân looked. Sure enough the other cart was carrying red-stoppered bottles.

It was getting dark by the time they reached their stop-off point. Seachrân smelt trees, and felt much cooler: the hot wind had died down.

'There's a stream here. If you wouldn't mind helping me fill up my bottles, I'll be on my way,' said Aytem.

They did so, and watched the sandcamel drink and drink until Seachrân thought it would explode.

'Do not forget, call in,' said Halig.

They were at the foot of a tremendous mountain. Its southern side was a bare and rocky continuation of the desert; but trees began to grow here on the western slopes, and on the northern side they were spectacularly huge. Halig's people had made a rough road for themselves, taking care not to harm any trees, and there was rarely any reason to venture far inside the forest. There were trees in there, it was said, that had never encountered human beings.

Seachrân, brought up in Kloster Hallow, knew which trees were friendly. After the drudgery of the kitchen followed by the heat of the desert, it was as if he was returning to see old friends after years away. In spite of his weak legs and the fact that they still had a long way to go, he wanted to run.

Halig walked slowly, however, and kept stopping. She wanted him to rest too, but he felt too full of energy; and instead of sitting with her he dodged about in the trees, examining as much of everything as he could, filling himself with the senses of home.

'Halig, look,' he kept crying, and Halig would have to admire a fluttery the colour of sunrise; or a rain-water pond formed inside the flower of a Forlornhope tree, with tiny malformed mubbles rising and falling within it; or a tree root so high that when he looked up at it he hurt his neck.

The temperature was dropping rapidly, and Halig stopped to take her scarf out of her pack once more.

'Look, Halig!' cried Seachrân again, climbing up on to the tree root and pointing through a gap in the trees. 'A n . . . new star.'

Halig smiled at him indulgently. From where she stood the sky was hardly visible.

'New star, my sweet? The sun is too bright for the stars to be out yet. Do you mean the Bane moon? But that will not rise for a while.'

Seachrân shook his head, annoyed that she thought he could mistake a star for the moon.

'L . . . l . . . look for yourself, Halig. Not a moon: a s . . . star. W . . . with a tail.'

It was only as the words left his mouth that Seachrân realized what he had seen. Slowly he withdrew his mother's necklace from inside his tunic and eased the string over his head. He held it up so that the dying sun made it glitter. As the tiny amount of light from the new star fell on it, the faintest of notes sounded.

His eyes met Halig's in awe.

'The comet has returned,' she whispered.

14

Solly woke to a world suddenly silenced. The storm was over. It was time to go.

Somebody was up before him, and had lit the oven, so getting out of bed wasn't as unpleasant as it might have been. He pulled on some of the clothes they'd found and opened the curtain that hung over the doorway.

Lalune was curled up in front of the oven. She must have been cold, got up in the night to light it, and fallen asleep in front of it.

He was tiptoeing around her to get to the leftovers of last night's meal when he saw that she wasn't asleep. She was crying.

'Lalune?' he said.

'Go away,' she said, waving a hand at him without raising her head.

Her face was puffed up, and her nose was red. Her breaths came in deep tremors. Clearly she'd been there for some time. Solly knelt next to her and put a hand on her shoulder. She shrugged it off half-heartedly, but he put it back and she didn't object again.

'We'll be gone long before they have a chance to get here, you know.'

'You may as well leave me here,' Lalune mumbled indistinctly.

'Don't be silly,' Solly said, drawing her up into a sitting position so that he could put his arm round her. 'It was a mistake, that's all.'

'No.'

'Yes, it was. Anyone could have done it. You said yourself, it was calling you . . .'

'I didn't mean . . . I wasn't talking about that. You're right. You could've done it, or Etolantie: not that she seems to have a pendant pass, just that bracelet. And they've got a long way to come.'

A tear rolled out of one sewn-up eye, and as she brushed it away the Book of the Key fell from her lap. Solly picked it up absently, and more tears fell.

'What is it then?'

'I read it,' she wept, as if she'd done something unforgivable.

Solly opened the book. The words meant nothing to him. And besides, without eyes . . . he knew she had some sort of vision, but had assumed that it was just enough to enable her to see where she was going. He rubbed her arm comfortingly.

'How?'

'I think I l-learned . . . the l-language it's written in . . . in the cyberclinic. You know, all that mind knowledge . . . pouring into us?' He had to concentrate to make out the words in between sobs. 'Turns out . . . was useful after all. Y-you wouldn't have thought they'd w-waste their time . . . knew all along what they were planning . . .' Her last words were lost altogether in a fresh bout of crying.

52

Solly found a piece of rag that didn't look too dirty and held it to her nose. She blew into it noisily.

'Is that what you read? What they really wanted the cyberclinic for? But we knew that already.'

She shook her head and made an effort to control her voice.

'No. It's a diary. Sort of. With other bits stuck in, from a printed news bulletin.'

'I thought it would be instructions,' Solly said.

'It was put together by one of the first humans to come to Clandoi. Except he probably never made it as far as here, it took three generations to travel . . .'

'Wait a minute: we don't come from Clandoi?'

'No . . .'

Lalune was interrupted by Etolantie bounding out of her bedchamber, dressed in a woollen sweater that reached her knees.

'The storm's stopped,' she shouted as she shot past them towards the privy. 'Hello, Sunguide. The storm's stopped.'

Lalune winced.

'I had a headache already.'

Sunguide had been perching in the porch for the night. Now he fluttered slowly into the room.

'How's the skyboat?' Lalune said.

'Prpr. Rrresting. I think he will be all rrright in time, but needs to be back in colony. And you need to eat. Must not lose any more time.'

'Sunguide, didn't you say something to me once about remembering when humans first came to Clandoi?' Solly said. He hadn't really noticed him saying it at the time. It had been when Sunguide had told him that human beings were being killed in the cyberclinic. He hadn't believed him then. He hadn't believed in a lot of things then.

'Prpr. Yes. Hrumans not always here. But I not know where they came frrrom.'

'Earth,' said Lalune. 'It's another planet, far away across the stars.'

'Prpr?'

'Lalune can read the Book that came with the Key,' Solly explained, uncovering a pot of leftover food.

'Can you?' said Etolantie, coming back in. 'What's for breakfast? What does it say?'

'It was called Earth,' Lalune said in a flat voice.

'What was?' said Etolantie. 'Oh, *not* leftovers.'

'If you want something else, you can make it,' said Solly, putting some of the cold meat into bowls. There wasn't much, and they didn't have time to warm it. 'Or I'm sure Sunguide can find you some wubberslugs.'

Etolantie stuck her tongue out at him.

'Carrry on, Lalune,' said Sunguide.

'Where we came from. It's another planet. It's so far away that the first people to be sent here, and their children, had died by the time their ship arrived, and it was their grandchildren who started to live here.'

'Two brothers together did journey away, across stars and mountains a year and a day,' sang Etolantie.

Solly stared at her, realization dawning.

'What?' she said. 'It's a nursery rhyme.'

'Prpr. Much trrruth hidden in nurserrry rrrhymes.'

'Aube collects them,' Solly said. 'Nursery rhymes and fairy tales. He must have been trying to find out.'

'It was a bit more than a year and a day,' Lalune said.

'And more than just two brothers. Hundreds of people. But that must be what it means. They came in a ship called the Queen of the Stars.'

Solly put some food into her hand.

'Why did they come?'

A tear slid down Lalune's cheek.

'They didn't want to. They were exiled. They were criminals and the families of criminals. The scientists had found a group of genes that they all shared, and the people of earth decided to rid themselves of them all . . .'

'So we all have this gene too?'

'Wayfarers do,' Lalune said. 'And Pelegians.'

'What about you?'

'Appaloosians weren't the criminals. They were the crime.'

15

Halig craned her neck, trying to see what Seachrân had seen, but the trees obscured her view, and she wasn't agile enough to join him up on the root.

'I can't see anything,' she said anxiously. 'What colour was it? You are *sure* it had a tail?'

Seachrân felt a little cross. There was just a tiny bit of sky visible through the trees. There was nothing there now. He wondered if he'd imagined it. He hunched his shoulders and looked again at where he'd seen the star. If he *had* seen it, it meant that he was the Holder of the Key.

'It *was* there,' he said stubbornly.

'Or *will* be,' said Halig thoughtfully.

Seachrân screwed his eyes up tightly to try and see it again; but it was no good. He jumped down.

Halig was muttering to herself.

'I will have to check. See it for myself. But . . . I shall need to find an accurate star chart, moon tables . . . Curious, there has been other no sign . . . there should be other children . . .' Her voice trailed off as she hastened on towards Kloster Hallow. The tall tower observatory could already be seen rising high above the trees in the distance, black against the gloomy sky.

Kloster was a collection of beehive-shaped huts in the

valley. Seachrân's mother had been taken there when she had been found dying in the forest, her new-born baby cradled in her arms. Though she hadn't told Halig why she had been so far away from help when her labour began, Halig had guessed. Seachrân was a 'half-skin': a racial mix of Appaloosian and Pelegian. Either her family had rejected her, or she had anticipated them doing so.

The people who lived at Kloster were a strange mix. Some, like Halig, were Pelegians in self-imposed exile: a protest against the extermination of the Wayfarers so many years before.

Others, like Seachrân, were outcasts because of their skin. Appaloosians were tolerated in the city because they would do the worst jobs. Pure-blood Pelegians were not supposed to breed with them, and when they did their offspring were shunned by both peoples. Their skins were bitonal but the colours rarely sharply defined, and the pupils of their eyes were round, so their parentage was obvious. Mostly the babies were taken into the forest to die, and that was where Halig Saw them and went to find them.

All too often they were already dead.

Others came for a variety of reasons. The disabled, those on the run from prison, from society, or from life. Halig never turned anybody away. Their lifestyle mirrored that of the Wayfarers, as far as they could tell. They believed in the Being, were devoted to history, and ate no meat. At first Halig had insisted that they lived in tents, as she said the original Wayfarers had done, but it hadn't been long before the tents became more substantial. Now, though even the really big buildings like the hospital and the observatory were still called 'tents', they were actually made of sturdy stone.

As they reached the outlying huts children ran to greet them, and Seachrân swung them in his long arms. Halig smiled at them, but stopped only to pick up a small girl who fell over in front of her.

'Is Kepler Coriolis in the observatory?' she asked them. Being assured that he was, she carried on, almost running across the Telling Place, where they gathered around the evening fire.

Halig *never* ran. Seachrân heard several people wondering what was going on.

'Halig, stop!' an Appaloosian woman called Si-Sef cried. 'You'll make yourself even more ill!' Si-Sef had been put in charge of the hospital tent, and was not afraid of ordering Halig around.

But Halig ignored her and carried on. By the time she reached the tower the people were crowding about behind her, wondering what she was about.

But she didn't satisfy their curiosity, only calling, 'Seachrân! You come too!' from the first storey window. They murmured in surprise as Seachrân slowly followed her up.

The stone tower was several storeys high, and the two of them had to stop frequently on the way. They arrived in the glass-domed loft at last, puffing, and there found Kepler Coriolis, a swarthy Pelegian who had taken it on himself to run the observatory. He taught advanced mathematics, and Seachrân was more than a little in awe of him. Normally he kept as far away from his instruments as possible.

Kepler had only just opened the blinds that kept the sun out during the day, but even so it was hot and stuffy in the small room, and like Seachrân he was dressed only in a short grey tunic. He'd even taken his sandals off to cool his feet on the stone floor.

'Welcome, Halig; welcome, Seachrân,' he said without lifting his eye from the telescope.

'Seachrân has seen something in the sky,' said Halig, not bothering with small talk. She held both hands over her heart as if it ached with all the running.

'He has, has he?' said Kepler. 'And what might this something be?'

'Seachrân?' said Halig.

'A n . . . n . . . new s . . . s . . . star.'

He stuttered more than usual.

'With a tail,' added Halig.

'Where?' Kepler said crisply.

Seachrân gave up trying to get his words out. It was always more difficult when he felt under pressure. He pointed instead over the treetops towards the horizon, where the ominous dome of cloud that was the Ne'Lethe squatted over the North Pole.

Kepler swung his telescope towards it and for a few minutes Seachrân and Halig watched him fiddling with the knobs as he focused in. Then there was silence. Seachrân jigged up and down, and Halig had to give him a look to make him stand still. He fiddled with his necklace instead, and squinted at Kepler so that he could see two of him.

'Well, well,' breathed Kepler eventually.

'Well?' said Halig.

'Well!' added Seachrân, and nearly laughed out loud.

Kepler moved over to let Halig have a look.

'Have you checked the star charts?'

'Not yet,' said Halig. 'We came straight up here when we got home. Where is it? That tiny hair? It's practically invisible.'

Kepler turned to Seachrân very suddenly and stared at him with glittering eyes.

'Seachrân. You're the boy with the necklace.'

Seachrân shrank back from him, unsure if he was angry with him.

'Here, Seachrân, have a look. You found it,' said Halig.

Seachrân looked nervously at Kepler, who nodded.

Kepler, who never let anybody near his precious instruments!

Seachrân bent over to stare through the telescope. For a moment he couldn't see anything at all. Then, far, far away, he noticed a tiny, insignificant scratch on the sky, with a pinpoint of a spark at one end. It was much fainter than when he'd seen it in the forest, but it was definitely the same.

'Where were you when you saw it?' asked Kepler.

'In the forest,' said Halig.

Kepler was astonished.

'And he saw it from there? From amongst the trees? You couldn't even see that from this observatory without a telescope.'

'If he is truly the Holder he may have Seen it with more than his physical eyes,' Halig said. 'He's been having dreams too.'

Kepler looked thoughtful.

'Seachrân,' said Halig, 'Kepler Coriolis and I have some

work to do. Go and get the children to build a good big fire for the Storytelling. And why don't you fetch some mallownuts to roast in it, and tell the cooks to make a toffee dip to go with them. I think tonight will be a special occasion.'

16

When they'd finished eating Lalune went to dress. Solly anxiously watched her go. *He* knew she wasn't a monster, but she wouldn't be convinced.

Etolantie tried to push the door open.

'It's stuck.'

'It was broken, remember?' said Solly, feeling around the edges to get a grip. 'Maybe we should just take the whole thing off. You pull that side. Got it? One, two, three . . .'

The door fell to the floor with a thud, but they were faced with another barrier, this one made of solid snow. Etolantie giggled, and Solly scrowled at her.

'Shouldn't you be getting dressed or something?'

'I *am* dressed,' she said. 'There weren't no children's clothes. Will we have to dig a tunnel to get out?'

'There should be an escape hatch in the roof somewhere,' said Solly.

'There,' said Etolantie, pointing to a small square door over the privy. 'An' a ladder.'

Solly climbed up and eased the hatch open. It was almost too heavy for him to move, until the snow slid off and he was able to lift it and poke his head out.

'I hope there's some spare snowskates,' he said, his voice muffled by the thick snow. 'We won't even reach the barn without them. Snow's all the way up to here.'

'These are snowskates, ain't they?' said Etolantie, holding up some very worn-looking round frames with leather woven across them, and straps to go over their boots. 'An' there's coats an' outside trousers here. But it's all for growed-up people.'

The house was so buried it was difficult to make out where it ended. To the north rose a mountain, a blue-grey glacier flowing down its side, and the Ne'Lethe grew ever darker. Nearby was a small stunted forest, right now almost concealed by a thick layer of snow. Two narrow lines of trees stretched from it right round to the west and east.

To the south nothing broke the whiteness for almost as far as he could see. Only the slightest change of texture showed where the snow stopped and the cloudy dome began. Birds were singing, and he could hear a vague buzzing noise. Probably stingwings.

Somewhere over there was Etolantie's house. That was the direction they had to go in. They'd left his snowcamel Star there, in the care of a fungus: not a Pruppras this time, but a guerdon.

'I supposed we keep going until we reach the Ne'Lethe, and hope Etolantie can work out where her house is from there,' he muttered.

The night before he'd wrapped their pendant passes in the poley skin. Now he flung it as hard as he could in the opposite direction. With any luck some wild animal would eat them.

The ladder was shaken from below; he clutched the opening to stop himself from falling. It was Etolantie. He glowered at her. 'You're the queen of annoying, Etolantie.'

'I want to see!' she said. A lump of snow fell on to her upturned face, and she spluttered.

'You'll see when we're ready to go,' Solly said shortly, descending again. 'Get your pack. And put some outdoor clothes on. I'll have a look at the snowskates.'

Etolantie pouted.

'Come on, Lalune,' Solly called. 'We've got to get a move on.'

She came out of the bedchamber wearing a red leather top with a knitted jerkin, and leather trousers. She'd also found a silk scarf to tie over her missing eyes.

'There's boots here,' Solly said. 'See if there's any that fit better than those huissier ones. And there's coats and over-trousers; proper leather ones, not that synthetic Appaloosian rubbish.'

He could have kicked himself. Her face looked stricken.

'I'm sorry. I didn't mean that Appaloosians are rubbish,' he said hurriedly.

'That's all right,' she said. But she stood still.

'These snowskates are usable,' Solly said. 'We're going to need them too.'

'Must hurrry,' flapped Sunguide.

'I can't see,' said Lalune. 'It's all gone now. I think the angels have abandoned me.' Solly felt his heart ache with compassion for her. She hadn't added 'because I'm a monster,' but he could tell she was thinking it.

He gently took her hand and sat her down. He found boots to fit, put them on her feet, and helped her into coat and over-trousers. She let him do it, pale and passive.

'Prpr. Is time to say farrrewell,' said Sunguide sadly.

Etolantie hugged the Pruppras.

'You will try an' catch us up, won't you?'

'Thanks for everything,' said Solly.

'Goodbye, Sunguide,' whispered Lalune.

Etolantie climbed up the ladder. Solly passed up her pack and she heaved it through the hatch.

'Use it as a sledge,' said Solly.

'She'll squash the food,' said Lalune.

'Got to get down somehow.'

Lalune was next up. Solly passed up the remaining packs, borrowed from the farm, and then climbed up himself. Sunguide came up too to wave goodbye.

Solly helped Lalune to strap on her borrowed snowskates before copying Etolantie and sliding down the snowy slope on his pack. Lalune attempted to walk down, fell over, and slid anyway.

Once she would have landed laughing, Solly thought miserably, as she got up and brushed herself down without a word.

'Yuck! What's that smell?' Etolantie said, wrinkling her nose.

Solly sniffed and made a face.

'Swag. Must be one in heat nearby.'

'Eeuw!' said Etolantie, and flapped the air in front of her face. 'I didn't know they smelled *that*—'

She was interrupted as Solly abruptly pushed her and Lalune to the ground.

'Ow!' said Etolantie. 'Why did—'

'Shut up!' whispered Solly. 'There's somebody up there.'

Far away to the south of them something glinted. It was a snow skimmer. It was still a long way off, but it was approaching the house at speed. The buzzing he had heard previously was growing steadily louder.

'What is it?' said Etolantie.

'It's a huissier skimmer,' whispered Solly in dread. 'I should have known the sound.'

Sunguide made a squeaking noise of horror.

'How did they get here so quick?' gasped Etolantie.

'Try to slide along the ground to the back of the house,' hissed Solly. 'They may not have seen us. And keep your heads down.'

'I *am*,' whispered Etolantie.

'Hurrry. Prpr. They'll arrrive in ten minutes. Less. Hrumans better get rrrunning. Get to forrrest. Hide. I stay here, find you when rrready.'

'What about our tracks?' said Solly, scrabbling to get his pack on.

'Leave to me. Rrrun!'

As the three of them began towards the trees there was a terrible trumpeting noise. Etolantie stifled a scream.

Lalune was struggling, holding her hands out in front of her, and tripping every few steps. Solly remembered that he hadn't taught her how to use the snowskates.

Etolantie tugged her hand, crying, 'C'mon, Lalune, c'mon!'

'Don't pull her, guide her!' hissed Solly.

Lalune stumbled; Solly seized her elbow.

'Swing your feet round each other,' he puffed.

'Can't,' she gasped. 'Go ahead . . . you hide . . . look after Etolantie . . .'

The trumpet blasted again, and Lalune almost sobbed with despair. They were only halfway to the forest.

'Not . . . leaving you,' Solly huffed, and he half lifted

her up and dragged her the rest of the way.

Etolantie was waiting for them under the first tree.

'Go!' cried Lalune. 'They're . . . just behind us . . . hear trumpets!'

'*That's* not the huissier,' said Etolantie, but she turned anyway, and trotted remarkably calmly into the forest.

Solly risked a look behind him. Something huge and odious was lumbering towards them, lifting its trunk and blasting rudely. It looked like a pile of rotting carpets on legs, and in front of it was fluttering a smaller, far neater pile of orange fungus.

'Sunguide!' In spite of everything Solly laughed. 'It's the swag we smelled! He fetched it to cover our tracks. What a *stink!*'

Even from this distance they could see where the snow had been flattened and yellowed by the passage of the foul creature. It was shambling towards them, swatting futilely at Sunguide.

The undergrowth was too dense to get through it at speed. The swag was crashing through the trees behind them, trumpeting at intervals. Etolantie was still in the lead, and Solly behind. Lalune was concentrating on her snowskates when Etolantie stopped abruptly, and Lalune bumped into her.

'What?'

'Why've we stopped?' said Solly.

'Something in the path,' whispered Etolantie in a terrified voice, and now that they had stopped Solly could hear it: a fierce growl, and a swishing noise, coming from in front of them. Solly pushed the girls aside.

'*Sacry inferno!*'

'What?' said Lalune from behind him.

'Lalune, Etolantie: very quietly step out of the forest,' said Solly, carefully taking his hand-held crossbow out of his bandoleer. He tried to take the solidity of the ground to steady his hands, tried to become one with the trees, as Brise had taught him.

'*What is it?*'

The swag was close behind them; Solly could hear the buzzing of the snow skimmer approaching the forest. And now, cutting off their path, was the fiercest creature he had ever seen.

17

Seachrân screamed in terror, and the children helping him to build the fire joined in with frightened squeals. Adults working nearby hurried to see what the noise was.

'What's wrong?'

'Help! *S . . . S . . . SAVE HER! NO . . . O . . . OH!*'

'Save who?'

'Who is he talking about?'

The bowl Si-Sef had been cleaning dropped to the ground and shattered. Ignoring it, she ran with the rest.

'What is going on?'

'There's t . . . two of them!' shrieked Seachrân. 'L . . . l . . . look out!'

Si-Sef caught hold of his hands and held them firmly. She had seen him like this before.

'Seachrân! Can you hear me?'

He could, but he couldn't centre on her. There was a man approaching, with a gun. He could see Si-Sef, but superimposed over her face was another one: his girl. And she was in danger.

'D . . . don't let it get close!' he cried. He could barely breathe.

'Stand back, everybody,' he heard Si-Sef saying calmly. 'Let him have some air.'

He saw the girl as if from above. Shadowy monsters were in front and behind her. It was *her* fear that made his stomach clench; *her* heart that pumped so rapidly.

He thought he might faint. Si–Sef made him lie down. She knelt next to him and made sure he couldn't bite his tongue or hurt himself.

Near the girl were two people, their faces so bright he couldn't make them out. He thought he'd seen them with the girl before.

Suddenly one of the monsters leaped.

18

The creature was the size of a large dog, snowy-white, with a hard umbrella. It had a short neck and huge teeth. It was growling and oozing saliva.

But most terrifying of all was its tail. It began in the middle of its back; it was at least three times as long as the beast itself; and it ended in dozens of snapping mouths full of wicked fangs, dripping something that burned the ground.

'It's a whippersnapper,' said Solly.

'A whippersnapper?' whispered Lalune.

'Watch that tail: it's poisonous.'

'I can't see,' Lalune said, almost too quiet to hear.

'Don't let it come close!' whimpered Etolantie.

'Move away slowly,' said Solly. He was holding his crossbow towards the creature, but his hand was shaking so much he doubted if he'd be able to hit it. 'Pa told me that when they start running for you they don't stop, even with a spear stuck in their chest. They just run straight up the spear and take your hand off.'

Lalune and Etolantie started to back away into the forest.

'Not that way, its nest is somewhere in there,' said Solly. 'Get out of the forest.'

He could hear the swag crashing about behind them. The snow skimmer was still buzzing around somewhere.

The whippersnapper's growls grew louder, and it started to paw the ground. Suddenly it snarled and crouched down, ready to pounce.

Solly braced himself.

There was an unexpected trumpeting from behind them. The swag had broken through the trees at last. The whippersnapper turned its attention away from the children and opened its mouth in a howl of rage.

'What stop forrr?' yelled Sunguide. He was flitting before it backwards, so hadn't seen the whippersnapper. 'Huissier come!'

'Whippersnapper!' cried Etolantie.

The swag lunged up at Sunguide, snapping furiously.

'*Oooowwww!*' bellowed Sunguide, shooting upwards just in time.

'Run!' shouted Solly, throwing himself sideways just as the whippersnapper leaped forward over their heads and on to the swag.

Lalune and Etolantie scrambled after Solly. They heard the swag screaming in pain as several of the whippersnapper's tail-mouths closed on it.

'*Rrrun!*' cried Sunguide, bouncing ahead of them.

Solly and Etolantie grabbed Lalune's hands. They put their heads down and pounded out of the forest.

The animals made a tremendous noise: the swag was putting up a good fight. The stench from it was even worse than before.

Solly stopped at the edge of the forest, gasping

for breath. He turned to the others, but his weak smile of relief froze.

A snow skimmer was parked next to the trees. A single huissier was leaning nonchalantly against it, seemingly unconcerned by the hullabaloo behind him.

19

'Halig?' Seachrân said. He felt confused.

Si-Sef moved to one side, and he heard somebody take her place.

'I am here, my sweet,' said Halig. She must have heard his screams from all the way up in the tower. 'You had another vision? The same girl?'

Seachrân nodded. Was the girl still alive? He shivered.

Si-Sef motioned for somebody to bring a blanket.

'Tell me, Seachrân: what does it look like where this girl is?' asked Halig.

Seachrân didn't know what she meant. A little boy ran up with a blanket, and Halig tucked it round him.

'Are there trees?' prompted Halig. 'Or grassy fields? Is it hot? Dusty? Near an ocean?'

'No,' said Seachrân, but he didn't elaborate. He fiddled with the fringe on the blanket.

'What, then? Seachrân, I think this girl is something to do with the Key. If you can tell me what it is like, we shall know where to look for the other Holders of the Key.'

'It's c . . . cold,' Seachrân whispered, moving his arms in a wide circle to indicate the whole world. 'Colder than n . . . night. S . . . so cold that the air has f . . . frozen into white blobs th . . . that fall from the sky. Everything is g . . .

grey and cold and hard. I d . . . don't know how anything c . . . can live, it's s . . . so cold. But she does.'

Clandoi was a mercilessly hot planet. The entire Southern Hemisphere was unexplored desert, forever turned towards the uncompromising sun. All known creatures were gathered in the North; most humans populated an enormous crater created by an asteroid centuries ago, or the huge canyons that from space had looked like scars. There was only one place on Clandoi that fitted the description.

They turned their eyes towards the shadow that always crouched on the northern horizon.

'They're *inside* the Ne'Lethe,' Si-Sef whispered.

20

'That wasn't nearly as hard as I'd been led to believe,' the huissier said easily.

At the sound of his voice Lalune thought her heart might stop.

'I thought at least you'd have been skulking in some cave or deep in the forest. I'd hoped for more of a challenge.'

The racket from the forest grew louder. The huissier ignored it.

'Three of you, though,' he said. 'That's two more than they told me. The Appaloosian girl and two unknown Waifs. Old Forcyef, or whatever she calls herself, should be pleased.'

The thrashing of the two beasts was getting closer. Lalune could feel the ground shaking beneath their feet.

'What kind of creature have you stirred up in there?' the huissier said. 'You wouldn't believe some of the things I've seen in this Being-forsaken land. I suppose I'll have to deal with that as well as you. Now then, who's first?'

Lalune heard a clunk as he prepared to shoot.

The swag was screaming, crazed with pain from the whippersnapper's poisoned fangs. The whippersnapper growled fiercely but weakly.

'Lalune, isn't it?' the huissier said nastily. Lalune shoved

Etolantie behind her. 'Odd name for an Appaloosian. You got a personal mention in the dispatch. They would have had somebody here sooner if it hadn't been for that *blizzard*.' He said it as if it was an unfamiliar word. 'Good for them I'd just come through the gateway.'

Solly stepped in front of her.

'How noble of you,' said the huissier. 'I had no idea you Waifs were so brave.'

Lalune's mouth went dry. She heard a tiny noise as the huissier's fingers started to squeeze the trigger on his gun.

But suddenly the swag plunged out of the forest. She heard Sunguide fluttering, teasing it towards the huissier. She smelt blood, and heard the swish and snap of the whippersnapper's tail. The creature bellowed and lurched forward several steps.

'*What on Clandoi . . .!*' gasped the huissier.

'Watch out! Its tail!' yelled Solly.

'It's bit his face!' screamed Etolantie.

The huissier screamed as the fangs clamped sightlessly on to his face. An acrid stink filled the air as the poison burned through his skin. He fell to the ground, blinded and in agony. The dying swag trumpeted for the last time. There was a thunderous shaking of the ground.

And then silence.

21

'Are they dead?' whispered Lalune.

'Yes,' said Solly shakily.

'I think I might be sick,' said Lalune.

'Me too,' said Etolantie. 'It was nearly as revolting as that snowcamel that we saw stuck in the Ne'Lethe.'

Lalune swallowed and put her hand to her mouth.

'Shut up, Etolantie,' said Solly.

'You shut up,' said Etolantie. 'I can see that mountain over there from my house.'

Sunguide buzzed up to have a look.

'I rrrecognize it,' he confirmed after some minutes. 'If you keep mountain always at this angle, you will meet rrroad, I think. About one day's walk for hrumans.'

'What time is it?' said Solly. 'I always could tell from the colour of the Ne'Lethe at home.'

'Prpr. Is still early,' said Sunguide. 'Not even middle of morning. Prpr.'

They had to say goodbye to him all over again. Etolantie cried a little. Sunguide fluttered back to the farmhouse, and though they were in a hurry, they stood and waited until he had disappeared into the trees.

'He's gone,' said Etolantie at last.

'I'm cold,' said Lalune.

'We'd better go,' said Solly with a little sigh, and Lalune wondered if he too felt as if they had been left without direction and without leader.

'Why don't we take the snow skimmer thing?' said Etolantie.

'I was *going* to,' Solly growled and stalked over to the machine.

'Swag face,' said Etolantie.

Lalune reached out and touched her shoulder.

'Don't worry about him. It was good thinking.'

'He's just annoyed cos *he* din't think of it,' Etolantie said.

'Any idea how to start one of these things?' Solly called.

'Is there anything that looks like a little drawer with a button in front?' said Lalune, carefully making her way towards him.

Solly fumbled about, and she heard a click and a hiss as a tiny drawer slid out.

'It needs a pendant pass,' he said. 'I got rid of ours.'

'Get the one off the huissier,' said Etolantie, leaning against Lalune to see inside the skimmer.

Lalune could almost hear him scowl at her, but he went without a word. He was gone for a few minutes, during which Etolantie climbed into the skimmer and Lalune thought she heard Solly retch. His returning footsteps sounded unsteady.

'Eeuw,' said Etolantie. 'You've got blood all over you.'

'I had to . . . to move the body . . .' Solly said. 'His stomach . . .'

Lalune was glad he didn't finish the sentence. He dropped the pendant into the drawer.

Silence. The engine didn't murmur.

79

'Try again,' she said.

'No, still nothing.'

'Kick it,' said Etolantie.

'Did it get damaged by the whippersnapper?' asked Lalune.

'It was nowhere near.'

'I'm sorry,' she said apologetically, as if it was her fault. 'I think it might use voice recognition. We'll have to walk.'

'Could have been worse,' Solly said.

'How?'

'It might have needed a fingerprint,' he said ghoulishly, making a snipping noise with his fingers and thumb.

'Eeuw,' shuddered Etolantie.

Solly tucked his hand under Lalune's elbow and they began to walk up what felt like a gentle hill. Lalune hadn't taken more than two steps in the unwieldy snowskates before she tripped and had to grab Solly to stop herself falling flat on her face.

'There's a technique to them,' said Solly. 'I'll give you a lesson.'

The snowskates were wide and round, designed to spread her weight over a large area, so that they didn't sink into the snow. Hers and Etolantie's, taken from the house they'd stayed in, were made of worn leather stretched over a frame made of bone. They had leather straps that fitted over their boots, and bone spikes underneath to help them grip the snow. The spikes pointed backwards and retracted slightly, so that if they had to go downhill on them they could use them like skis.

'Yours are nicer than mine,' Etolantie said admiringly to Solly.

'Pa made them for my birthday,' said Solly. 'Now, watch me, both of you.'

'I already know how to use 'em,' said Etolantie, and her feet made a steady *swish-thump, swish-thump* away from them.

'See how I swing my feet out wide like this?' said Solly.

'I can't see.'

'Uh . . . sorry . . . you have to make them go in wide semi-circles around each other,' he explained. 'That way your feet don't catch on each other. I'm going to move away from you a little, or we'll trip each other up.'

'Don't leave me.'

'I won't. I'm right here next to you. Hold your hand out, and I'll guide you.'

'It's hard work,' puffed Lalune after a few awkward steps.

'It gets easier,' said Solly. 'Get a rhythm going.'

They made their way slowly up the slope in the direction Etolantie had gone. Lalune started to sweat from the unaccustomed exercise. After a while, though, she started to match her pace to Solly's, and the steady *swing forward, step, swing forward, step* began to feel quite natural, and less tiring.

'Are we near the top?' she puffed after a while, hoping it wasn't going to be uphill all the way.

'Etolantie's just ahead,' said Solly. He didn't sound out of breath at all. 'Then it's down for a bit before the next slope.'

They caught up with Etolantie at the top of the slope. Lalune couldn't bring herself to slide down it without being able to see, so she and Solly carried on walking while Etolantie skied.

They carried on like this for a couple of hours: up a gentle slope, down the other side; up and down; up and down. They had odd gulps of water, but nothing more.

'I'm hungry,' Etolantie announced.

'Is it time for a rest?' Lalune said hopefully.

'It's quite sheltered here at the bottom of the slope,' said Solly. 'Take your packs off: we'll have something to eat. But we mustn't stop for long.'

'There's a funny noise,' said Etolantie, dumping her pack on the ground.

'Don't be silly,' said Solly.

'No, she's right, there is a funny noise,' said Lalune, rolling her aching shoulders. 'A sort of grinding, roaring. It doesn't sound like a skimmer, though.'

It was very quiet still. Solly's hood rustled as he pulled it back to listen.

'I can hear it now. It sounds like an animal.'

'It's over there somewhere,' said Lalune, pointing.

'Is it Sunguide?' said Etolantie.

'I wouldn't have thought he'd catch us up for some time,' said Lalune. 'It could be Aube.'

'Skyboats don't make a noise,' said Solly. 'Besides, it's something on the ground. The snow's being pushed up by something.'

'I see it,' said Etolantie. 'It's like a tunnel growing underneath the snow.'

'What is it?' said Lalune, her hands suddenly sweaty. The others didn't seem frightened though.

'I can see something at this end of it,' said Solly. 'Some kind of jagged curve.'

The noise grew louder.

'It looks like a mouth,' said Etolantie. 'With lots an' lots of teeth.'

'It's a tubal worm,' said Solly suddenly.

'As in tubal worm tracks?' asked Lalune.

'Yes,' said Solly. 'The hunters use the tracks to sledge on. The worm charges through the snow eating up vegetation and rocks and stuff, whatever gets in its way, and leaves a smooth straight track of ice. That's why we make our sledges with those big curves underneath: to fit over the tracks.'

'You go ever so fast on a tubal worm track,' said Etolantie.

Lalune sensed the noise change direction.

'What's happening now?'

'It's just turned a bit,' said Solly. 'It's . . .'

Etolantie screamed.

'What?' cried Lalune.

'Jump!' bawled Solly, grabbing hold of her and throwing them both down the hill they way they'd come. Lalune fell face-first into the snow.

But Etolantie's screams just went on and on; to Lalune, it seemed that the girl wasn't moving at all.

'*Etolantie!*' spluttered Lalune thorough a mouthful of snow. She tried to get up, but fell over her snowskates. 'Solly!' she cried, but all she heard was a muffled cough. He must have landed in a snowdrift too.

She heard the tubal worm thundering closer and closer. She tore off her snowskates, and tried to struggle blindly back up to Etolantie, knowing she wouldn't get there in time.

'Lalune!' Solly gasped indistinctly from somewhere down the hill. 'Etolantie!'

A sudden trumpeting split the air, and the world filled with light: and with the light Lalune's vision returned.

Part of her wished it hadn't.

She saw the long line of ice the worm left in the snow behind it; she saw the way the line led directly towards Etolantie; she saw its pointed teeth bearing down on her mercilessly.

Etolantie held her arms up in the air pathetically. Lalune, all hope gone, struggled forwards, icy tears burning her cheeks.

The teeth of the tubal worm were half a hand's width from Etolantie when the light became painfully bright. There was a loud rushing noise. A glowing, brassy being seized Etolantie's hands and wrenched her upwards, out of the way.

Gulping down their packs, the tubal worm stormed past them, on down the slope.

And the blindness returned, worse than ever.

22

An eager hush progressed through the gathering as Halig made her way to the Speaking Platform. Nobody yet knew why this unexpected feast was being held, but from the nudges and pointed fingers, speculation about Seachrân was widespread.

Seachrân had felt very self-conscious the whole evening. Halig had told him to sit near her, and everybody could see him. Si-Sef was nearby too, eyeing Halig anxiously and looking cross. She always looked cross. Perhaps it was just the way the Being had made her face.

Seachrân didn't know what was expected of him, so he applied himself to his food until Halig told him what to do. Usually the cooks made him eat roast vegetables and rice first; tonight they had let him take whatever he wanted, and his plate was heaped high with mallownuts and toffee sauce. Si-Sef did not look impressed.

Halig reached the Platform and climbed on to it, orange firelight spilling over her face, giving her a fragile look. She held up her hands for quiet.

'My people,' she said. 'People of Kloster. We should begin in prayer.'

There was a rustling noise as everybody put down their plates and knelt, or raised their arms, or simply sat contemplatively. Prayer happened all the time in Kloster.

Seachrân swallowed his mouthful and shut his eyes.

'Great Being,' Halig prayed, 'we have waited for many years for this time. Now it seems that you once again step into the affairs of men . . .'

She spoke for a long time. Seachrân preferred short conversations with the Being. But this was Halig's way.

He tried to attend as best he could, but when his eyes were shut the girl's face appeared to him. She was holding her arms up in the air, her mouth open in a round scream of fear. There was a loud rushing noise and a painfully bright light.

Whoever this girl was, she seemed to attract danger.

At last Halig ended her prayer. There was a distinct letting-go-of-breath from the crowd. Halig's eyes were wet, Seachrân saw, and she leaned heavily on her staff.

'For many years we have been awaiting a sign,' she said, her voice shaky. Seachrân had never seen her get so emotional about anything. 'Sixteen years ago one was sent among us bearing the Key of Being. She died, and her son inherited it. We did not know whether he was one of the three Holders, or would hand it on again.'

Seachrân bit into the crunchy outer skin of a mallownut, and let the sweet curd inside seep into his mouth.

Halig went on.

'My friends: the comet Wanderer has been sighted!'

There was an excited murmur.

'Not only that, but the one who discovered it Saw it before even our dear Kepler Coriolis had observed it through his telescope. You all know Seachrân . . .'

Seachrân swallowed hastily again and grinned sheepishly as he felt many eyes turn to him.

'Chew your food properly, Seachrân,' muttered Si-Sef irritably from next to him. 'You'll end up choking to death in front of everybody.'

'. . . you all know how he came to us, born in the forest, his dying mother's necklace − the Key − clutched in his tiny fist,' Halig continued. 'My people, I name him to you tonight as the one who Saw the Wanderer: Seachrân the Holder of the Key of Being!'

Everybody cheered, and somebody thumped Seachrân vigorously on the back. Halig dabbed her face with her scarf and waited for quiet.

'We belive that one of the other Holders of the Key, maybe both of them, will come to us from beneath the Ne'Lethe. Yes, I know that sounds absurd. It is cold. It is inhospitable. The only people in there were deliberately frozen on the orders of the Imperator's ancestor.

'But Seachrân has for some time now been having visions of a girl, and it has become clear that she is in there, and she is not frozen. Seachrân is the Holder of the Key. This cannot be coincidence.

'All depends on finding these others. This planet is dying. We know from prophecy that soon the Great Migration will begin. The Three Holders will save us from climate disaster, and lead us back to the land of our ancestors. We cannot let the Wanderer pass us by and not use its light. We must keep watch. We must be vigilant. We must be ready for them.'

She paused, her eyes raking the silent throng. Her face was pale, and unusually sweaty. She took a sip of water.

'But now, we must sing.'

There was laughter and more cheers, and Tallis Silchip took out his guitar. Halig moved aside for him, and he began to sing.

> *When the Wanderer you see*
> *Make you ready, for the Key*
> *Calls its Holders, calls all three:*
> *All glory to the Being*

The crowd joined in.

> *All glory to the Being! All glory to the Being!*

Tallis paused for a dramatic hush to fall before singing the second verse.

> *The sunset with its fiery glow,*
> *Moon of blue, oh these we know,*
> *Now the Wanderer green does show!*
> *All glory to the Being!*

> *All glory to the Being! All glory to the Being!*

Halig began to descend the platform steps. Seachrân glimpsed her face, and wondered if she was well. Her jaw looked rigid, as if only willpower kept her mouth smiling.

Nobody else seemed to notice though. Not even Si–Sef. Tallis had begun the third verse of his song.

When the Wanderer does sail
Bringing healing in its tail,
Holders three, you must not fail!
All glory to the Being!

But before the people could join in the chorus there was a crash as Halig fell from the last step.

23

'What happened?' shouted Solly hoarsely, brushing snow from his face as he floundered back to them. 'That thing . . .'

'An angel!' said Lalune, her face shining. 'It was an angel. She's all right.'

'You saw it?'

'My vision came back. For a moment.'

Solly remembered the creature that had saved him from the ravenous Janus tree at the centre of the Great Darkness, waiting for souls to stray anywhere near. He knew about the angel that had guided Lalune when she first came out of the cyberclinic.

Etolantie was running towards them, laughing and crying at the same time. He hadn't seen her being brought back to the ground. There was no sign of the angel any more.

'I'm all right,' she yelled. 'The angel saved me.'

While Lalune held out her arms for Etolantie and the girls hugged each other, recounting what had happened in loud animated voices, Solly looked around him, and his heart sank.

'Did you see it?!' Etolantie yelled excitedly. 'An angel! It pulled me out of the way! I never seen an angel before!'

The tubal worm had ruled a neat line through the place they'd been standing. Their packs were gone. Their food: gone. Their clothes; their tent; their bedding: all gone.

'I saw it, Etolantie! Big and bright and beautiful! Oh, Etolantie, I was so afraid!'

A pitiful few things had miraculously rolled clear: a bag of tent pegs, a small jar of caviar and the storm kettle.

'Did you see its eyes? They was goldy coloured.'

It wasn't enough for them to survive one night.

'I saw, I saw!'

'At least we've got my bandoleer,' Solly said drearily. He never took it off except to sleep.

'Well, that's all right then,' said Lalune, releasing herself from Etolantie. She had seen the angel, but she couldn't see everything that they had lost.

'No,' he said. 'That's *all* we've got. The worm ate everything else.'

'Everything?' Lalune said, touching her scarf-covered eyes nervously.

'It can't of ate *everything*,' said Etolantie.

'Just about,' said Solly, gesturing towards the tubal worm track. 'All the packs. The blankets, tents and spare clothes, and most of our food.'

'Well,' said Lalune uncertainly, 'if you've got the bandoleer still you can hunt, can't you, and light fires? And didn't you put the Janus mirror in there? We can tell Aube to hurry.'

'No,' Solly said. 'I put it in my pack.'

'Oh,' she said. 'What about the Book of the Key?'

'In my pocket,' he said. He wondered why she had

mentioned it. She'd read it, and had been so upset. Maybe she was hoping it had gone.

'We could go back to the house an' fetch more things,' said Etolantie.

'It would take too long,' said Solly. 'There can't be much time left until dark. And besides, the huissier might be there by now.'

'Sunguide will be all right, won't he?' said Etolantie.

'He'll stay still in a corner and they won't even notice him,' Lalune reassured her.

'We should get going again,' said Solly. 'Can you find your house from here, Etolantie? We don't want to miss Aube.'

'I *told* you, I can see them mountains from it,' she said, waving at them. 'So it must be somewhere over there.'

'How far d' you think it is?'

'I spec it's really close,' she said confidently. 'We could be there by tea-time.'

Solly wished he shared her confidence. They wouldn't survive a night in the open.

'Better get going, then,' he said.

'But we haven't had anything to eat,' objected Etolantie.

'There *is* no food,' said Solly. 'Well, a little caviar, but that's all.' He picked up the pot and opened it. 'A *very* little.'

'We should eat,' said Lalune. 'We need the energy to walk.'

Solly doubted it would give them much. There wasn't much more than a couple of mouthfuls each.

'We'll have to scoop it out with our fingers,' he said, offering the jar to Lalune first. They stood up to eat, stamping their feet to keep warm, an icy wind turning their bare fingers blue. Then they melted some water in the storm kettle. They had to take turns drinking, but the lukewarm water did a little to ease the hunger pangs.

Solly led the way in what he hoped was the right direction, instructing Etolantie to walk next to Lalune so that she could guide her around any obstacles. He kept looking around for Aube, but there was no sign of a skyboat anywhere.

Etolantie wasn't very good at leading Lalune, and she kept falling. Solly found a stick for her to wave in front of her, which helped; and she assured him that she was fine. Their progress was slow, though, and by the time they reached the top of the hill his stomach was complaining almost as much as Etolantie.

'I can see it!' cried Etolantie.

'Your house?' Lalune said.

'Yes!'

'Where?' said Solly.

'Look, see the road over there: that's our field, an' that bump there is just behind my house, and there's the scarecrow Pa an' me made.'

'I can't see the road,' Solly said doubtfully. 'Are you *sure*?'

'Ye-e-es,' said Etolantie, rolling her eyes. 'I know where I *live*. Come on!'

She let go of Lalune's arm and raced down the hill. Solly started to stalk off after her, muttering something about spoilt brats.

'Solly?' called Lalune. 'I need some help.'

'Sorry, Lalune,' he said. He ran back to her. 'Sorry. I forgot.'

'How far is it?'

'As far as we've already walked since lunch,' he said. 'But downhill this time.'

'I'm so hungry!' said Lalune.

'We'll find food there,' said Solly. 'Can you go any faster? Etolantie's at the bottom already.'

'I can't,' gasped Lalune. 'Not downhill. I keep thinking I'm going to fall. I'm sorry, it must be really annoying.'

'No, it's fine. Just keep on walking as you are, and I promise we'll eat something soon, even if it's the leather off the chairs!'

This didn't appear to cheer Lalune up much.

At last the ground levelled up, and Solly said, 'We're practically there now. Just a little bit more.'

'He's here!' shouted Etolantie. 'Star!'

Solly's heart lurched.

'Star!' he cried, letting go of Lalune's arm and beginning to run.

Star was still in the field backing on to Etolantie's house. He had grown fat, and his coat was glossy. His tail thumped the ground, and he *huffed* loudly.

Solly flung his arms around him, and his snowcamel licked his face affectionately. The guerdon that had been set to guard him wrapped around Solly's shoulders.

'Oh, Star, I've missed you so much,' Solly said.

He drew in the sweet green scent of snowcamel.

There was another smell too. Fresh and soapy.

He was trying to work out what it was when an icy voice cut the air.

'Well, isn't this a nice surprise!'

24

Solly yelped in fright.

Sybilla Geenpool was standing, hands on hips, next to a snow skimmer. It was her perfume he had smelled.

Pa wouldn't have been surprised. I should have been practising hunting skills more.

She had a look of mingled anger and triumph, which was quickly masked by a frigid smile.

At the sight of her, Star, always uneasy around strangers, started to yowl, '*Hoo-hoo-hoo,*' and Solly patted his trunk reassuringly.

Sybilla looked paler than last time he had seen her: her once golden skin was unhealthy-looking, and her dark eyes had shadows underneath. She was dressed in a black synthetic cloak, and her dark curls had glints of grey at the roots.

And she was wearing a gun in a holster at her waist.

'Solly! You decided to return!' she said, with a brittle smile for him, and a brief glance at Lalune, who was approaching them gingerly, swinging her stick.

Etolantie she ignored.

'Hello, Thybilla!' said Etolantie cheekily.

'Hello, Sybilla,' Solly said, still stroking Star's trunk. Etolantie had undone the long rope they'd used to tether him, and he had the grey, fuzzy rope-like guerdon wrapped around his neck.

'And you must be Lalune, the runaway,' Sybilla said. She held her hand out to Lalune for some reason: Lalune couldn't see it, of course, but Solly and Etolantie both stared at it, puzzled. Sybilla put it down. 'My name is Sybilla Geenpool. I expect Solly has told you about me.'

Lalune fingered her scarf nervously.

'Hello,' she said to a space slightly to the side of Sybilla.

'I was rather surprised when you left so suddenly, Solly,' Sybilla said. She wasn't troubling to hide the gun. 'But I knew you'd return. Belenus Dollysheep told me you had nowhere else to go. Besides, I heard your animal howling in the night, poor thing. I was sure you'd come back for it. I would have offered to look after it for you if you'd asked. Still, you're back now, and with another guest. I'm sure we can begin where we left off. Now, Solly, Lalune, I'm sure you could do with a drink? Something to eat? I think I can squeeze you all into the snow skimmer.'

Her lip curled as she said this, and for the first time her eyes flickered towards Etolantie.

'That would be lovely, thank you,' said Lalune.

'What about my snowcamel?' Solly said.

'Can't you just cut him loose and let him follow?' Sybilla snapped.

'He won't know the way.'

'You'll just have to leave him then,' Sybilla said smoothly, her fingertips almost unconsciously brushing against her gun.

Solly was shocked. *She wouldn't shoot Star? Would she?*

'I'll have to tie him up near fresh food,' he said, his

mouth dry. His heart lurched at the thought of leaving him again, but if she killed him . . .

Lalune plucked Solly's sleeve and murmured, 'What's going on?'

'She's got a gun,' Solly said under his breath.

Lalune paled.

Solly untied Star and led him to the other side of the house, where Etolantie's mother had planted a garden. The huissier had tried to burn it, but new shoots were coming through, and there was plenty for the snowcamel to eat. He tied him to a broken plough.

'Please look after him,' Solly whispered to the guerdon. 'Please.'

Star seemed to sense that he was being left again, and began to howl.

'Hurry up,' Sybilla called impatiently.

'I have to tie him properly,' Solly said, checking the knot. He picked up what had once been a tree branch, and now was just charcoal. He gave Star a last hug; behind the snowcamel, where Sybilla couldn't see, he scratched on the plough. Writing was awkward without a bubblescreen, and he had to be quick, so he just put an arrow, a house shape, and 'L' for Latrium.

'Please understand, Aube,' he muttered.

Then he left Star, and tried not to look back.

'Go and get into the skimmer, then,' Sybilla said. Her voice sounded perfectly pleasant, without a hint of menace. But there was the gun. 'The sooner we get back to my house, the sooner we can eat.'

Solly took Lalune's arm and led her to the skimmer. He wondered if it would do any good if he grabbed the controls somehow when they were in the air.

He started to help Lalune into the back when Sybilla said, 'The blind girl had better go in the front with me. She'll be more comfortable there.'

Solly swallowed. *Can she read my mind? I can't do anything from the back.* Sybilla closed the door after them. She opened a small drawer in the control panel and dropped a round blue key into it.

'Latrium,' she spoke into a microphone. The snow skimmer growled into life and sped away.

25

'Let me get to her,' said Si-Sef, pushing everybody aside, tying back the greying curls from her striped face as she turned from partygoer to professional in three strides. Frightened, Seachrân knelt next to her.

Halig was never ill. She was supposed to help others, not need help herself. She was a rock of stability in Kloster Hallow. What would he do if he lost her? What would any of them do?

Si-Sef squeezed Halig's wrist and looked in her mouth. She pulled back her eyelids, keeping up a constant stream of muttering as she worked.

'Come on Halig, you can fight this. I *told* you this would happen. You should never have made such a long journey, being so ill. Come on, woman, show me you're still with us. All that visiting the sick, looking after those children, it's a wonder you didn't fall ill years ago. You knew you were too weak to go.'

Seachrân swallowed. 'Sh . . . she said she'd b . . . been ill. I th . . . thought she meant j . . . just a little bit ill.'

'She's been sick for months now,' Si-Sef said. 'She should have been resting, but she worried about you. Worried about everybody, didn't you, Halig?'

Halig's eyelids opened a little. She looked dazed.

'That's right, woman, you *should* be feeling guilty,' Si-Sef went on fiercely, though she stroked Halig's face gently enough. 'Worrying's bad enough, but travelling to the city? Made you ten times worse. I'm sending you straight to the hospital tent for a week. No arguing now. You and you!' She jabbed a finger at the crowd. 'Go and get a stretcher. *Now!*'

Halig closed her eyes again. Seachrân couldn't believe how ill she looked. Her dark skin had lost its glossiness, and her lips were purplish blue. And he noticed for the first time that she had lost weight. How had he not seen it before?

'What's wrong with her?' said Kepler Coriolis.

'Same as what's wrong with all the sick on Clandoi,' Si-Sef said, lifting Halig's head up to put a folded shawl under it. 'Tree sickness.'

Several people gasped in shock at this.

'Tree sickness?' said Seachrân falteringly. The Imperator had tree sickness. The cook, Ninurtus Worldweb, had said that he was going to die of it.

'Yes, this sacry tree sickness!' snapped Si-Sef. 'This wasting illness; this curse with no cause.'

'Most of the visits she made were to people with the disease,' said Kepler. 'She's not indestructible, whatever she may have thought.'

'How can it have no cause?' said Seachrân.

'Well, obviously it *has* a cause,' said Si-Sef. 'Where is that stretcher? We just don't know what it is, or how it's passed from person to person. We only know that more and more are succumbing all the time, turning up here with wasted muscles and failing organs; and that we have no idea how

100

to cure it. Halig acted like she thought she was immune, *damny* woman.'

She wiped her eyes with the back of her hand.

'Why is it called tree sickness?' said Seachrân.

Kepler snorted.

'Some stupid belief that humankind has been cursed by the trees,' he said.

The stretcher arrived.

'*If* and *when* it is proved otherwise, it's as good a theory as any,' said Si-Sef, standing back to let the men get to Halig. 'We know that whenever a tree became diseased, they would recover when a human became ill and died.'

'I didn't even know she was ill,' said Kepler. 'She didn't tell me.'

'She played it down,' Si-Sef said. 'Pretended it was a seasonal cold. I guessed it was tree sickness because I've seen the early symptoms so often. Now, I need to go and make sure she's comfortable. You can all stay here. I can do without hordes of people getting in the way.'

Seachrân's face must have looked as forlorn as he felt, as she added, 'You may visit in the morning, Seachrân. She'll probably be awake then, and the company *might* make her stay in bed.'

26

As Solly led her into the house at Latrium, Lalune was startled to hear her boots ringing hollowly on a wooden floor. She had never walked on wood in her life. She paused doubtfully. The Wayfarer houses she'd been in had stone floors; her own house was tiled. Wood was far to precious to walk on, certainly in boots. She took them off.

'Go on in and sit down,' Sybilla said, taking her coat from her as if they'd come to a dinner party. 'Make yourselves at home.'

This is surreal, Lalune thought. *She seems so pleasant. I can hardly believe she's really holding a gun on us. But Etolantie would never be this quiet if she wasn't.*

Still feeling intimidated by the floor, Lalune felt her way through an inner door into the warm main room. She still had the stick, and when none of the others showed her the way she waved it until it bumped against something soft, which she thought might be an armchair. It smelled new, and was made of some woven fabric. She sat down on it cautiously.

'Good,' said Sybilla. 'Now, I shall get you something to eat.'

She moved away from them, and Lalune heard the clattering of crockery at the other end of the room.

Etolantie whispered, 'Did you see what she done with the old stuff from the house?'

'What?' said Lalune.

'Huge pile of rubbish outside the house,' Solly said briefly. 'She's thrown it all away, put all new stuff in.'

'*An*' all the mubbles in the lake are dead,' Etolantie added. Lalune could hear the pain in her voice. This had been the home of her friends, after all. 'An' look at the floor!'

'Is it wooden?' said Lalune. 'It sounds like wood.'

'Yes,' Etolantie said. 'It's all gold–coloured an' patterned like water. It used to be stone when this was Rayon's and Nuit's an' Tornesol's house. An' the walls are all mirrors now, an' there's glass things everywhere, not doing anything, jus' to look at.'

Lalune heard Sybilla's returning footsteps.

'Now, I have bread and soup warming up. No spices this time.'

'That's very kind of you,' Lalune said politely. The mention of soup made her feel even hungrier than before, though she heard Etolantie very faintly making a noise of disgust behind her.

'Why did Dr Dollysheep thay we had to come back here?' Etolantie asked.

Solly had to repeat her question before Sybilla answered. Lalune couldn't imagine why Etolantie was lisping, or why Sybilla was ignoring her.

'To get you out of the mess you've got yourselves in, of course,' Sybilla said impatiently. 'Belenus Dollysheep always did have a weakness for Waifs. Though you will stay here for a while first.'

103

'Why?' demanded Etolantie, dropping something that sounded like a wooden bowl with a clatter.

'Leave that alone, please,' Sybilla snapped. 'I'm not going to give you another chance to steal my things.'

Lalune's heart nearly stopped, thinking she meant the Key. But then Sybilla added, 'I hope you've brought that dolly back. It's an antique.'

Lalune knew this wasn't true. Etolantie and her ma had made it for Rayon, the little girl who'd once lived here.

Etolantie said, in a *very* meek voice, 'I'm thorry, Thybilla. Tholly thaid I had to bring it back, only it fell out of the thkyboat into the thnow, an' I couldn't find it. *Pleathe* tell uth why we have to thtay.'

Sybilla snorted.

'I'm following orders.'

'Whose orders?' asked Solly. 'Who gave them to you?'

'Ha!' said Sybilla resentfully. 'You may well ask. I was sent to be the gatekeeper. Latrium has been the gateway for centuries. Though it hasn't been used for a while. The people living here always used to be gatekeepers, but of course they'd forgotten. Now that the work has begun again somebody who understood had to take over again, and . . . well, somebody had to be sent.'

She sounded angry as she said this, and Lalune wondered if she'd been sent – whatever that meant – as some kind of punishment. The smell of soup began to drift through the house, and her stomach clenched in hunger.

'Somebody who understood what?' Solly asked but Sybilla ignored him.

'How could it've been a gateway an' Tornethol an'

Nuit an' Rayon din't notithe people coming through?' said Etolantie.

'I'm afraid I don't have any idea who you're talking about.'

'They wath the people who uthed to live here. My friendth.'

'Oh, them,' said Sybilla dismissively. 'There hadn't been much call for traffic for a while. And when there was, it would have come through another gateway by the barn. There was an earthquake that brought some of the roof down. That's why we had to remove your friends and have a new passage built, where the original road had been three hundred years ago. I had them install the bathchamber at the same time. You Wayfarers might be used to squalor, but I certainly am not.'

Etolantie gave a choking cry of rage and Lalune felt for her hand to try to calm her down. Sybilla carried on speaking as if nothing had happened.

'Now, I expect that food will be ready by now. Please come and sit at the table to eat, and then I will show you your rooms.'

27

The table was wooden as well, but with no covering.

The soup was delicious. Solly cut some bread for Lalune, and for a few minutes they ate in silence. Etolantie gobbled hers down noisily as if she didn't know when she was going to eat again.

At least that's one problem solved, thought Solly gloomily. *I wish I knew why Sybilla wants to delay us, though.*

After the soup Sybilla brought them salty biscuits, some tangy stuff she called *cheese*, and sweet pastries.

'Thethe are almotht ath nithe ath toffee,' Etolantie said with her mouth full. 'Can I have another?'

· 'I'm so glad you like them,' Sybilla said dryly. 'Please, help yourself.'

When they had finished Sybilla stood up.

'And now I will show you your rooms. You are to stay here for three nights, and then I shall take you—'

'*Who* thayth we have to thtay?' said Etolantie.

'Dr Dollysheep said you'd know somewhere we could go where Forcyef would never find us,' Solly said. 'Does he give you the orders?'

Sybilla's eyes flashed angrily, but she didn't answer.

'If you've got somewhere safe for us, as he said, we really *would* rather go sooner,' Lalune said, fiddling with her scarf.

'We've already had one huissier nearly catch us.'

'Oh, he did catch up with you, then,' said Sybilla in surprise. 'When you turned up here I thought he must have missed you.'

'You thent him!' Etolantie said accusingly.

'No. But he did come through here.'

'You *thent* him!'

'He came through *here*?' said Solly.

'Of course,' said Sybilla. 'This *is* the gateway.'

'She thent him to get uth.'

'No I didn't. He had orders too.'

'Then there could be more of them,' Solly said, scraping back his chair in alarm. 'We *must* go. As soon as we can.'

'No,' said Sybilla quickly. 'You'll be perfectly safe here.'

'He tried to kill us,' Lalune said. 'He *would* have killed us.'

Sybilla's demeanour changed abruptly.

'Ah, well, if you must go, you must,' she said, her shoulders sagging. She suddenly looked a lot older, and pathetically vulnerable. 'It would have been such fun to have cooked properly for once, and had friends to eat with. I used to live at the Palace you know, with hundreds of others around me all the time. Life can get very lonely here on my own. But I completely understand, if you can't spare the time even for a drink of mulled mallownut wine.'

'Of course we could spare a few minutes for a drink, thank you Sybilla,' Lalune said, and Solly silently cursed Appaloosian etiquette. Even if Sybilla hadn't sent the huissier – and he couldn't be sure about that – where one was, another was bound to come.

'We need to go,' he said.

'We're very tired, Solly,' Lalune said. 'A few minutes won't make much difference, will they?'

'I suppose not,' Solly said reluctantly. Next to him Etolantie sniffed, and got up again to prowl around the room.

'Splendid!' said Sybilla, pitifully grateful.

Maybe she really is just a sad, lonely old woman? thought Solly. *Though I doubt it. She made me leave Star.*

Sybilla opened the oven door and dug a poker into the heart of the flames. 'Most people just heat it over the stove these days, but I think plunging a red-hot poker in it gives it a special flavour all of its own, don't you?' she said, taking a jug of milky liquid out of a cupboard.

'I've never had mallownut wine before,' said Lalune.

Solly had never even heard of it.

Sybilla turned away from them to fit four tall glasses into silver holders.

'It's a children's drink, really. Hardly any alcohol in it at all, very rich and sweet. You needn't worry about the little girl being too young. She seems to be fond of sugary things: I think she'll rather like it.'

Etolantie made a noise that Solly interpreted as suppressed outrage. He could see her narrowed eyes following Sybilla's movements through one of the many mirrors on the walls, and tried not to grin. She only needed to contain her temper until they were out of here, and that wouldn't be long now.

Sybilla took the poker out of the oven and quenched it into the jug of liquid. There was a delicious seething of steam, and a wonderful honeyed aroma filled the room. When the hissing died down she poured the frothy, steaming drink into the glasses, and put three of them on to a silver tray to carry over to them.

There was a sudden crash and a shriek, and Solly nearly leapt out of his skin.

Etolantie had knocked over a tall shelf of ornaments. She stood in a pool of glass fragments looking subdued.

'Etolantie!' shouted Solly.

'You stupid child!' spat Sybilla, any trace of benevolence evaporated. 'Some of those are extremely valuable!'

Solly got up to help Sybilla pick up the pieces, and Etolantie sidled away quickly in case Sybilla decided to smack her.

'I think you'd better say sorry,' Lalune told Etolantie, wringing her hands. 'And go and help.'

'*No!*' Sybilla almost shouted. 'Stay away.'

'Thorry,' said Etolantie meekly.

When the mess was cleared up Sybilla gave Solly and Lalune their drinks from the tray and picked up her own without bothering to serve Etolantie. She took a long gulp as if trying to calm herself down. Lalune put hers on the floor to cool a little.

Solly sipped at his cautiously at first and almost gasped at the sensation that filled him from head to toe. He had never tasted a drink like it, not even the time he and Lalune had stolen some watered-down mead wine and drunk it together behind the snowcamel barn. He licked the frothy moustache from his lip contentedly. The warmth of it dispersed quickly through his body, energizing and relaxing at the same time.

'May I have mine, pleathe?' said Etolantie, looking suitably downcast.

'All right,' said Sybilla coldly. 'Not that you deserve it.'

'I'm sure Etolantie didn't mean it, Sybilla,' said Lalune.

'All the same, she should be more careful,' said Sybilla.

'That is so good,' Solly murmured comfortably. His limbs began to feel heavy, not uncomfortably so, but the kind of feeling you get as you fall asleep in a warm bed after a day in the open air. Perhaps they would stay after all. Just for one night. He lifted his glass again, and was surprised to find that it was already empty.

'She will be *very* careful from now on,' said Lalune in a severe voice. 'Won't you Etolantie?'

'Yeth, Lalune,' said Etolantie demurely.

Since Sybilla hadn't made a move to fetch Etolantie's drink the girl got up to fetch it herself; but somehow she managed to trip over, spilling Lalune's untouched drink over Lalune's feet.

'Ouch, Etolantie!' cried Lalune, aghast. 'What on Clandoi's got into you?'

Through half-closed eyelids Solly watched Etolantie slowly picking herself up. When she spoke her voice came from a long way away.

'Nothing like what's got into them.'

The last thing he saw was Sybilla slumping over in her chair. Then everything went blank.

28

'What've you done?' Sybilla slurred. '. . . dare you . . . come intomy . . .'

Then her glass fell to the floor and shattered.

Lalune's mouth hung open.

'Solly?' she said waveringly.

He answered with a snore.

'Solly!' she said more loudly, feeling her way to him. She found his wrist and was relieved to feel a steady though slow pulse.

'He'll be all right,' said Etolantie cheerfully. 'She din't want us *dead*, after all. She jus' din't want us to go *yet*.'

'How did you know?' said Lalune in amazement, making her way to Sybilla and checking her as well.

'Saw her in the mirror,' said Etolantie smugly. 'She put summink in *our* glasses but not in hers.'

Lalune began to laugh shakily.

'So you tipped the cupboard over and swapped them when she wasn't looking.'

'An' knocked yours over too, but Solly's such a greedy swag he'd already finished his. Want to try some of this one? It should be all right.'

'I'd rather not,' said Lalune. 'Just in case.'

'I've never had mallownut wine,' said Etolantie

regretfully, but she put the glass down.

'What do we do now?' said Lalune, crawling back to Solly and rubbing his hands in a vague belief that it would wake him up.

'Go through the tunnel of course,' said Etolantie. 'That's where she was going to take us.'

'The tunnel?'

'Into the Beyond,' Etolantie said with highly exaggerated patience. 'Solly found it last time. It's through there. Oh, I forgot, you can't see. The bathchamber. There's a sort of stairway, an' at the bottom there's a door an' a tunnel.'

'What about Solly? We can't carry him. We need a sledge, or a set of wheels, or *something*.'

'The baby cart!' exclaimed Etolantie.

'The what?'

'When Solly found me in my house he put my stuff in my brother's baby cart,' said Etolantie, dancing around the room in excitement. 'He made me go in it too, but only 'cos I hadn't eaten for ever so long. Soon as I could I walked, like him. We left it here. I bet it's still here. I bet it's in that pile of Rayon an' Tornesol an' Nuit's stuff that she's thrown away outside. I—'

She was interrupted by a thunderous knocking on the door. Lalune's stomach lurched.

'Huissier!' squeaked Etolantie in terror. She tiptoed to the window and drew back the curtain with a rustle.

'It's Aube!' she cried in relief. 'An' he's got Star with him!'

Lalune took a deep shaky breath.

Etolantie opened the door.

'Oh, Aube! You're here! We thought you was a huissier! We nearly got caught by one, only a whippersnapper ate him. We've drugged Sybilla, only Solly's asleep too, an' we've got to find the baby cart to put him on, an' go into the Beyond—'

'Slow down, slow down,' Aube said with a chuckle. 'It's good to make your acquintance after all this time, but these old ears work slowly, hmm. Let me shut the door and sit down, and then you can tell me. There, Star, you stay outside for the present. And good to meet you too, moon-girl, hmm. Well, well.'

Lalune heard the sound of a walking cane tapping towards her.

'How is your leg?'

'Better than it was, much better, thank you,' Aube said as he cased himself heavily into a chair. 'The Pruppras devised a most interesting splint for it, of woven wood fibres and fungus. Now there's the thing. A sort of living splint, as it were. Still wearing it, but I have to walk on it now, build up the strength, you know. Now, tell me your adventures. I tried to call you up on the Janus mirror, but you didn't reply.'

'It got ate by a tubal worm,' Etolantie said breathlessly, prancing around the room again.

'Whippersnappers *and* tubal worms?' Aube exclaimed. 'My, my, you have had a time, hmm?'

'How did you find us?' said Etolantie.

'Somebody left me a message at your house,' Aube said. 'Scratched on the plough where you'd left Star.'

'Must of been Solly: he tied Star up,' said Etolantie. 'Sybilla made us leave him. She had a *gun*, an' she—'

113

'Please,' Lalune interrupted, wringing her hands, 'we haven't time to talk. We have no idea how long Sybilla will sleep for. We have to go. And we need food, blankets . . . I don't want to steal, but we have no choice—'

'Certainly, certainly,' said Aube, patting her arm. 'What can I do?'

'The tubal worm ate almost everything,' she said. 'I don't know what we need. I just don't know, Aube . . .'

She ended with a sob.

'Etolantie and I will find a bag and fill it,' Aube said gently. 'You can sit there and calm down, my dear, and put Solly's boots on him. Do we know where we're going?'

'Down there,' said Etolantie. 'There's a tunnel. It goes through the Ne'Lethe. That's what Sybilla said, anyway. How are we going to get Star down?'

Lalune let Etolantie's chatter wash over her head, and laid her head down. She was so thankful that Aube was there, but she couldn't help wondering how he could so accepting of a monster like her.

At last they were ready to go. The front door was large enough for Star to squeeze through with a little persuasion, but getting him down into the bathchamber was nearly impossible.

First they bumped Solly down on the baby cart. Star howled miserably at yet another separation, but stubbornly refused to follow him down the narrow staircase. His ears flattened, and his nostrils flared at the sulphurous fumes.

'Come *on*, Star,' said Etolantie, pulling his rope.

'Solly's at the bottom,' said Lalune. 'You don't want him to leave you again, do you?'

'Come down, there's a good boy,' said Aube.

'Oh, *no*!' giggled Etolantie.

'What's he doing?' said Lalune.

'Trying to back out again,' said Etolantie. '*No*, Star, you only just got through the first time.'

'Now then,' Aube said. 'A little psychology should do it. This rope's long enough, I should think. Push Solly out of the way a little, Lalune. Take him out of sight.'

'*Hoo-hoo-hoo*,' yowled the poor snowcamel.

'Now, Etolantie, you go too.'

'Bye-bye, Star,' she said, and trotted out to join Lalune.

Aube followed with the rope, ushering the girls along the passage.

Star gave a howl of distress and almost tumbled down the stairs after them.

'Oh, no,' said Etolantie. 'He's stuck in the door . . . oh, look!'

A great wrenching sound echoed down the tunnel.

'Silly old Star,' said Etolantie affectionately.

'He's brought the doorframe with him!' said Aube.

Lalune rubbed her empty eye sockets in disbelief. Here, in the tunnel, she could see. Just a little.

They appeared to be inside a white tubular structure. There were no shadows. Purplish patches of mist washed through them as if they weren't there. Far, far away in the distance something dark sparkled. It was slightly warm in the passageway, and there was a strange feel to the air, as if the air they were walking through was solid, not gas. A low humming noise was coming from somewhere ahead.

Etolantie tried to push Solly.

'He's heavy,' she huffed, ''cos he's such a greedy swag.'

She moved jerkily, her voice and mouth unsynchronized.

Lalune took the baby cart from her and stroked Solly's forehead. How long would he sleep? What would she do if he never woke up?

She shook herself.

'Come on,' she said. 'Let's go.'

It was the strangest journey she'd ever taken.

29

There was only one way to go: towards that dim light that could be an hour away, could be a day away. Etolantie went first, leading Star. The tunnel was just big enough for the snowcamel, with not a finger's width spare. Lalune pushed Solly, who never stirred. Her feet sometimes hit the ground before she thought they were going to and sometimes after. Aube walked behind Lalune.

They never found out how long it took. Time was an ocean, with tides that raced in to overwhelm them and then dragged them backwards again; waves that broke over them and receded. Sometimes their steps were so fast that they were covering a day's walk in a second; at other times it seemed as if a single stride took an hour.

They were detached from themselves, viewing their bodies from outside, from above, meeting themselves coming in the opposite direction. They thought that they were travelling in silence, but afterwards remembered long conversations.

The walls of the tunnel were smooth and rough. The floor was uneven and flat. Lalune's eyes were blank, but her vision was perfect. It was dark, but they could see for miles. They could see nothing, but it was as bright as day.

They didn't feel like eating, but whenever they felt thirsty they found little basins set into the walls, with a constant trickle of water running into them. Or perhaps they saw the basins and

117

then felt thirsty. The water was cold and refreshing, with the same smell as the water in Sybilla's bathchamber. It was yellow and cloudy.

Sometimes they dreamed somebody else's dreams, talking out loud, their eyes open but seeing somewhere else.

30

Seachrân was ill. They brought him into where Halig was resting in the hospital tent.

'Probably just a virus somebody brought with them,' Halig said weakly, though it didn't seem like an ordinary illness. 'But not the tree sickness, thank the Being.'

His mind was filled with visions: not clear events, but impressions that made him shake and moan. Even if he'd had the ability to speak clearly, there was no way to describe the strange hallucinations that filled his head, his soul, his whole being.

He felt as if waves of time were constantly breaking over him and receding. People walking past him so fast that they were gone in a flash, then took an hour to make a single stride.

He felt detached from himself, viewing the camp from above. His conversations with Halig and with the other children sounded muffled in his mind, as if they were in a different room.

'He w . . . will be taken,' he moaned, though he wasn't sure who 'he' was: he saw uniforms, a flash of weapons.

'Hush, my sweet.'

His bed was soft and hard. The floor was uneven and flat. It was too dark, but the light hurt his eyes.

He was terribly thirsty, and whenever he was, somebody would bring him water before he asked for it. Or perhaps he saw them coming and then felt thirsty. The water was cold and refreshing. It was yellow and cloudy. How could he tell that in the pitch blackness? But it wasn't dark: it was the middle of the day.

He held his mother's necklace tightly clenched in his hand, and it strengthened him. His thoughts were drawn to the Ne'Lethe, though Halig wouldn't let him out of bed to see it. The comet troubled him too, giving him a sense of deep unease, as if it heralded dark happenings.

31

The only part of the journey any of them remembered clearly happened in the middle of the tunnel. There was a bright light somewhere round a bend. The humming was louder. The ground beneath them was strewn with rocks, to Lalune's non-eyes looking as if they floated just above the ground; and the baby cart tipped over. They had to stop to tie Solly on to it, and perhaps this interruption made it easier later to recall.

They came to a large pile of rubble, big enough to fill the tunnel to halfway up. They could hear trickling water.

'Now what?' said Etolantie. 'We'll never get Solly over this. It must of been that earthquake Sybilla told us about. We'll be stuck here forever an' ever. D'you think more rocks'll come down?'

'I don't *want* to think about it,' said Lalune. She had to climb with care, as somewhat disturbingly the rocks gave the illusion of movement as she put her hands on them.

'Will Star fit?' said Aube.

'I think so. It looks like these rocks were once the roof, so there's enough room.'

Lalune clambered cautiously down the other side. There was an alarmingly unstable-looking piece of rock hanging down from the hole, big enough to crush them all if it fell. To her it looked as if it wasn't attached to the roof, but logic told her that it must be. There were jagged cracks down the walls, and a rivulet of water had eaten a course across the tunnel, to disappear into a fracture on the other side.

'If we try an' move the rocks it'll take days an' days,' called Etolantie cheerfully.

'Don't touch anything yet,' said Lalune.

'No, indeed,' Aube agreed. 'We don't want to make things worse.'

Their voices boomed and echoed down the passage.

There was something glinting under the rubble. Lalune bent down to look. It looked like some kind of fabric; leather perhaps, decorated with metal disks, tarnished with age. It was trapped under the biggest piece of rock.

'I found something. A boot, I think. There must have been people here when this happened. It's, oh . . .'

'What?'

'Nothing, just a boot,' said Lalune. Her fingers had found what was unmistakably a bone, sawn off to free the owner.

Etolantie shouldn't see this, she thought.

She saw a flat stone that wasn't supporting anything, and lifted it to put over the amputated foot. Underneath it she made another discovery.

'Can one of you come here?'

Etolantie scrambled over the rocks, causing a small avalanche.

'Careful, young lady,' said Aube.

'Look at that,' said Lalune, pointing. 'I think it might be

122

a shield. Could you help me dig it out? We might be able to use it as a sort of sledge, to drag Solly over.'

'Why'd they leave it here?' said Etolantie, brushing aside the stones from the shield energetically. It looked ornamental rather than functional, with loops and curls of silver decorating the front. A chain of some heavy dark metal was still intact, attaching a dagger in a sheath, but the dagger was too rusty to be of any use.

'I expect they were more concerned to get out of the tunnel if there was an earthquake.'

They cleared most of it quite easily, but a large heavy rock weighed down the last bit, and they couldn't shift it.

'I bet Star could pull it out,' said Etolantie.

'Good idea. You stay here, I'll go and lead him over.'

Lalune struggled back over the rocks to where Star was stamping his feet impatiently.

'Come on, Star, over the rocks.'

He put his ears back, and at first she was afraid that he was going to refuse; but suddenly he bent his knees and galloped past her, dragging the halter out of her hands, and slithering down the other side in a heap of stones. Dust flew up into the air, and there was a shudder from the roof above.

Lalune sneezed.

'Everything all right over there?' asked Aube.

'There was a noise from the roof.'

'So I heard.'

Without waiting for the air to clear, Lalune carried their bag awkwardly over the rock pile. Star was prancing a little way down the tunnel, frightened by the noise.

'Here's the rope,' coughed Lalune. It was the one Solly

had used to tether him when the snowcamel had been left at Etolantie's house, and was very long. 'Catch Star, tie it on to him.'

Lalune tied the other end on to the shield's chain and tugged to make sure it was firm. Etolantie slapped Star's rump, and he hauled, and with a clatter the shield tore free.

Several small stones fell down from the roof, and the hanging rock shuddered.

'Hmm. I think the quicker we do this the better, my dear,' Aube called.

Lalune dragged the shield to the other side of the pile of rocks, still tied to Star. Aube helped her to lift Solly on to it. His feet dragged on the floor.

'Can you get the baby cart over?' Lalune asked Aube, with a worried glance at the roof. More dust was falling from above.

'Hmm. I shall try, m'dear.'

'Get Star to pull Solly, and I'll guide him at this end,' shouted Lalune when Aube was over.

They had reached the top and were just about to slide down the other side when there was a deafening rumble from above.

'Pull!' screamed Lalune.

'I can't,' cried Etolantie. 'The rope's got stuck.'

It was caught under a rock. Lalune scrambled down to free it.

'Pull!'

Star hauled.

The rope came undone.

'Damny thing!' sobbed Lalune.

A trickle of powder turned into a torrent of small

stones. Lalune yanked at the front of the shield, and together she and Solly tumbled down the slope. Large rocks bounced around them.

'*Run, Lalune, run!*'

With a strength she didn't know she had, Lalune lugged Solly, now slipping off the shield, dragging him just a second in front of a billowing red cloud spiked wickedly with rocks. The ceiling above them began to crack. The hanging rock groaned. Lalune heard Etolantie shriek, heard Star howl, felt the thunder of falling rocks all around them.

Etolantie's hands reached out and pulled her sideways. Dust surged past them, ahead of them, but somehow they were safe.

For a few minutes the sound of falling rocks continued to deafen them, and the air thickened. It became difficult to breathe.

At last the noise stopped.

Dust still swirled about them. They were covered from head to foot in it. Their hair was red, their faces, clothes, hands and boots: all were enveloped in the stuff. Great circles of white showed where they had screwed their eyes tight shut.

Star was huddled shivering against a wall.

Etolantie was the first to speak.

'Did you see, there was somebody's foot still in that boot?'

They began to giggle, and soon they were rolling about, unable to stop laughing.

32

They had come down one leg of a forked junction. Etolantie had pulled them back into the other leg.

There was a great chasm above them. Light was pouring down it, cloudy and red at the moment from the dust, yet still enough to hurt. Really hurt. Lalune's non-eyes felt terribly sore, and now she couldn't see anything at all.

The humming they'd heard previously was much louder here too: part of the light, as thunder is a part of lightning.

'What is it?' said Etolantie.

'Maybe it marks the middle?' said Aube. 'Or some kind of power source?'

'To power what?' said Lalune, rubbing her eye sockets.

'I spec it's why you can see in here,' said Etolantie.

'I hope not,' said Lalune. 'I won't be able to see when we get out if it is.'

They brushed themselves down as best they could, shaking the dirt from their hair and brushing it off their clothes. Star stamped his feet, sending red spirals of dust up around them. They had a drink of water from one of the nearby basins, lifted Solly back into the baby cart, and carried on walking.

Now they were on their way again, time began to ebb and flow strangely once more. They didn't feel tired or hungry. They trudged on and on. When the light pouring down from the chasm was far behind them they found a switch for the electric lights, and turned them on. They weren't generously spaced, and before they'd walked past two more they turned off again. After a while there was another switch for the next three lights, and they also turned off too soon.

Lalune rubbed at her blank eyes. Her vision was no longer returning when it was dark. Etolantie must be right – there must have been some kind of power source that had made her see again for a while.

I don't want to be blind, she thought. *Why has the Being allowed it? Perhaps it's because of what I am. Because I don't have a soul. Why did he allow me to see at first?*

They had been going for a day or an hour when they felt thirsty and stopped for a drink.

'I think Solly's waking up,' said Etolantie.

'Solly?' said Lalune.

Star licked Solly's dusty face, and spat in disgust. Solly flickered his eyes open briefly.

'Hello, Lalune. We're coming to save you now,' he murmured.

'Ha!' snorted Etolantie. '*Him* save us?'

'He did once,' Lalune pointed out. 'You *and* me. I don't think he's quite with it yet, though.'

They walked on. After a while Lalune felt Solly take her hand.

'What happened to your hair . . . clothes . . . everything?' he said in amazement, struggling to get out of the baby cart. 'And mine? And how did I get here? And Star! I thought I'd lost you!'

His voice was slurred.

'Hello, Solly,' said Etolantie. 'I'm here too. And Aube.'

'There was a cave-in,' said Lalune. 'Do you want a drink?'

They stopped and drank from one of the basins. Lalune gave Solly a brief outline of what had happened.

'Well, I suppose I should thank you then, Etolantie,' he said, still dazed.

'That would be nice.'

'I feel like I've been asleep for a week,' he groaned. 'What was *in* that stuff? I've got a headache worse than when I had concussion. And, *ow*, bruises everywhere. Bruises on my bruises. How much further d'you think it is? How long have we been in here?'

'Difficult to say,' said Aube. 'I'm not sure time's exactly the same here.'

'Sybilla will be awake too,' Etolantie said, and Lalune's stomach churned.

'I hope she's got a headache like this as well,' said Solly.

'We've got no time to lose,' said Lalune. 'She might come after us. Or contact somebody on the other side. We have to keep going.'

'We can't,' said Etolantie.

'Why not?' said Lalune.

'There's a wall in the way.'

'Now what?' said Solly.

'I would imagine that we go upwards,' said Aube. 'Look at that. A lift, perhaps?'

'There's a lever here in the wall,' said Solly. His voice receded as he walked away from them. He grunted with effort; there was a grating noise, a rush of air, and a clang as the lift landed heavily. A door screeched open, and they entered.

Lalune could tell immediately that they were in a far smaller area. Echoes she hadn't even registered suddenly ceased. They were standing a lot closer together, as if there wasn't quite enough room. With Star, there probably wasn't.

She reached out and found a hand close by. Solly's.

'This is it, then,' said Aube. 'The Beyond. Now there's the thing. Never in my life did I think I would be seeing it with my own eyes.'

'I wonder what it'll be like?' said Etolantie. 'The sun an' the moons an' the stars an' the sky an' everything.'

The lift rose slowly and noisily on un-oiled cables.

'I seen pictures of stars,' said Etolantie. 'They had five points. An' the moons had faces, the Blue Moon had a happy face an' the Bane Moon had a cross face. Not real faces, ones made of crates an' things.'

'Craters,' said Lalune.

'I wonder if it's day or night,' said Solly.

'Night, I spec,' said Etolantie with a yawn. 'We been walking all day.'

'We didn't start off until the end of the day, nearly,' Lalune said. 'And anyway, I couldn't tell how long we were down there. Don't you think it felt strange, like it took no time at all, but at the same time it could have been fifty years?'

'Fifty years!' said Etolantie. 'How old's my brother going to be when I see him again? Or will we catch up?'

'Oh, I expect we'll catch up, m'dear,' said Aube.

The lift kept rising. The cables *tick, tick, ticked* softly. Star shuffled his feet, and *huffed* gently.

'We must of been a very long way down,' said Etolantie with relish. 'Look, I can see all the way.'

She moved, and made the lift sway. Lalune held Solly's hand more tightly. She didn't need to see to feel just how long the drop would be if they fell.

'We're nearly there,' said Solly. The noise from the cables became louder. There was a scraping, clanking noise, and the smell of oil and iron, and suddenly the door opened, and they were falling out of the lift, and gulping down clean air and standing on ground that didn't move.

'Oh,' said Etolantie in great disappointment. 'Another tunnel.'

'But you can feel a breeze,' said Solly, patting Star and helping Lalune to her feet. 'It can't be far to the outside.'

'The wind's *hot*,' said Etolantie.

'What does it look like?' asked Lalune.

'It's more a cave than a tunnel,' said Aube. 'There's a forest of dripping stalagmites and stalactites. Beautiful, beautiful. Rather like the ones in the Glimmering, if you've ever been.'

'Come on then,' said Solly. 'We won't see it standing here.'

He took Lalune's hand, and they followed the tunnel cautiously. Lalune's hands were sweating.

The Beyond, she thought. *The most momentous occasion of my life, and I'm going to miss it, because I'm blind. Perhaps that's no more than a monster can expect.*

They turned a corner, and suddenly they were out in the open, with the wind lifting their hair. They stood in silence for a few moments, staring and staring, unable to take it in.

'What's it like?' said Lalune. 'It smells . . . *wonderful*.'

But nobody replied straight away. Lalune thought that they must be too simply overwhelmed with this new world – until Etolantie spoke. Lalune could hear the tears in her voice.

'But it's jus' the same! There's no sun or moons or stars or anything! It's the same Ne'Lethe as before! It was all lies!'

33

'Solly! Lalune!'

Solly woke with a start. He was stiff, and the headache was still there, though it had shrunk to a pain behind his eyes.

'Come out here and see!'

It was Etolantie, whispering loudly from somewhere outside. Lalune was still asleep. They still had the tent pegs, and they had made a tent in the dark by bending a flexible sapling over and draping blankets over it. The four of them made it very warm. Too warm.

'What?' he mumbled, trying to focus. He couldn't have had more than an hour's sleep.

'Solly! Lalune! Come out, quick!'

'You don't want to miss this, m'dears,' Aube said.

'I'm coming, I'm coming!'

He sat up and groaned as his head throbbed. Lalune mumbled something in her sleep, and he nudged her until her forehead creased and she realized that she was awake. She sat up quickly.

'What is it?' she said, alarmed. 'What's wrong?'

'I don't know,' Solly said. 'Whatever it is, Etolantie and Aube want us to go and look at it.'

Lalune touched an empty eye unconsciously, and Solly

felt a pang of remorse. Whatever it was, Lalune wouldn't be able to see it anyway.

'Here are your boots,' he said, tossing them to her.

She wriggled out of her blanket.

'Do we need them?' she asked. 'The ground was dry last night. I'm so tired my fingers won't work properly.'

'Didn't you hear the wind in the night? Could've brought more snow.'

'It's not very cold, for snow.'

He tied her boots for her, and they crawled out of the tent. It was grey outside, the sort of grey when it's still night, but you know it won't be for much longer. There was no snow. Not far away was a cliff, gleaming eerily with a weird blue light, but blacker where the mouth of the cave was. They hadn't camped as far away from it as he'd thought. Solly rubbed the sleep from his eyes. *Pa wouldn't have been so careless. We could've been caught.*

'Where's Etolantie?' said Lalune, and Solly took her hand and pointed it in the right direction.

She and Aube were lying flat on their backs a few steps away, gazing straight up with rapt attention.

'Look up, look up!' Etolantie said.

Solly looked up.

'What is it?' asked Lalune. 'What can you see?'

The cliff rose high above them, higher than any cliff Solly had ever seen.

He felt his breath catch in his throat.

The cloud they had seen overhead last night hadn't been the Ne'Lethe after all; just ordinary cloud. The wind that had kept him awake had driven it away, and where it had been was an immeasurable expanse of blue so deep Solly felt

133

that there was nothing to stop him from tumbling up into it. He felt so dizzy that he almost fell over.

'*Stars?*' he whispered incredulously.

'Stars?' repeated Lalune. 'Tell me.'

Handfuls of silver sparkling shimmering dust had been flung into the infinity. Each tiny pinpoint shimmered and twinkled and danced, and the blue went on and on and on.

'It's so *real*,' said Etolantie softly. 'It's like it's realer than anything else ever.'

'I never imagined it would be like this, Angelus,' Aube murmured. 'Oh, Being, that you let me live long enough to see this! Makes fire dust look like a child's drawing, hmm. Begging your pardon, Etolantie.'

'If you lie down you feel like you're floating in it,' said Etolantie in awe. 'Imagine living an' never seeing this.'

Solly winced. He took Lalune's hand. Her face was wet.

'I can't see anything,' she said. 'Nothing at all. It's just white, everywhere.'

Solly felt a surge of hatred for those who had taken her eyes away. What had she done to deserve missing this? He wanted to be her eyes for her, but knew that there were no satisfactory words to describe their first ever sight of the sky.

'Imagine a blue so blue that it's one shade away from being black, and one shade from purple,' he said. 'Imagine the hunters out camping, and they've lit fires, but so far away that they're just pinpricks of light. Imagine those fires over and over, millions of them, scattered all over the blue. Imagine looking down on to it, so that you feel you might fall into it forever, and never stop falling. Only we're looking up, not down.'

Lalune dug her fingers into his hand, too emotional for words.

Through some trees near the horizon something larger than the stars was shining. Solly craned his head to see a gibbous moon hovering there, bright and cold as an ancient glacier. Its silver-blue glimmer was a net catching a little stream, the cliffs, trees and boulders, and the four of them in its magic.

'The Blue Moon,' he breathed. 'It's like a glacier lit up from inside.'

'So bright,' Aube said. 'I never thought it would be so bright.'

'What's that funny star with a line behind it? It's green.'

'A comet, m'dear.'

'Where's the orange one, the Bane Moon?' said Solly.

'I spec they take turns,' said Etolantie. 'So as they don't get tired.'

Lalune's breath suddenly thrust out of her chest in a huge sob. Solly took her in his arms and held her while she cried away the hurt, and Etolantie got up to hug her from behind.

A clear whistle suddenly split the darkness. Lalune turned her head to hear better.

'Is that a morning joy bird?' she whispered.

'Yes.'

Soon it was joined by another, and another, until they could hardly hear their own thoughts. Though it was still dark, dawn was bearing down on them fast.

'And the sky? What does it look like now? Tell me.'

'The blue's going grey,' Etolantie told her. 'It's lighter over there, like the Ne'Lethe's always lighter on one side in

135

the morning. There's a bit of cloud, wispy like Aube's eyebrows, only black. When I grow up I'm going to have eyebrows just like Aube's.'

'Gracious heavens!' Aube exclaimed, as the clouds suddenly flamed red.

'What is it?' begged Lalune. '*Tell me.*'

'For a moment it seemed that the clouds themselves had caught fire, m'dear. So many colours.'

'The stars are winking out,' Solly said. 'And the sky's definitely purple now.'

'It's still a little bit blue,' Etolantie said. 'An' a little bit pink an' orange.'

A family of ground rutters crept out of their hollow and hopped towards a stream for their morning drink. The hunter in Solly thought about having a go at shooting them, and stretched his fingers towards his bandoleer.

But he withdrew his hand. It seemed wrong, somehow, to kill on this first morning.

There came a moment when the birds paused in their singing. The rutters sat on their haunches, watching and waiting. The world held its breath.

A sliver of bright orange flared along the horizon, and as if this was the signal, the birds began to sing again, a great chorus to welcome the glorious sun. The sun thickened and lifted gradually out of the mountains. It quivered for a second, and broke free from the ground.

The sun had risen.

And Lalune wept.

34

Lalune tried to forget what she couldn't see and concentrate on her other senses. The birds were singing as if there was only good in the world. She could smell the same fruity fragrance as she had coming out of the cave, strong and sun-warmed.

An energetic breeze dried the tears on her cheeks. She lifted her face to the sun, feeling healing in its rays.

I wish I could see the sun.

'You can't look at it,' Etolantie said.

Lalune hadn't realized she'd spoken out loud. Solly rubbed her arm comfortingly.

Etolantie carried on.

'It hurts your eyes. I never want to do anything ever again,' she added with a little dreamy sigh. 'Jus' watch that again an' again.'

Lalune nodded. *And I shall never see it,* she thought bitterly. *It is only what a . . . a thing like me deserves.*

She felt Solly's body jerk next to her.

'Ow!' said Etolantie. 'What was *that* for?'

Solly didn't answer. At least not in words that Lalune could hear.

'Well, I should like to eat,' said Aube.

'I'm starving,' Etolantie agreed. 'We never ate last night.'

Aube chuckled.

'Let's have a look at those boxes of food from Sybilla's house,' he said. 'And work out how to cook the rice.'

'Solly,' said Lalune, 'I'd really like to wash. I can hear a stream nearby . . .'

'I'll take you,' he said. He didn't mention that she wouldn't be much help anyway, but she knew he was thinking it.

He led her over stony ground. The bubbling of the streamlet grew louder, and the fragrance was almost overpowering.

'Mmm. Fruit,' she said, sniffing the air.

'There's some great big orange fruits on a tree right by the stream,' Solly said. 'They look like cups.'

'I thought I recognized the smell. Orbal trees. They used the oil in the pods.'

'They use the oil in everything.'

Lalune splashed water on her face and used the corner of a blanket as if she could scrub away the anguish in her heart along with the dust.

She wondered again why had she couldn't see angels any more. They had been there showing her the way when she came out of the cyberclinic and was all on her own. They had helped her to run from the clinic and back to Aube's cave with Solly. She had seen them quite clearly when Etolantie was saved from the tubal worm.

But now she was completely blind. What had happened? Had the angels been so horrified about what she had discovered about herself that they had left her?

'Hello,' came Etolantie's cheery voice, breaking her gloomy thoughts. 'Solly said I was getting in the way, so to come an' wash with you.'

Lalune managed a somewhat wobbly smile.

'How deep is this water?' Lalune asked. 'I don't think I'm making much difference like this. And it's warm enough to go right in.'

'I *had* a bath when Solly and I was with Sybilla that first time,' Etolantie said indignantly.

'I should think it's much more fun to bathe in a stream,' Lalune said.

'We-e-ell,' Etolantie said doubtfully, 'there's a stony splashy bit where you are, an' like a deep pool bit on the other side, where them trees are. Will we have to take all our clothes off?'

'Can't bathe with them on.'

'Will Solly an' Aube see?'

'Not if we hang blankets up like a curtain.'

After some fuss hanging the blankets up, the two of them stripped off their clothes and hobbled over the smooth stones, gasping and squealing. The air may have been warm, but the water certainly wasn't. Lalune splashed the smaller girl and got splashed back, and forgot a little of her pain.

When they had warmed up – or at least had got used to the cold – Lalune sat down in the deeper part of the pool and leaned against a long tree root.

'What wouldn't I give for some soap right now,' she said. 'I'd really like to wash my hair properly.'

'I *hate* having my hair washed.'

'Have I still got dust in mine?' Lalune asked, bending her head over.

'Yes, loads, all in the curls.' Lalune heard water rushing

against Etolantie's legs as she waded back out of the pool. 'I'm going to see if the food's ready yet.'

Lalune ducked under the surface and rubbed her scalp vigorously. She found a smooth stone and scraped her limbs clean.

'I wish I could see,' she said under her breath. 'Oh, Being, I wish I could see. Why did you give me back my sight just to take it again?'

Because you are the only one who can see the world of angels: my world.

Lalune gasped, and staggered down with a splash.

'Who was that?'

Don't you know me, Lalune?

The voice was . . . in her head.

'Being?' she breathed. '*Being?*'

The Being laughted softly.

Though evil happens, there is good to be found in everything, Lalune. Even in losing your sight. Nobody else can do what you will do.

There was a disturbance in the air, as if some huge creature had moved, and Lalune knew she was alone again.

35

News of the arrival of the Wanderer spread fast, and hundreds of people began to arrive at Kloster Hallow. They came from small villages, they came from isolated farms. They travelled by sandcamel cart, skimmer, and on foot. They came in convoys of creaking carts; they came alone.

Some of them had their own telescopes, though by now there was no real need. The comet could clearly be seen chiselling its way across the hard night sky, and even in the day, the sun's rays were caught in its tail. The comet had been spotted in Peleg City too. The Imperator had issued an Edict ordering everybody to attend a special celebration to mark the astronomical event. Anyone mentioning prophecies fulfilled, or the Great Migration, however, was to be punished. Those coming from the city had fled before they could be stopped.

Seachrân was constantly being asked about the comet, or his visions, or where he was going to lead the people in the Great Migration. The worst people were the ones who wanted him to tell their fortunes, and simply would not believe that he couldn't.

'Just be polite, but firm,' Halig told him when he complained. 'They will soon learn that you have nothing to say to them. How many cartons of grain are in each crate, my sweet?'

She was in the stock barn, completely against Si-Sef's orders, counting their stores. Si-Sef was hovering nearby, tapping her foot and scowling.

'Five h . . . hundred and t . . . t . . . twelve,' Seachrân said, letting his queggel explore the barn on the long leash he'd made for it. 'It . . . tried that. Th . . . there's always somebody else I haven't been p . . . polite but firm *to* yet.'

It was the hottest part of the day, when most sensible people were asleep; but it was the only time he could escape the pilgrims these days. Halig should have been resting too, but the only concession she made to her illness was to sit while she worked.

'I do not understand why these travellers think that we have an endless supply of food,' said Halig, coughing into her handkerchief as she scribbled down the number. 'Hardly any of them bring any with them. We have five crates left, and a sixth one with a single layer of cartons left, so that's . . .'

'T . . . two thousand, six hundred and t . . . twenty-four.'

Seachrân thought he saw blood on the handkerchief, but Halig folded it too quickly for him to see.

'Thank you, my sweet. Where would we be without you?'

'Halig, I must ask you to drink your medicine,' said Si-Sef firmly. 'And to take a rest. I really don't see why somebody else can't do this.'

'W . . . w . . . why do they think *I'm* s . . . so special?' Seachrân said, flapping his tunic to cool himself down. 'I saw the c . . . comet, that's all. I c . . . can't tell the future.'

'You give them something to believe in,' Halig said, grimacing as she drank. 'You will take them to a new wonderful land. We are getting through more than a crate each day. It is no use: I shall have to send out for more food. People need belief, Seachrân. Especially when times are hard, as they are now. Thank you, Si-Sef.'

'T . . . today some people t . . . tried to tell me I *hadn't* seen the c . . . c . . . comet,' said Seachrân grumpily, watching the queggel gnaw the corner of a carton. 'They s . . . said it was s . . . something c . . . caught up in the trees, and it was just c . . . coincidence that it was seen a few d . . . days later.'

'That grain is for humans, not for queggels, Seachrân,' Halig said sternly. 'It is strange how those with the least faith are often the most zealous in their beliefs. Now, I have to speak with the cooks.'

Si-Sef snorted.

'Just this one last thing, Si-Sef. Seachrân, do you not have a mathematics lesson to be going to?'

'Kepler is making us get up in the night to do astronomy instead,' Seachrân said, even more grouchily. He wanted to do some *real* maths, not all this looking and looking and looking.

But he scooped up the queggel and went off to find Kepler anyway. At least he'd be out of sight of the pilgrims.

He found Kepler in the observatory. The shutters were down against the sun, but it was still stifling.

'I have something for you,' said Kepler, mopping his face. He was holding a leather and steel contraption. Seachrân's face fell.

'L . . . leg braces,' he said glumly.

Kepler looked in surprise at the leg braces, as if he'd forgotten about them.

'Oh, those; yes, well, Halig insisted. I'm sorry. No, that wasn't what I meant. The blacksmith saw me and gave them to me for you. No, I meant this.'

He held out a long parcel. Seachrân opened it eagerly, the queggel perched on his shoulder. Inside was a fat brass telescope and a stand, a miniature version of Kepler's.

Seachrân tried to make his face look grateful, but it was difficult. He was sick of the comet, and just wanted things to be ordinary again. It didn't look as if that was going to be possible, though.

'Now, then,' said Kepler, who didn't seem to have noticed his lack of enthusiasm, 'we have enough data from our nightly observations for you to begin to track the path of this comet, Seachrân. And, more interestingly, to *back*track it. You see, a long time ago the crater that currently houses the capital city was made by a collision with this very same comet . . .'

Seachrân knew this already. The Palace where he had worked for the Imperator marked the exact point of impact. He had been told this almost every day that he'd been there. He raised the new telescope to his eye and focused it on the horizon, well away from the sun so that he didn't burn his eyes.

'. . . revisits us regularly. It coincides with another astronomical event: the Encompassing In Equal Degree. The Sun dawns at zero degrees longitude, and the Blue Moon sets at one hundred and twenty . . .'

There were even more pilgrims on their way: on foot,

with a sandcamel dragging a tiny cart. Seachrân wondered how the dazed-looking old man with alarming eyebrows could bear being out in this heat.

'. . . in other words, the three celestial bodies will arrive at the horizon at exactly equal distances. It's a pity that we can't be in the observatory in Peleg City, the one they call the Queen of the Stars: that is where these measurements were taken from . . .'

Seachrân focused the telescope on the smaller of the travellers: a girl of about seven or eight years, hair the colour of honey. She too looked disorientated.

'. . . only for a few minutes after that the sun will set, and the Bane Moon will rise, appearing to take its place . . .'

Seachrân realized that he was holding his breath. The girl . . .

'Now, you'll have to factor in the gravity of each . . . Seachrân?' Kepler looked about him wildly. 'Seachrân! Where did that boy go?'

36

The rice was not a success. Somehow it had expanded to three or four times its size and had burst out of the storm kettle. What remained was hard and burned. They left most of it for the birds. The boxed meat was tough and too salty, but at least stopped them feeling hungry.

'Do we know where to go from here?' asked Lalune.

'There appears to be but one way,' Aube said. 'A road of sorts. I think we're in a canyon or some such thing. The cliff appears to block us off on three sides. Since we cannot fly, and didn't bring a skyboat with us, I suggest that we take the only available option, hmm?'

'Where's Sunguide?' Etolantie said as they began to walk. 'He said he'd catch us up.'

'He will,' said Solly. 'He'll just follow the spores.'

He held Lalune's hand to guide her, but despite this Lalune kept stumbling on loose stones. Clouds of dust swirled up from their footsteps.

'I've only just got clean,' she said crossly.

'Can I take off some clothes?' said Etolantie. 'My boots hurt, an' I'm *dying* of hotness.'

'You're only wearing underwear as it is,' said Solly.

They all were. They had decided before they started out that it was the only bearable way.

'And your feet'll hurt even more if you take your boots off,' he added.

They all had similar boots: knee-length and lined with poley fur, designed for trekking through the snow.

'It is *horribly* hot,' said Lalune. 'Can't we do something about them?'

'May I suggest that we try unlacing them and letting them trail on the ground behind us?' said Aube. 'It will be a lot cooler.'

'We'll keep treading on them,' Solly said, but they did it anyway.

Etolantie and Solly also took off their tops. Lalune wasn't sure what Aube did about his – she could hear him puffing and panting along behind her – but there was no way she was removing hers. She did tie her hair up away from her neck with a bit of leather ripped from her sleeve, though, and did the same for Etolantie.

The sun grew hotter and hotter, and there was no shade. Lalune had never imagined that the sun could be so uncomfortable. Her feet itched. Her long underwear chafed against her legs. Her leather top clung to her back, and her hair stuck to her face and neck.

In no time at all they'd drunk their water. They stopped for a rest, and Lalune didn't object when Solly took out a knife and sliced the sleeves off her top.

'Poor old Star, you can't take off your clothes,' said Etolantie.

Lalune could hear the animal flailing his leathery umbrella, trying vainly to cool down.

'Is there no stream or anything he could wallow in?' she said.

147

'There has been no water of any kind for a while,' said Aube.

Lalune wondered if her own voice sounded as faint.

They walked and walked and walked. Now the road began to slope upwards, and Lalune tripped over every third step. She didn't think they could be making much progress at all. Her mouth was so dry she couldn't make any spit, and her skin felt as if it was burning.

'I'm thirsty,' said Etolantie at intervals.

But there wasn't any more water, and they all felt too exhausted to do more than concentrate on the next step. Lalune started to feel a little sick and dizzy, but she didn't say anything: she didn't want to slow them down any further.

After a particularly bad misstep, Lalune put her hands on Solly's shoulder to haul herself up again.

'Ow,' he said.

'Your shoulder's gone all spongy,' she said hoarsely.

'You have blisters,' Aube said.

'*Ow*,' Solly said again. 'My head hurts when I try to see.'

'My head hurts too,' said Etolantie. '*An*' I'm thirsty.'

'We all have blisters,' said Aube wearily

'But there's nothing rubbing his shoulders,' said Lalune.

'Oh my, but my head is sore, Angelus,' said Aube.

'So is mine,' Lalune said. 'What's wrong with us?'

'It must of been Sybilla,' said Etolantie, starting to cry. 'First she tried to poison us, then she made us ill. My head really, *really* hurts.'

'But only Solly drank anything,' said Lalune. 'And she didn't even meet Aube or Star.'

There was a heavy noise as Star lay down on his side, panting.

'Oh, Star,' sobbed Etolantie. 'Don't die, Star.'

'He's not going to die,' said Solly. 'Look, there's water down there.'

'A pond,' murmured Aube. 'Now there's the thing.'

'How far?' said Lalune, her voice quavering. She didn't think she could walk another step.

'An hour, maybe?' said Solly. 'And downhill.'

Star took some persuading to get up. Etolantie and Aube walked with him, half pulling, half using him as support. Lalune and Solly followed, hand in hand, under the ferocious sun.

Thunder rumbled a long way away.

'Thunder means rain,' said Solly in a cracked voice. 'Rain means water.'

'What?'

'That's what we need: water.'

But the rain never reached them.

'I *need* a drink . . .' whispered Etolantie. 'I can't walk . . .'

Solly tried to speak, but his voice was too dry for Lalune to hear him. She pulled his mouth to her ear.

'They went the wrong way,' he said.

Lalune was too confused to work out what he meant.

'Never mind,' said Solly. 'They'll find . . . the pond . . . somehow. Got to . . . keep going.' His voice sounded as if his tongue had swollen.

'Solly . . .' said Lalune thickly. 'Trees.'

She could smell the leaves. Trees needed water.

'Flowers look like . . . bathtubs . . .' Solly murmured.

Lalune missed her footing again, and this time it seemed so much easier just to let herself carry on falling.

Somebody grabbed her hand and tugged at her. Far

away she heard Solly whispering, 'Get up, you have to get up . . .'

But instead she fell down inside herself, and she knew she hadn't made it through the tunnel, she hadn't even made it out of the clinic, but she was being forced back into her pod, and they were filling her lungs with orbal oil once more, and she was choking, choking, choking . . .

37

'Halig! Halig!'

Seachrân stuffed the queggel inside his tunic, and ran until his trembling legs forced him to stop and rest. The pilgrims looked at him curiously, obviously wondering if he'd had another vision. Seachrân ignored them. He had to find Halig.

He set off again, walking this time, making sure that his face was cheery but urgent in case anybody stopped him. He hadn't put on his leg braces, and soon his legs were aching, and his heart thumped so that he thought everybody must hear it.

'Halig!' he wheezed again, putting his head through the hospital door.

But she wasn't resting there, or in her tent. He tried the cookhouse, and the stock barn, and finally found her with a group of carters who had dropped off their passengers and were returning to the city. Si–Sef was nearby, glaring at them so hard it was a wonder they couldn't feel themselves getting scorched.

'. . . requests to every farmer, dairy, and merchant in the vicinity,' Halig was ordering them when he arrived. 'And if you bring more travellers, *please* remind them that my resources are not infinite.'

She was leaning on her staff and sounded very weary. Seachrân tapped her on the shoulder.

'Halig.'

'Yes, my sweet?' Halig said in a distracted way. 'Oh, you had better take invitations to all artisans and labourers. Kloster is becoming quite overwhelmed with the need for smiths and tailors. Now, Seachrân?'

The carters turned away, more interested in earning coin than in what the strange half-skin might have prophesied now.

'I s . . . saw her,' he said, still a little breathless. 'The girl.'

Halig dabbed her sweating forehead with a damp cloth, and Si–Sef handed her some water.

'My, I have never known it to be so hot. Thank you, Si–Sef. Another vision, my love?'

'No. She's here. Well, c . . . coming here. An . . . another pilgrim, I think.' He pointed east, to where he had seen the girl. 'Kepler g . . . gave me a t . . . t . . . telescope, and I s . . . saw her.'

'At this time of the day?' said Si–Sef, whose mouth seemed constantly turned down. 'Surely she would have found shelter until this heat lifts?'

'C . . . can I go?' said Seachrân.

'I think that you should,' Halig said with a smile. 'It will be a suitable welcome for this girl who has haunted you for so long. Take a sandcamel cart. But do not push the animal too hard.'

Seachrân didn't waste a moment. Ignoring the stares of the pilgrims, he scurried away to the shady paddock where the sandcamels were snoozing away the day. There was always a cart ready there, in case of some emergency. He dragged it into the rutted track, whistling to his favourite sandcamel, Modya. She heaved herself obediently to her feet, strolled over to him, and stood patiently blowing through her long trunk while he harnessed her on to the cart.

He pointed her in the right direction, as far as he could remember it. He couldn't see the girl from ground level.

'C'mon, Modya!' he urged, but even she would not do more than an accelerated amble on this, the hottest of days.

He hummed to himself as they went, glad of the chance to rest his legs. He waved to his friends swimming in the lake. Soon they were out on the road that ran around the Ne'Lethe. Here Seachrân let Modya walk on at her own pace. She wouldn't leave the road unless he told her to.

The sun glared down ferociously. They went slowly, stopping at every tree to cool down. There were few streams on this side of the lake, but the cart had a full water barrel, which he, Modya and the queggel all drank from.

It was well over an hour later when Seachrân saw another human being. Not the girl, but two rough-looking men some way ahead. They were looking around them as if lost. Obviously they were strangers to the area. Then he saw them point up a steep mossy slope; and he saw his girl up there, poised motionless out in the blazing sun as if she'd been turned to stone.

'Th . . . there she is, Modya!' he cried. 'G . . . go on, girl.'

Modya gave him an indignant look and carried on at exactly the same pace.

The slope the men were climbing was too steep for Modya. Seachrân stopped her as near to the girl as he could, left the Sandcamel to graze in a small copse, and

153

hopped out of the cart to follow the men up the slope, the queggel clinging to his neck like a scarf.

Voices floated down towards him, but it was difficult to make out the words. The men were obviously asking directions, he guessed to Kloster Hallow: though the only word he heard clearly was 'Solly', which he thought was an ancient word for the Sun.

Then they went off, in completely the wrong direction. Seachrân didn't care much. It was two fewer pilgrims to question him.

He continued to climb up the slope, and at last reached the top. He couldn't see the girl. There was an untidy heap of clothes lying on the dry earth. He prodded it with his toe, and heard a moan.

Seachrân pulled back the top layer of cloth, and recognized the old man who had been with the girl. His skin was terribly burned from the sun. But he opened his eyes and murmured something that sounded like 'Angelus,' so Seachrân knew he wasn't too late.

He looked around, but there was no sign of the girl, and no shade to leave the man in. He crouched down, pulled the stopper off his water bottle, and held it to the old man's lips.

The man's tongue, dry and swollen, scraped out and licked a few drops of water.

'Most kind, hey Angelus, hmm?'

Maybe the girl is called Angelus, thought Seachrân.

He looked around again, and saw the cart that the sandcamel had been pulling, and beyond it a heap of black fur. Leaving the water with the old man, he went to look. The animal was exhausted, but alive.

Then he saw the girl.

At first Seachrân thought that he was too late. She was lying motionless on the barren ground. She was wearing nothing but a pair of thick-looking shorts and leather boots. Her skin wasn't just red: it was horribly blistered.

Please Being, may I be in time, he prayed, holding his necklace.

He grabbed the bottle from the old man and ran to her side. Sitting so that his shadow fell over her, he dripped a little water on to her mouth.

She licked her parched lips, and took a shallow breath.

Seachrân gave her some more water, and suddenly she seemed to wake up. She grabbed the bottle and took a long, long drink.

Then she opened her dry eyes and looked at him.

'You was in my dream,' she whispered.

38

. . . darkness all around, as if she's at the bottom of a well . . . can't hold her thoughts steady . . . the cyberclinic, she's been cybernated again . . . thoughts keep drifting off into blackness . . . where am I? . . . not in the cyberclinic, there's movement, she's in a cart . . . heavy weight lying across her feet . . . somebody squeezing her hand . . . fading away again, must stay awake . . . must stay awake . . .

. . . the cart stops . . . random thoughts haunting her like ghosts . . . memories of when she was a girl, her father's face, smiling . . . her father was dead . . . the cyberclinic, ten thousand people imprisoned, waiting to die . . . voices nearby, meaningless voices . . . must stay awake . . . people waiting to die . . . what can I do? . . . must stay awake . . . Solly, are you there? . . . Etolantie? Aube? . . . we have to do something . . .

. . . looks up and a tiny white disk of consciousness swims above her like the top of the well . . . fighting to breathe . . . why can't I breathe properly? . . . force upwards towards consciousness . . . the white disk grows larger . . . suddenly Lalune felt as if her head was breaking through the surface, and she was groggily awake. A sack had been pulled over her head. Panic washed over her as she tasted a greasy rag in her

mouth, and for a few moments she struggled not to gag on it. She took several deep breaths through her nose to calm herself down, and felt her heartbeat slow a little.

We were walking, she thought, trying to ignore the pain in her wrists. *Where were we? It was so hot.* Her hands had been bound so tightly that her fingers had pins and needles. Her head was throbbing. Her body was on fire.

I remember voices. Somebody found us.

It was oppressively hot. Her clothes were sticking to her back. Her feet were numb. Something heavy was lying across them. She tried moving them. It felt like a body. *Solly? Etolantie? Aube?*

Whoever it was didn't move. She wondered if they were still alive. She tried to shift her legs again. Her feet weren't tied. She eased them out: whoever was lying on them rolled off and she heard a small moan.

Solly! He's still alive!

'What was that?' said a voice sharply.

'They shouldn't be awake yet,' said another voice.

Lalune lay very still.

'We didn't have enough of the drusian for two,' whined the first voice. 'Nobody said nothing about two of them.'

Two? Then Etolantie and Aube weren't picked up.

She didn't know if that was good or not. Her head pounded.

'The boy had her hand so tight I couldn't leave the girl behind.'

'They'll wake before she gets here, you'll see.'

'We'll just bang 'em on the head if they do.'

'Not damaged, she said. Not even bruised.'

157

'The boy, yes. Not the girl. She didn't say nothing about no girl.'

'I gave the boy more drusian, anyway. He should be out of it for a few more hours at least. If the girl wakes, hit her.'

Lalune remembered more now. Solly being dragged away from her as she lay almost unconscious on the ground. His hand gripping hers, so that rough hands had to lift her on to the cart as well. A bitter drink being forced down her throat.

The drusian. It must be a drug of some sort.

Solly hadn't let go for a long time. *He has now, though. The drug must have relaxed him.*

Lalune shifted her head slightly, and felt the gag around her mouth slacken a little. Perhaps she could free it some more. Very carefully, so as not to make any sound, she flexed her neck so that the back of her head rubbed up and down. The gag was definitely shifting. She rubbed it some more and felt it come loose. She pushed the rag out of her mouth with her tongue and breathed deeply through her mouth.

If they were careless with the gag it's possible that they were with my hands as well, she thought. She twisted them this way and that, but though they loosened a little bit she couldn't release them.

Damny! I probably just tightened the knot.

Lalune lay still, concentrating on breathing. The sack smelt disgusting, like mouldy grain.

She could hear the men murmuring and laughing a short way away. Woodsmoke drifted through the sack. A night creature howled and several others answered.

And something else. Something very faint. In

the distance she could hear the ugly buzzing noise of the skimmer.

The men had heard it too. She heard one of them say something, and whatever she was lying on rocked a little as if they were sitting on the other end and had got up suddenly.

She held her breath as her captors leaned over her again, and hoped they wouldn't somehow notice through the sack that she'd removed the gag.

Closer the skimmer came, and closer, high up overhead. As it descended towards them the noise grew deafening, and she could feel the roar of its engines vibrating underneath her. The sacking on her head flapped wildly in the wind the skimmer created.

Then the wind dropped suddenly as the skimmer landed. The engines cut. She heard her guards walking to greet whoever it was that had arrived. There were murmured voices, and as they drew nearer Lalune recognized them.

Sybilla Geenpool and Dr Belenus Dollysheep.

39

Si–Sef stayed with the strangers most of the night, giving them drinks and applying healing lotions. She had stripped off their ridiculous fur clothes. The girl had been wearing a bracelet, and the man a pendant. A Seer's pendant, Halig had thought.

'What kind of person wears such clothes in this heat?' Si–Sef was muttering crossly when Seachrân came in. 'And doesn't shield such fair skin from the sun, or carry spare water?'

She didn't know that they had come out of the Ne'Lethe. Seachrân had been too anxious about their condition to tell her.

'I b . . . brought you some more b . . . b . . . boiled water and fresh herbs,' he said softly.

It was still dark outside: the birds had not woken. Seachrân had already slept, but something had woken him, and he knew he wouldn't get any more rest that night.

Si–Sef sniffed and took the new supplies from him.

The girl and her companion were both too burned to be dressed again yet, and lay under cool sheets. The old man's skin was so pallid it was obvious that he'd never seen the sun. And the girl, though she had darker hair, was freckled, and freckled skin was more easily damaged. She was lying on her front, her back covered in a poultice of herbs. Seachrân knelt down and stroked her head.

'How is the sandcamel?' asked Si-Sef, mashing the herbs vigorously in the hot water.

'S . . . sleeping. T . . . tomorrow we'll c . . . cut off his fur.'

'It's simply cruel to let a sandcamel's fur get so long. But at least it stopped him burning, like these two. Make sure he drinks plenty.'

She finished preparing the herbs, and put the bowl down to cool.

'I have to do my rounds now,' she said.

'C . . . can I s . . . stay and watch them?'

'Call me if they wake,' Si-Sef said, 'Don't touch their burns.'

Seachrân settled back to watch over the two strangers, wondering who they were.

I know that I'm one of the three Holders, he thought. *Somewhere on Clandoi there are two others. But not these two. Kepler said that all three have to be born on the same day. She's only about eight, I think, and the man must be at least sixty.*

So why did he feel such a strong link to the girl?

She was fidgeting a little in her sleep. Si-Sef had given her something for the pain, but she probably still felt uncomfortable. He'd never seen anybody with such bad sunburn.

Who doesn't know about the sun? thought Seachrân. At Kloster they were taught about its dangers before they could walk, and not even the tiniest child would forget to go out without something to shield their skin, and plenty

161

of water. These two hadn't had any protection, and their water bottles were dry.

But he thought about the visions he'd had, and how cold it had been. He looked at the pile of fur coats and blankets. How cold would it have to be to wear such things?

To pass the time Seachrân drilled himself on all the prime numbers up to a thousand. He counted them backwards, and practised multiplying them together in his head. He took the queggel out of his pocket and let it run around the tent.

A morning joy bird started its dawn herald nearby. Soon the cooks would be waking. Seachrân's stomach growled. *It* thought breakfast time was long overdue.

'Hello,' said a voice, and he whirled round.

It was the girl. She had lifted her head and was regarding him with wide, dark eyes.

'H . . . hello,' he said.

'I'm hungry,' she said. 'An' I need to pee. But I can't get up. It hurts when I move.'

Her voice sounded funny, as if she was speaking from the back of her throat. Perhaps it was burned too?

Seachrân grinned at her.

'Si-Sef will h . . . help you,' he said. 'And the c . . . cooks will be up soon. If she says you c . . . can eat I'll b . . . bring you something.'

'I seen you before,' she said.

'I found you.'

She shook her head, frowned, and winced as the skin on her face cracked.

'Before that,' she said. 'I think I had a dream, an' you was in it.'

162

'I saw you t . . . too,' Seachrân said. 'In a d . . . dream.'

'My name's Etolantie.'

'Seachrân Pythagoras.'

She lowered her head again.

'Sybilla had two names as well.'

'S . . . Sybilla *Geenpool*?' said Seachrân, startled.

'Yes. D'you know her?'

'Sh . . . she used to b . . . be the Imperator's accountant,' said Seachrân. 'H . . . Halig said she s . . . s . . . stole his money and g . . . got sent away. I was . . . supposed to have her job but she gave me to the cook instead, and he b . . . beat me, and Halig brought me b . . . back here.'

'She talked like you,' said Etolantie. 'Like she was holding her nose.'

Holding my nose?

'Well, y . . . you talk like you've got a m . . . mouth full of m . . . marbles,' he retorted, and felt ashamed immediately for speaking to a guest like that.

But Etolantie giggled.

'I din't like her.'

'I never m . . . met her,' said Seachrân, grinning again. 'B . . . but I don't think Halig liked her much.'

He went to the door to find Si-Sef, and almost bumped into her coming back in.

'She's awake,' he said. 'C . . . can she eat?'

'I expect so,' Si-Sef said. 'Something light, mind. And get rid of that queggel, will you?'

Seachrân nodded, caught the queggel, and left her to tend to Etolantie.

40

Sybilla was speaking as they came within range.

'. . . was with a girl when they passed through Latrium. Two girls, in fact. . . . The Appaloosian that escaped from the cyberclinic and an obnoxious Wayfarer brat.'

'This one's definitely Appaloosian, Ma'am.'

'I'm surprised the Waif wasn't with them too. But I didn't tell you to take the female. I have no use for it.'

'We did see another girl,' one of the kidnappers said fawningly. 'Very helpful she was, too. Showed us exactly where to find these two.'

Lalune was horrified. *Etolantie showed them?*

Sybilla sniffed.

'Can't be the one *I* met then. I hope you didn't bring *her*. Most odious child I've ever come across.'

'What should we do with this girl?' said Dr Dollysheep, plucking at the sack that covered Lalune's head. He didn't remove it, though, to Lalune's relief. 'Do we know who she is?'

There was an ominous grumble of thunder.

'It doesn't matter who it is. We'll kill her,' said Sybilla crisply.

Lalune had difficulty stopping herself from crying out.

'We should find out whose clone she is first,' Dr

Dollysheep said.

'Why?' said a third voice, a female. 'They can always have another made. I agree, kill it.'

'It never fails to amuse me how little sympathy you have for your own kind, Toobe-ef,' Sybilla said in an amused voice.

'I may be Appaloosian,' said Toobe-ef in a dangerous voice, 'but that doesn't mean that I have to embrace my heritage. You know I have my own clone too, just mature enough to begin harvesting.'

'You'll always be Appaloosian on the inside, Toobe-ef,' said Sybilla.

'If she belongs to somebody of influence there could be repercussions,' said Dr Dollysheep.

'Technology has moved on,' Sybilla said. 'Soon individual components will be able to be made, at a fraction of the cost of an entire body clone. And if we *don't* kill it, and it falls into Halig's hands, she and her people will have even more of an excuse to make trouble. We cannot afford for her to poke her great nose in. Not right now. Not until we can present the Imperator to all the people, fully healed, and they can see for themselves the benefits of the program. When will you be ready to begin the procedure, Belenus?'

'If you'd given me a mite more time, Sybilla . . .' Dr Dollysheep answered her.

'I would have,' Sybilla snapped. 'I tried. I put enough drusian into their drinks to fell them for three days but . . . but . . . they would't drink it.'

'You still could have got a message through sooner,' Toobe-ef pointed out. 'We should really have got the room secured *before* they arrived.'

'When does the Imperator get here?' said Sybilla, neatly ignoring this. Lalune guessed that she wasn't prepared to reveal exactly why she hadn't sent a message sooner. She'd been knocked out by her own drug – this 'drusian' they kept mentioning.

'Some time in the next two or three days,' said the other woman.

A few raindrops had begun to fall.

'Two or three days,' murmured Dr Dollysheep. 'Well, that should give me sufficient time. Now, I'm going in before this storm sets in. I need to rest. It is a complicated procedure.'

'Just make sure that you are ready for it, Belenus Dollysheep,' said Sybilla.

'I think I shall find my bed too,' said Toobe-ef stiffly. 'Will the cargo be safe in the cart overnight?'

'You two!' snapped Sybilla. There was a scramble as the two kidnappers stood to attention. The rain grew harder.

'Y-yes, Sybilla?'

'Ma'am?'

'Keep guard. If I find that you've fallen asleep on the job you'll be frozen and packed off to the cyberclinic before you realize you've got frostbite. Oh, and I want the female killed, and the body gone before the morning.'

Thunder growled again, this time a lot closer. The rain suddenly became heavier and soaked through the sacking. The noise of it on the cart was like stones bouncing on a drum.

'We never have rain at this time of the year,' shouted one of the kidnappers in disbelief. 'Not like this. And we've got to stay out in it?'

Lalune could hear the rain thrashing against his plastic poncho. Sybilla and Dr Dollysheep had plainly gone.

'More to the point, she wants us to kill the girl in this rain,' shouted the other. 'I say we wait until it stops. We can carry her into the forest and do it. *I* don't want to clean the cart out after.'

She heard them retreat to what she guessed was the covered front end of the cart, and felt it sway as they climbed in.

Thunder crashed again, this time nearly overhead. She felt the cart roll a little from side to side: it had given the men a fright. And no wonder. It was far more violent a storm than anything she'd experienced before. If she hadn't been so terrified of what they were going to do to her she'd have been scared too.

She started trying to prise her hands apart again, but it was no use. Perhaps she could wriggle out of the sack? Wouldn't the men feel the cart rock? She explored her surroundings with her foot. She already knew the cart was open to the sky. She could feel one side of it under her feet; her head was jammed against the other. Solly was on her right.

But to her left the cart was open. Carefully Lalune shifted herself until she was right on the edge. The next time thunder smashed open the skies she dropped off the cart on to the ground below.

The cart must have shuddered like crazy, but nobody came to check on her and Solly. For a while she lay there, winded.

When she had recovered she tried to get rid of the sack. Her head thumped against a cartwheel. She bunched the sack up in her hand and pushed it under the wheel as far as it would go, writhed about until she had pulled it around the wheel a little, then wriggled her way out of it.

She gulped down the clean air thankfully.

What should she do now? She was blind, and her hands were tied.

'Solly?' she whispered. 'Solly? Can you hear me?'

But of course he couldn't. Even if he *was* awake, and there was no guarantee of that with all the drugs they'd given him, she'd have to shout to be heard in this rain.

Raindrops were hammering the ground furiously, bouncing up again, puddling wherever there was the slightest dip. The cart was parked on a sloping road that was rapidly becoming a river. If she didn't move soon she would be swept away.

Lalune crawled out from under the cart with difficulty, using her elbows instead of her hands, scraping the burned skin painfully. She stood up cautiously and leaned over the back of the cart. She felt sacking, but Solly was too far away for her to touch.

And if I could reach him, how could I pull him off the cart and carry him away, blind and single-handed? She pulled again at the cords that bound her wrists. *No-handed, in fact.*

'What should I do?' she whispered. 'Oh, Being, what should I do?'

This time there was no answer. It looked as though she was on her own. She leaned over the side of the cart and whispered to Solly.

'Solly, I don't know if you can hear me. I hope you can forgive me: I'm going to have to leave you. You see, it's you they want. If I stay they're going to kill me. They want to

168

keep you alive for some reason. They don't even want you bruised. I can't get my hands untied, and I can't carry you. I have to go. I'll get help, and I'll come back for you.'

Solly didn't move. She knew he couldn't hear her. She laid her head down on the cart for a moment and let the rain mingle with her tears.

And she left him.

She had no idea in which direction to go. She knew she had to get away from Sybilla though, so holding her tied hands out in front of her she walked in a straight line away from the cart, leaning in low in case the men happened to look out. Maybe she would come across a house and could ask for help.

Her fingers met something rough. Tree bark. And the rain was pattering on to something overhead. Leaves. She was in a forest. That was good. The trees would hide her. She hoped.

Her clothes were saturated. The wind was growing stronger every minute. She bent down and scrabbled about on the ground until her hands closed on a fallen branch. This she held out in front of her so that she could feel her way.

It was horribly slow. She moved her feet gingerly, expecting to trip up every step. Wet branches slapped her face. Once the wind gusted so hard that what sounded like a whole tree creaked and crashed down nearby.

The ground was slippery and stony underfoot; she kept turning her ankles. She struggled on and on, hoping she was getting somewhere, terrified that she was going round in circles and would end up where she started. With Sybilla.

Stop panicking, she thought crossly. *If I keep going downhill*

I have to be heading away from her.

She didn't know how long she had walked when she splashed into a shallow stream, and realised how thirsty she was. How long had it been since she drank? Or ate? She was so tired too. Surely she was far enough away now to stop for a drink and a rest?

But drinking from a stream with her hands tied was nearly impossible. She tried to cup them and scoop the water up, but the water escaped before she could get it to her mouth. In the end she lay down awkwardly, her belly on her arms, hanging her head over the stream and lapping.

It was uncomfortable lying on her hands, so when she had finished drinking Lalune rolled on to her back into the shelter of a tree. Strong gusts of wind drove the rain like steel rods almost horizontally, but the tree sheltered her from the worst of it. She could smell mushrooms, and she was achingly reminded of Sunguide.

'Oh, Sunguide, my friendly Pruppras,' she murmured. 'What would you do? Why did you ever leave us?'

She was shocked to find herself jerking awake with no idea how long she'd been asleep.

She sat up in a fright and scrambled to her feet. It was still raining hard, and the wind was howling more than ever.

'I fell asleep! I mustn't sleep! I have to . . .'

Lalune suddenly realized that she had stood up with no difficulty at all.

Her wrists were no longer tied. The ropes that had bound them had rotted away, their remains dangling from her arms, mushy and useless. Her exhausted mind tried to make sense of this when somebody spoke.

'Prpr. You are awake. Is good.'

41

Solly saw a carriage arrive from the tiny cell where he had been imprisoned. The window was barred, though it wasn't really necessary. The moment he had woken Sybilla Geenpool had appeared, fully recovered from the drugged wine and had made him drink something that made him feel so weak and helpless that if he'd tried to stand up he'd have collapsed.

He knew because he'd already tried.

Now he just lay there, staring out of the window, wondering where he was and which room Lalune was being held in.

First out of the carriage was a huge Appaloosian woman wearing some kind of uniform. Perhaps she was a nurse. She had that kind of air about her: orderly, efficient and authoritative. She was carrying a black leather bag and a small case, which she put into the arms of a waiting servant. Solly knew he was a servant because he'd been the one they'd ordered to pick Solly up when he fell. But he'd also seen him striding about the building as if he owned the place. Perhaps he did, and Sybilla had appropriated it.

The servant scurried into the building with the bags. The nurse turned back to the carriage where a sandalled foot had emerged. This was followed by an emaciated leg clad in short crimson breeches so richly hued that Solly wondered how the leg didn't break from the intensity of the colour.

The nurse held both arms up to receive the rest of the person into them: obviously walking was out of the question. She lifted her patient out. Solly saw a russet-coloured sleeveless tunic embroidered with copper thread, over a ruffled silk shirt the same amber colour as the stone of the Key of Being.

Solly barely had the energy to groan at this memory. These people, whoever they were, had kidnapped and drugged him. They had taken his clothes, his bandoleer, and the Key, and had dressed him in a rough white robe.

He heard a querulous voice speaking. It was feeble, but for all that it was the voice of a boy who'd never been disobeyed in his life.

'I want to see it. Right away.'

The nurse turned, carrying her burden, and Solly could see from her face that she didn't think this was a good idea. Presumably she knew the consequences of insubordination however, for she said nothing.

The servant had returned, and bowed down so low that his hair flopped into a puddle.

'Imperator, perhaps first a drink, and a short rest—'

'Who is this?' demanded the boy. 'How dare he address me uninvited?'

'A menial, Imperator,' said the nurse. 'He is of no consequence. Shall I have him sent away?'

The man, still bowing low, began to protest.

'I apologize . . . merely wished to welcome . . . humble abode . . .'

'I will not be spoken to by menials,' shouted the boy. He sat up in the nurse's arms for a moment, then sank back, worn out by the effort. Solly glimpsed a blur of lank blond hair, and a gaunt, white face.

The nurse nodded to a huissier, who came hurrying out, grabbed the servant roughly by the arm and dragged him out of sight.

'Take me to see it,' said the boy.

The nurse marched towards the building, and Solly shut his eyes, thinking that was it. Then he heard voices murmuring outside his room, and the door opened.

'Put me down,' ordered the boy.

Solly heard a scuffle and soft footsteps, but his eyelids felt too heavy to open just yet.

'It is sunburnt.'

'Superficial burns, Imperator. They will be gone in a few days,' said Sybilla.

'Its hair will have to be cleaned and cut.'

'Yes, Imperator.'

'Suitable clothing must be found. I will not be seen in common cloth.'

'It has already been ordered, Imperator.'

The boy shuffled around into Solly's view, and Solly forced his weary eyes to open to see the face of this tyrant.

He found himself staring at himself. Was it some kind of mirror? If so, it was a horrible distorting mirror. Either that or he'd been ill without realizing it. The face was so thin Solly could almost see the texture of the bones under the stretched skin. The hair was the right colour, but looked limp and lifeless. The eyes blazed brightly, as if he had a fever.

Then the face smiled a thin satisfied smile, and Solly knew that his own mouth hadn't moved. This wasn't him after all. It was the sick boy from the carriage.

'It is perfect,' whispered the boy. 'Perfect. You have done well, Sybilla.'

'I am indebted by your clemency, Imperator.'

'When will the procedure begin?'

'Immediately, Imperator. We await your pleasure.'

'And this doctor – he is able to do it?'

'Of course, Imperator. He is an expert.'

'An expert, yes, Sybilla Geenpool, but not the only one. Let him know that. Nobody is irreplaceable.'

'I shall inform him at once. Now, if you wish, Imperator, we can start to prepare the subject immediately.'

'I wish it.'

There was some movement behind him, and Solly heard the creak of a door being opened in the passage outside the room. Moments later the nurse appeared carrying a syringe full of clear liquid.

'What will that do?' said the boy.

'It will destroy the subject's self-awareness, Imperator,' she replied, swabbing Solly's arm. 'The person inside this body will shrink until there is nothing of him left. Then, when the doctor is satisfied, perhaps tomorrow, he will begin the next stage, of inserting your Imperial Soul into this healthy body.'

Solly couldn't even struggle. He couldn't lift his littlest finger to help himself. He could only watch as the nurse held the syringe up to the light.

He prayed. For the first time in his life, he prayed.

Help me!

And he heard a voice in his head, as loud as if the speaker were standing behind him.

Remember the lessons your father taught you. Build a walled stronghold inside yourself, so that you can be safe within.

Nobody else looked up. They hadn't heard it.

The nurse squeezed the syringe and a filament of liquid flashed out of it.

Solly concentrated on steadying his heartbeat. He breathed once, as deeply as he could in his feeble state. There wasn't time for any more. He imagined his father's voice instructing him

Think about the walls. Think like the walls. Think cold and strong and solid and immovable.

Now the nurse was approaching him.

Draw the walls into yourself. Draw in their solidity, their immovability, their strength, their coldness. Draw it into yourself.

The nurse had hold of his arm now, the needle poised. She was stroking the inside of his elbow, but he hardly noticed it. He was busy building a wall in his mind, drawing it up out of the cell walls. Up, up it rose, strengthening and thickening, and when the needle entered and he felt the cold liquid surge into his veins he was ready for it. The drug raced through his body, but Solly was already locked away inside a secret room. His body was no longer his own, but he clung on to his mind.

Then the Being spoke again.

It is not for long. Soon comes the end, one way or another. The final days begin, and Clandoi will be freed.

'Sunguide! Oh, Sunguide!'

Lalune felt for him, and there he was in her arms, all rubbery and comforting, blowing through his flaps soothingly while she cried.

'Prpr,' he said at last. 'Must go. Storrrm is getting worrrse.'

'Where will we go?' said Lalune, feeling hysteria rising from deep inside her. 'We can't go back up the hill. They've got Solly up there, they want him for something, but they were going to kill me. I don't know what they want him for. I didn't want to leave him, but I had to. I had to, Sunguide—'

'Prpr. Shhh,' Sunguide said. 'Do not distrrress yourrrself, moon girl. We must find shelter. Prrriority.'

Lalune took a deep breath and tried to calm down.

'Good,' said Sunguide approvingly. 'I will fly here in frrront of you. Put yourrr hands on me, and I will be yourrr eyes.'

The rain stung Lalune's face, and the wind grew ever more powerful. With Sunguide there Lalune could go faster than before, but he couldn't stop her feet from finding roots to trip on, or the branches from whipping her legs. She was wet through, and although it had been far colder under the Ne'Lethe she shivered in the dreadful wind.

When they had walked for what seemed like hours she sensed that she had reached the end of the trees, or at least a large clearing.

A mighty blast plucked her from the relative shelter of the trees and flung her out into the open, away from Sunguide. She landed in a muddy puddle.

'Prpr. Are all rrright, moon-girl?'

The wind howled so loudly that she could hardly hear him. She nodded and sat up, groaning. Her shoulder hurt, and she could feel warm blood trickling from her sore knees.

Something hit her hard on the arm.

'Ouch!'

'Quick, moon-girrrl,' Sunguide shouted urgently. 'Move out of open place.'

Then there was a thud on the ground next to her, a splash in a puddle, and suddenly she was in a battleground, with cannonballs hurling at her, smashing through the trees, bouncing off the ground.

'What is it?' Lalune screamed as she was hit repeatedly on her head, arms, legs and body. 'What's happening?'

'Hail!' bellowed Sunguide.

As she scrambled up Lalune's hand closed on a hailstone as big as her fist. Every moment she stood in the open was a moment she could be knocked out. She had to find shelter, and quickly. She ducked her head down and scurried back under the trees, where the ice balls were slowed slightly by the leaves.

But even here she was soon ankle-deep in ice and

bruised all over. The wind howled and the noise was deafening. Shivering and grasping Sunguide so tight she must have hurt him, Lalune hobbled across the uneven ground, slipping and scraping her elbows and knees.

'In here!' Sunguide yelled, tugging her to the left.

She followed, and gasped as she moved from the maelstrom outside into a warm hollow place . . .

. . . and stopped, amazed. She could see again, properly this time, in true colours. She felt her face glow with a sense of wonder. Was she dreaming? Were her eyes really back?

43

Seachrân was prodded out of sleep by the sound of muted voices and feet running in the direction of the hospital tent.

His first thought was of Etolantie. Aube had woken the previous day. Both were healing excellently, Si-Sef assured him: but he knew that burns could get infected, and with such large burns . . .

Grabbing a tunic he scrabbled into it as he ran, not caring who saw him half naked. But when he reached the hospital it wasn't Etolantie's bed surrounded by Si-Sef and several assistants; nor was it Aube's.

'Just concentrate on breathing, Halig,' Si-Sef ordered. 'Ninem, see to the line, please. Kiel, take this to be tested.'

'Yes, Si-Sef,' said the two helpers meekly. They didn't exactly run to do what she said, but Seachrân did have to dodge out of their way in case they knocked him over.

He approached the bed anxiously, and Halig's eyes widened when she saw him. She started trying to tell him something, but her voice was muffled by the oxygen mask.

Si-Sef hadn't seen him yet.

'Hold still, Halig! Really, woman, you are quite the worst patient I've ever had to deal with!'

'Seachrân!' gasped Halig, pulling the mask off.

179

'What are *you* doing here?' said Si-Sef crossly, replacing it. 'Out of the way, please.'

One of the assistants moved him firmly away from the bed and carried on working on the Seer.

'W . . . w . . . what's wrong with her?' said Seachrân, frightened. 'H . . . her eyes are y . . . yellow.'

'Her organs are shutting down,' Si-Sef said shortly, plugging some wires into a bubblescreen. The other ends snaked under Halig's night-gown.

Halig disliked bubblescreens: the only one in Kloster Hallow was one Kepler had brought with him. Kepler thought nobody knew about it, but here it was, attached to Halig.

She must be really, really ill, thought Seachrân, and he tugged on his necklace and prayed desperately.

Halig shook her head and tugged at the mask again, gesturing at Seachrân to come closer. Si-Sef held it over her mouth, but let her remove it when she saw that Halig wasn't going to give up.

'I suppose I won't get you to relax until you've said what you want to say,' she sighed, examining the zigzags dancing over the bubblescreen. 'But quickly.'

'I have Seen somebody,' Halig wheezed, and sucked at the mask again. 'In the forest.'

'Don't you think it's about time you stopped worrying about other people and started showing a little concern for yourself?' Si-Sef said, rapping the bubblescreen aggressively. 'Kiel, come and make this thing work!'

'You sent him to the lab,' said Ninem, motioning another assistant to take over from him. 'I'll do it, Si-Sef.'

'A girl,' said Halig. 'Your age . . . Do you understand

180

what . . . I am saying, Seachrân? . . . *Exactly* your age.'

Seachrân nodded. He didn't know if he imagined the sudden hush, broken only by the hiss of oxygen.

'The Being be praised,' whispered Ninem. 'Another Holder of the Key of Being.'

Halig took the mask from her face again.

'You have to find her. She is in the . . . Glade of Janus Trees.' She had to inhale oxygen every few words. 'She is burned too . . . take lotions . . . and water . . .'

She finally allowed Si-Sef to replace the mask. The bubblescreen beeped into life.

Seachrân backed away as Halig's bed was obscured by a flurry of medical assistants.

'W . . . will you be able to h . . . help her?' he said.

'We'd do a lot better without all these interruptions,' said Si-Sef sharply, but she looked up as she said it, and he saw the look in her eyes. She was just as scared as he was.

He turned and almost knocked Etolantie over. She was wrapped in a sheet and staring into the room with huge eyes.

'I bet she means Lalune,' she whispered.

'You heard her?'

Etolantie nodded.

'She an' Solly came through the Ne'Lethe with us, but when the men came they took her an' Solly, an' left me an' Aube. She din't say she Saw Solly. Why din't she?'

Seachrân towed her out of the room.

'I d . . . don't know. Seeing's a f . . . funny thing: it d . . . doesn't mean he's n . . . not with her.'

'Can I come? She won't know you. An' I'm better from my burns now.'

181

'G . . . go and wake Aube. I'll get K . . . Kepler C . . . Coriolis and find some stuff for her b . . . burns. I'll c . . . come back here for you.'

He looked at the room where Halig was one last time before leaving.

44

She is inside a hollow tree. Sunguide is resting on the ground next to her.

The terrifying noise outside is muffled. The air is warm, soporific, and Lalune leans against the wall of the tree.

It is surprisingly soft, covered in velvety fibres that secrete a sweet, warming essence. She strokes it.

Her mind fills with memories, each evaporating as soon as it arrives. As if they are being taken from her. At first she struggles, but it is easier to let it happen, and before long she has forgotten about the storm, about Solly, about everything but this.

She has even forgotten that there was ever a girl called Lalune.

This is where she has always wanted to be, here inside this tree.

There is a pile of orange fungus nearby. Something tells her that it has a name, but it isn't important enough for her to remember it right now.

There is a creaking sound, and the far side of the tree begins to open up. She can see a tunnel, and she knows that at the end of the tunnel she will find the most beautiful place in the world. She wants to go there, but the opening is too narrow. She will have to wait.

Perhaps she will sleep. When she awakes the opening will be wide enough and she can go through.

The door she came in by makes a slight noise. Very slowly it *starts to ease itself shut. One door closes, one opens.*

Something is going on outside, in the place she came from, a storm perhaps. If storm is the word. There are hailstones. What are hailstones? It doesn't matter. In here is what matters.

She stretches luxuriously against the smooth, soft trunk. In here, and what is through the second door.

Such a beautiful place waits on the other side.

Such a beautiful place.

Such a beautiful . . .

. . . beautiful . . .

A crash from outside. She jerks awake, annoyed. A branch has been blown in to the closing door, and it can't move any further. If it doesn't shut perhaps the other won't open, then she'll never be able to go through.

She drags away from the trunk. Strands of it stick to her, trying to hold her back, but they are still too flimsy. They float in the air around her, a magical haze. Some have penetrated her skin. She can see an iridescent fluid moving lazily through them.

How strange.

She will think about this later. For now, she must make her way through the thickening fronds to free the branch from the doorway. Nothing must stop her from going through the other doorway.

What a long way away it is. She walks and walks, but never reaches it.

There is a brassy shout, and she snaps awake.

She fell asleep! She was only dreaming about walking!

Now which doorway was she heading for?

They are identical.

A branch blocks both of them.

She considers them carefully. A second branch blocking the second door? It must be an illusion designed to deceive her.

Both branches are stuck diagonally across the doorways.

But surely one doorway is expanding little by little? The branch doesn't quite touch the edge: that one is the mirage.

She approaches the other and takes hold of the branch.

There is a flash of blue and brass that travels up her arm and through her body and into her head, and the strands that pierced her are suddenly severed.

A whiff of smoke: the tree around her quivered.

She remembered there was a girl called Lalune.

She remembered that she was that girl.

She remembered what the Being had said: only she could see the world of the angels. His world. She was sure she'd had eyes again, but they had gone now. She must have dreamt it.

Another deception.

It was peculiar though, she *could* see a little. Her vision was in negative again, but it was definitely back.

More memories came back.

She remembered Solly . . . and Sunguide.

'Sunguide! Wake up!'

A strand from the tree snaked around her wrist, and she felt a tiny prick.

'The tree! It's killing us!'

She yanked it out of her arm and grabbed Sunguide, tearing the fibres out of his little body too. Still clutching the branch she stumbled out of the open door. The sun was blazing down, the birds were singing, steam was rising from the ground, all the colours reversed but *she could still see it all.*

She raced as far away from the tree as she could before

185

throwing herself and Sunguide down on the ground in the hot, hot sun, and weeping for relief and joy.

45

Lalune felt the heat from the sun on her bare arms, and was shocked to see how raw they looked. Streamers of skin flapped from old blisters. Tiny punctures showed where the tree had pierced her.

Sunguide lifted himself unsteadily from the ground. He too was covered in pinpricks.

'Prpr. What is?'

'We went into a tree for shelter. I think it was carnivorous. Look at my arms.'

Sunguide didn't look at all well. He lurched towards Lalune to look, and was barely able to maintain his hover.

'Prpr. Arrrms already like that when I found you. Looks more like burrrn from the sun. But the holes . . . yes could be a carnivorrrous trrree.'

He let himself sink to the ground again, his flaps dropping.

'The *sun* did this?'

Lalune looked up. But it seemed that the sight she had regained didn't extend as far as the sky. It was a fiercely hot day again, now that the rain had stopped; but all she could see beyond the trees was blackness.

She sighed. At least she could see the trees, even if their leaves did look blood red instead of green. But the forest looked the same in every direction.

'We're lost,' she said. 'Sybilla's got Solly: they're going to do something to him. And Etolantie, Aube . . . we got separated from them.'

The pain in her heart was bigger than the whole world.

'Prpr,' said Sunguide faintly. 'Spores will help us . . .'

He made a noise that could have been a snore. Lalune sat down beside him and put the branch down on the ground.

Immediately her vision vanished.

She picked up the branch again, and her negative sight returned.

She tried it again. It was definitely the branch that was affecting her. She looked at it more closely. It was a strong, slender limb, maybe a sapling rather than a branch. It was the thickness of her wrist, and about the same height as she was. The wood was very dark, almost black, and very shiny. One end was a little wider, and ended in a lump with dry leaves wrapped around it. She pulled at them, peeling away layer after layer. Roots were revealed, spiralling around something that glinted.

Lalune's hands began to shake.

'I know what this is!' she whispered. '*I know what this is!*'

This was no sapling torn from the ground in a storm. It was a polished staff. Caught in its roots was a stone that gleamed and twinkled with an inner fire. And there were letters carved down the side.

'*The Staff of the Key of Being,*' she read in an awed whisper. '*One its owner finds.*'

46

Lalune eased the stone gently though the roots and held it in the palm of her hand. It quivered as if it were alive, and emitted a pure, clean note that resonated deep inside her. Yellow flames circled her without pain, cool and refreshing on her burns. The colours, still seen in reverse, became even more intense. She could pick out the detail on a tree the other side of the clearing, seeing minute insects without straining. She felt a strong desire to get up and run, and keep on running. There was something she had to do . . .

Abruptly she slid the stone back into the staff. She remembered what Solly had told her. If she held on to it for too long it would take over her will.

Lalune sank to her knees, humbled. Here she was, soulless, a monster, part of a Wayfarer prophecy. Was there some mistake? Didn't the Being actually mean for a *proper* Wayfarer to have the staff?

'Oh, Being,' she whispered, 'I don't deserve this.'

They wind whispered in the trees above her head, and the stone in the staff shone. She remembered how the staff had blown into the door in the tree, stopping it from closing.

It had saved her life. There was no doubt that it had

saved her. And somehow it enabled her to see, even though she had no eyes. She touched her empty sockets, and once again remembered what the Being had told her. *You are the one who will be able to see the world of angels: my world. Nobody else can do what you will do.*

She was still kneeling there when she heard voices. Her heart began to beat rapidly. Had Sybilla caught up with her? She stayed very still, hoping that she was well hidden.

'. . . long gone by now . . .'

'Perhaps we can track her?'

'The storm will have obliterated most signs.'

'Halig Saw her . . .'

Halig! Sybilla had mentioned that name. If this Halig was one of Sybilla's enemies, maybe she could help.

But being against Sybilla doesn't mean she's on my side. Sybilla seemed fairly angry with the huissier as well. How do I know who I can trust?

She picked up Sunguide, who blew through his flaps without waking, and crawled into the bushes to wait. She was too tired to run.

'We got to hurry, Aube,' said a familiar voice, full of fear and anxiety.

'Etolantie!' Lalune said. 'Aube!'

'Lalune!' shouted Etolantie.

'She's somewhere over there,' said another voice.

'Where? I can't see her . . .'

'There! In the bushes!'

There was the sound of running footsteps, and Lalune was nearly flattened.

'Lalune!' sobbed Etolantie. 'I thought I'd lost you! I thought you was dead . . .'

'I'm here now,' said Lalune.

'An' Sunguide! You found us! Sunguide? What's the matter with him? Is he asleep?'

'I think so. We had to shelter from the storm, only we chose the wrong kind of tree.'

'Where's Solly?' said Etolantie in a quavery voice.

Lalune's chest heaved. *They said that you told them where to find us, Etolantie. Why?*

And now they had Solly. She didn't know what to say.

But she didn't have to say anything right now, as other people had arrived. Aube was there, walking stiffly with his stick; a thin boy wearing braces on his legs, some fuzzy creature around his neck; and a crowd of others too. Hands pulled her into the clearing, and somebody put a blanket around her, though it wasn't cold. Everybody was talking at once.

'Quite some burns you've got there, dearie.'

'Wh . . . what's the orange thing?'

'Best get her back as soon as we can.'

'He's one of the Pruppras. Most interesting creatures. Most. Fungi, you know?'

'He can talk an' all. Least he can when he's awake.'

'I expect you're hungry aren't you?'

'How did you find me?' said Lalune.

'It was Halig,' said Etolantie. 'She's a Seer, jus' like Aube. She Saw you in the forest, an' we came an' found you. She does it all the time, Seachrân says. Where's Solly? What happened?'

She touched Lalune's face and caressed her eye sockets, as if to make sure she was really there.

She can't have meant to tell the kidnappers.

191

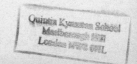

Etolantie was smothered in thick goo, black to Lalune's eyes where the sun had burned her. Somebody was applying the same stuff to Lalune.

A bottle of water was put into her hands, and she drank thirstily before answering.

'Sybilla caught us.'

Etolantie gasped.

'Sybilla! Has she got Solly? How'd she find you?'

'We got separated from you,' Lalune said. 'Some men came along and kidnapped us. They said you told them where to find us, Etolantie. Did you?'

Etolantie paled.

'I thought they was going to help us. I din't know they were bad men. Then they left us, an' we would've died, only Seachrân came and found us. They asked if I knew where Solly was. What do they want him for?'

'I don't know,' Lalune said as somebody dabbed something cool on to her shoulders. She looked around. Who could she trust?

Somebody pushed a piece of bread into Lalune's hand, and she took a bite. She couldn't remember when she'd last eaten.

'We'll go back to the camp,' said a swarthy-looking man. 'You need to have those burns properly treated.'

He didn't mention Solly.

47

Seachrân led them to the edge of the forest, where they had left a sandcamel cart.

'Star?' said the girl. 'He looks different. Was he burned too?'

Seachrân was astonished. The girl had no eyes, and her eyelids had been sewn together. How on Clandoi could she see the sandcamel? His eyes slid to the staff she was gripping so tightly, and he felt a shock of recognition. It was part of the Key of Being, he was certain. He felt under his tunic for his mother's necklace: the first part of the Key. He wanted to ask, but for some reason felt tongue-tied.

'She's called Modya,' Etolantie said in a small voice.

'They call them sandcamels here,' Aube said. 'Star's back at Kloster Hallow, being looked after and making friends with the other sandcamels.'

Seachrân helped the girl up into the cart. There was just enough room for her, Etolantie and Aube. Etolantie held Sunguide, the funny little mushroomy thing she said could talk. The rest of the rescuers would walk.

'When will Sunguide wake, Aube?' Etolantie asked anxiously. 'I know when he tears himself you can mend him with toffee an' sticky tape, but I don't know any other medicines.'

'We shall just have to wait and see, hmm,' Aube said. 'But don't worry yourself. Most resilient, these Pruppras; most.'

Seachrân perched unsteadily on the front ledge of the cart, the queggel digging its clawed toes into his neck. He snapped the whip in the air above Modya, urging her into a fast trot. He was torn between his desire to get back to Halig and his need to speak to this girl. Did she know who the third Holder on the Key was? Or where they were to lead the people in the Great Migration?

But she was behind him, and that alone would have made conversation difficult, even without this overwhelming shyness.

It also took a certain amount of concentration not to fall off the cart.

Etolantie was unusually subdued. The girl had said something to upset her, though Seachrân didn't know what. Their journey was consequently almost silent.

He knew what had happened the moment they clattered into Kloster Hallow. Without saying a word to his passengers – without even waiting for Modya to stop – he slithered down from the cart and loped, stiff-legged, into the hospital tent.

'H . . . Halig!' he cried, but was met only by sorrowful faces. 'Halig!'

He found Si-Sef sobbing into a pile of sheets. She lifted her swollen face to him. She had clearly been crying for a long time. Normally so severe, she held out her arms to him, and he rushed into them.

'She was the only mother I ever knew,' she whispered hopelessly. 'I was orphaned when I was two, and nobody wanted me.'

194

'W . . . when did she d . . . d . . . die?'

'About an hour ago. It was very sudden . . . everything just gave up, all at once. I couldn't save her . . .'

Seachrân left her and pushed open the door to Halig's room. The bubblescreen had been turned off. The room felt chilly. The air smelt unfamiliar, disinfected.

Si-Sef's assistants were busy washing and re-clothing the Seer, but when they saw Seachrân they stood back, dabbing their eyes.

'Halig!' cried Seachrân. 'W . . . why?'

He threw himself down next to her and held her hand. It wasn't as cold as he thought it would be, and was bony, as if it had no muscle left at all.

'I wasn't h . . . here,' he said. 'I w . . . wasn't here.'

'You were doing as she asked,' said one of the assistants gently. 'That was more important.'

'You couldn't have done anything, Seachrân,' said Si-Sef from the doorway. 'And I think once she had told you to go that was it. Her job was done. She could leave us.'

'Her last prophecy,' said another assistant, picking up a hairbrush and running it through the old woman's thick hair until it lay around her like a veil.

Seachrân sank to the floor and sobbed and sobbed.

Some time later, when the tears had stopped, Si-Sef pulled him to his feet.

'We have to ready her for burial,' she said firmly but kindly. 'Go outside. Your friends are waiting for you, and there's food.'

'I d . . . don't want t . . . to eat.'

'No,' said Si-Sef. 'But your body needs it.'

Seachrân's legs had cramped up, and he staggered, giving

one last look to the woman who had been his whole world for so long.

Lalune, Etolantie and Aube were sitting under the shade of a large tree, eating bread and cheese. The mushroom, Sunguide, was awake, though groggy, and Etolantie was squirting honeyed water over him at intervals.

He could see that they knew what had happened. Etolantie stood up to shake his hand.

'That is a very interesting gesture,' Aube said, wiggling his eyebrows comically. 'I have seen a number of people doing it, but I can't quite work out its meaning, hmm?'

'It's called shaking hands,' Etolantie said. 'Seachrân told me. It means ever so many things: "hello", an' "goodbye", an' "sorry", an' "I promise", an' all sorts of things. This one means, "I'm sorry".'

Seachrân had to smile at this, if a little wanly.

'What a useful thing,' said Lalune, making a place for him at the table. 'How do you know which one it means?'

She had a lovely voice: the same accent as Etolantie, low and guttural, but more polished.

'I spec you use different hands, or waggle your fingers, or something,' Etolantie said, passing a plate of bread to Seachrân. She sounded as if she had been crying too.

Seachrân took a hunk of bread and nibbled it, to please Si-Sef, but it refused to go past his throat, so he fed it to the queggel instead. He was thirsty, however, and drank cups and cups of tea, hot and comforting, while he listened to the others talking about life under the Ne'Lethe, and how different it was to here. Apparently they lived in proper houses, not tents at all. And it was so cold you could see your breath, all the time.

But they only succeeding in distracting him from Halig for a short while. And when he thought about her, he couldn't help the tears spilling out again.

Etolantie got up at once and hugged him; Lalune patted his knee.

'I lost my ma an' pa,' Etolantie whispered. 'If you cry about it, you feel better quicker. An' Lalune's pa, I mean her father, he's lost too.'

'We've all lost so much,' Lalune said softly.

'Sh . . . sh . . . she was so p . . . precious,' Seachrân said. 'The most p . . . precious thing in m . . . my life.'

In the midst of their whispering together and comforting each other, they became aware that Aube had stood up, and was staring into the distance in a strange way. He was a very short man – almost a dwarf – but Seachrân had the distinct sense that he was looming over them as he intoned in a loud voice:

'*The ice shall grow, many shall starve, and many shall sleep. Hard times are coming. But when times are at their hardest, and each has lost that which is most precious, the time for journeying shall come. They must find the Key, and that Key shall turn back the ice. The boy is the Sun, for by him we shall see the Sun again; and the girl is the Moon, for by her we shall see the Moon again; and the other is the Visitor, for by him we shall see the Visitor again. They shall journey together yet alone.* This was the Prophecy, given on the day you all were born. Each of you has lost that which is most precious. The time for journeying alone is passed. The Visitor has returned in the form of a comet. Solly is the sun, and Lalune is the moon. Seachrân is the Visitor: known as the Wanderer, the comet that streaks across the skies. When these three

197

celestial bodies encompass the Queen of the Stars in equal degree, that is the time to use the Key, and turn back the ice.'

Seachrân stared at him in awe.

'W . . . was that a p . . . prophecy of the B . . . Being?' he asked.

'He *is* a Seer,' said Etolantie.

Aube mopped his forehead.

'I do believe it was.'

'The first bit: that's what you said on the day Solly and I were born,' said Lalune.

But it was the second part that interested Seachrân more.

'Th . . . the Encompassing in Equal D . . . degree,' he said.

'Prpr. I have heard of this occurrence,' said Sunguide.

'Now there's the thing,' said Aube. 'Sometimes these words come out and I have no idea what they mean. No idea at all. Still, it's not my job to try to understand. That is for the people involved. Which in this case—'

'But *I* kn . . . know w . . . what it m . . . means!' said Seachrân. 'I n . . . need t . . . to ask K . . . K . . . Kepler w . . . w . . . when . . .'

He stuttered to a halt. Kepler had definitely mentioned it. Seachrân couldn't remember if he'd said when it would happen. He tried saying it again, but couldn't get past Kepler's name.

'Ah, your astronomer,' said Aube. 'Most interesting man, hmm.'

'S . . . s . . . s . . . sorry . . .'

'Hold on to your Key,' said Lalune, touching her empty

198

eyes. 'It might help you get the words out. Mine helps me to see.'

'B . . . but you have no eyes,' Seachrân said.

'It's the angels,' Etolantie explained. 'Ain't it, Lalune? The Being sends them, an' then she can see without any eyes.'

'Something like that,' said Lalune. 'Try it, Seachrân.'

Seachrân grasped his necklace and shut his eyes. Taking a deep breath and concentrating on speaking slowly, he said, 'Kepler t . . . told me. There's an as . . . as . . . astronomical event. The s . . . sun, the Blue Moon and the c . . . comet all set at th . . . the same moment, equal distances apart. You have t . . . to be in the right place t . . . to see it exactly. B . . . but I don't know when.'

'What is the Queen of the Stars?' asked Lalune.

Seachrân took another breath.

But before he could get his words out, a cart pulled by a sweating sandcamel thundered into Kloster Hallow and pulled to a halt right in front of them.

48

'News!'

It was Aytem Sixty-Nine, the carter who had taken Seachrân and Halig along the sandcamel trail.

'News! A public proclamation from the Imperator himself!'

He was waving a spray can, and standing up in his cart so that everybody could hear.

'News! All must hear the message. All must be told. News!'

His eyes fell on Seachrân, and he gave a beaming grin.

'It's the Wise One's young charge! You made it back here all right, I see. And how is Halig? I haven't forgotten the invitation she gave me. Though that's not why I'm here. I've been sent, by the Palace. All the carters have. Got a proclamation to show. It's WASP footage of the Imperator himself, for a wonder. We all thought he was dying, but it seems not, as you'll see. Never saw a healthier boy. But everyone must see it, I've been told. Where is Halig? I need her to get everybody together.'

Seachrân seemed suddenly unable to open his mouth, and Lalune stood up and took his hand.

'Halig died today,' she said, fiddling with her scarf.

'Died!' said Aytem, shocked. He pulled his hat off his

head respectfully. 'I'm sorry, my lad. That's really sad news, that is. How did she die?'

Seachrân cleared his throat.

'Tree sickness.'

'Now that's even more of a shame, that is,' Aytem said, shaking the can. 'As you'll see when you watch this. Anywhere I can spray it where everyone will see?'

There weren't many people about.

'I'm not sure people are quite in the mood,' Aube said. 'What with Halig dying and so on.'

'I still have to show you all,' said Aytem, scratching his head. 'It's the Imperator, you know. Anyone else and I'd say leave it for another day. It can't be that important. But it's the Imperator.'

'Well, show it to us here, an' then go an' find other people,' said Etolantie.

'It's meant to be you all at once,' said the carter doubtfully. 'But I don't suppose anyone will find out. I just need somewhere big enough to spray it. This'll do.'

He indicated the hospital tent.

'Ah, not there, I think,' said Aube. 'Not quite the thing, with Halig still in there, hmm. How about that one?'

The carter nodded and carefully sprayed a large rectangle on to a different building. The film of liquid shimmered a little away from the surface of the wall. And just as Seachrân had once seen on somebody's bald head, a picture began to resolve itself in it. It looked like the film was flowing into place, organizing itself in a lazy spiral that became two figures. There was a tall black-haired woman and a blond young man, caught in mid-sentence by the look of it. Their faces were still too blurred to make out properly, but the building behind them was very familiar.

'Th . . . that is the Queen of the S . . . stars,' he said. 'At the Imperator's P . . . palace, where I used to w . . . work.'

Lalune made a strange noise and put her hand to her mouth. Etolantie was standing with her mouth wide open. *I know it's an impressive building* thought Seachrân, *but it's not that impressive.*

'They say that was built on another planet altogether,' said Aytem.

Gradually, gradually the image sharpened. The boy's face loomed close, and his mouth began to move. There was no sound yet.

Seachrân saw Lalune feeling for a chair and sitting down heavily. Before he could puzzle out why, a voice boomed out of the screen.

'People of Peleg City, of the whole of Clandoi, and of Kloster Hallow. I stand before you today whole and healthy. A cure has been found for the cursed tree sickness. You will know that I have been unable to leave my bed for many months; but this very morning, I ran a mile!'

There were faint cheers in the background. The WASP panned in closer. The Boy looked directly at them.

'Oh, Solly,' whispered Lalune. 'What have they done to you?'

49

Solly felt completely helpless.

His mouth moved, and words came out of it: they weren't his words. His arms gestured: they weren't his gestures. This morning his legs had made him run a pointless circuit of a field, dressed in what appeared to be his underwear, and accompanied by armed huissier and fawning servants who called him 'Imperator'.

And he could control none of it. His body was no longer his own. This Imperator was living inside his head, using him; he, Solly, was imprisoned behind a wall of his own making.

He wanted to howl. Another thing he couldn't do.

He tried to concentrate on the words his mouth was saying. Something about a new era for Clandoi. Sybilla Geenpool was called forward to explain the purpose of the cyberclinic; its presence under the Ne'Lethe came as an obvious shock to many, as cries of horror could clearly be heard beneath the dutiful clapping.

Then the Imperator spoke again, announcing amnesty to all who swore fealty to him, and the new cure, these clones in the cyberclinic, offered as a cure for all sufferers of the tree sickness. The people were ordered to hold a double celebration: the Imperator's recovery, and some astronomical event.

That wasn't the whole story, Solly knew. He had been there at the meeting with Sybilla and Dr Dollysheep, after all.

Dr Dollysheep! No wonder he'd been so keen to help him and Lalune to escape. Solly wanted to clench his fists, but of course he couldn't. Though surprisingly the Imperator chose that moment to punctuate his words by thumping the stand in front of him.

Those who opposed the Imperator – that was, anybody found *not* celebrating, and anybody heard to speak of something called the Great Migration – were to be frozen and sent immediately to the cyberclinic. They were to *be* the cure.

A name had been mentioned: 'Halig'. Apparently Halig led some sort of opposition group.

Solly could feel the Imperator's hatred for this woman. He could feel all his emotions, all the time. He despised almost everybody he met, and since he was some kind of prince he seemed to think he didn't have to hide it. He was rude and dictatorial, and there seemed to be nobody who dared to stand up to him. Even Sybilla was scared of him.

Ha! I bet she's not used to that!

The speech finished, and the crowd cheered. The huissier standing around the edges made sure of that. There were WASPs all around, and the Imperator took a few minutes to show off his new body to them before snapping his fingers at Dollysheep.

'Come. I wish to ask you something.'

He led the doctor into the Palace grounds. From here the Ne'Lethe could clearly be seen, brooding on the northernmost horizon. Over it the returning comet, the Wanderer, burned a greenish streak across the sky.

Pride of place had been given to a tower that reminded Solly of a picture he had seen long ago in Aube's cave. It was tall and pointed, with many windows, and it was made of some kind of shiny metal: it didn't match the rest of the Palace at all, which was yellow stone with a great deal of wood.

'That is the observatory,' said the Imperator. Solly felt momentary confusion. His arm lifted to wave away the many attendants who had entered with them, and they drew back to a respectful distance.

'And that is exactly what I wish to ask you about,' continued the Imperator.

'The observatory, Imperator?' said Dollysheep, startled.

'No, imbecile! About my treatment. This . . . body you acquired for me. You are quite sure that there is none of the original . . . person left inside it?'

'As sure as I can be, Imperator,' Dr Dollysheep said cautiously. 'Remember that it is an extremely new therapy.'

'But you are assured of its safety?'

'Of course, Imperator. As long as you follow the instructions I gave you: exercise well, avoid intensities of light and sound, and so on. May I ask: have you had any worrying symptoms?'

Solly's finger pointed at the observatory.

'The Queen of the Stars. The most recognizable building in the city. Everybody knows it, even if they have never been to Peleg City. I must have seen it every day of my life. And yet, when I saw it just now I felt . . . curiosity. And this morning, when I was out exercising, one of the

205

menials tried to run backwards and bow at the same time, and fell. And I noticed. And I laughed. I became angry during my speech, and struck the stand, though there was nothing for me to feel anger over.'

'I'm not sure that I understand, Imperator.'

The Imperator stamped Solly's foot in exasperation.

'Emotions, Dollysheep! I am experiencing unaccustomed emotions. Why would *I* wonder what the tower is for? Why would I heed a *menial* making a fool of himself?'

'There have been reports of patients who undergo heart transplants having similar occurrences, Imperator,' said Dollysheep. 'It passes.'

'You ran trials?'

'We used some of the clones in the cyberclinic, but we didn't wake them to see if there had been any psychological effects—'

'You had better be sure that there will be no more, Dollysheep,' said the boy. 'My death without an heir would cause considerable unrest. Clandoi acknowledges your role in my . . . healing. I had been considering rewarding you. I would not like it if anything happened to me that made me change my mind. I have given orders that if anything happened to me, the same should happen to you.'

50

They buried Halig the same day, as the sun set. It seemed very quick to Lalune and Etolantie, but Aube explained in a whisper that the heat would make her body smell very quickly.

The three of them were standing awkwardly to one side with Sunguide: not part of the mourners, but aware that they were the subject of many nudges and pointed fingers. Lalune had wanted to stay at the back, out of the way, but Seachrân had asked them to stay close to him, and he looked so sorrowful she couldn't say no.

From here they could see the Ne'Lethe, brooding on the northernmost horizon. Over it the comet, the Wanderer, burned its greenish streak across the sky. It was now close enough for the people to see the swirling patterns on its icy surface: it too was under much discussion. The sun set behind the trees, but Lalune was able to see the sky. Even *in negative*, it was better than nothing.

There were more people in Kloster Hallow than Lalune had ever seen in her life. Halig had been a great Seer and leader of her people, it seemed. Lalune wished very much that she had met her. People had been arriving for days, even before Halig had died, because of something they called the Great Migration.

Because burials happened so quickly here, the normal mourning period was a week. As this was Halig's funeral, it was likely to be nearer a month.

'How many will come?' asked Lalune, amazed.

'P . . . probably everybody living against the N . . . Ne'Lethe,' said Seachrân unsteadily. 'They are all N . . . New Wayfarers. And lots from P . . . Peleg City, t . . . too. Everybody on C . . . Clandoi knew Halig. And there's the G . . . Great Migration t . . . too.'

The Great Migration again.

'I was meaning to ask you about that . . .' Lalune began, but was interrupted by Si–Sef coming to fetch Seachrân to say goodbye to Halig. Etolantie went with them.

Kepler Coriolis stayed to keep them company. Aube had been explaining a great deal about the Wayfarers' way of life. Kepler was most intrigued.

'So you don't bury people straight away, under the Ne'Lethe?'

'For the Wayfarers it is very much dependent on the season, hmm,' Aube told him in a low voice.

A line of people was processing past the coffin that held Halig, and he didn't want to disturb them. Not that they were being quiet about it. There were wails and cries, and some even threw themselves in front of Halig's coffin and tore their clothes.

'The ground is too hard in the winter,' Aube went on, 'and we are not allowed to use wood for a pyre, so many people just wait until the spring. Or have a water burial, if they live near to the ocean. Now there's the thing. A sea burial is a moving event. Very final, you know: no grave. I buried my Pa that way. Makes you say your farewells properly. I confess, I don't really know what the Appaloosians do.'

'We cremate them,' said Lalune.

She watched Seachrân, who was weeping for the woman who had been a mother to him, and felt almost envious. She might never be able to say goodbye to her own parents. Etolantie was holding his hand, her thumb in her mouth. Lalune had never seen her suck her thumb before. Sunguide had fluttered forward too. Maybe he could heal grief; the Pruppras were good healers.

Si-Sef had her arm around Seachrân, and she was very nearly howling with sorrow. The musicians were playing something that made Lalune's heart feel as if it would tear in two.

'Kepler,' she said suddenly, 'what exactly does the Prophecy on this side of the Ne'Lethe say?'

'I can't remember the precise wording,' Kepler said, scrutinizing her with his intense black eyes. 'It's all to do with timing. The comet comes. The one who inherits the Key is revealed. That's Seachrân, of course. Two strangers appear with their Keys. You're one of them: you have the staff.'

'Solly is the other,' said Lalune, suppressing a huge sigh. 'But he's been taken by Sybilla Geenpool.'

'Then the Keys are used,' said Kepler. He too was thoughtful. 'Unfortunately the Prophecy doesn't specify how.'

'And then what?' asked Lalune.

'The ice is turned back,' said Aube, wiggling his eyebrows.

'Our Prophecy says the Ne'Lethe will disappear,' said Kepler, nodding emphatically.

'Probably the same thing, hmm?'

'And then comes the Great Migration.'

'People keep mentioning that,' said Lalune. 'What does it mean?'

'You don't know?' said Kepler in surprise.

'There is nothing of that mentioned in our Prophecies,' said Aube.

'Dear me,' said Kepler carefully.

'Is it important?'

'It is the return of the people to the land of our ancestors: a paradise called Earth,' Kepler said.

'I know about Earth,' said Lalune. 'It's in the Book that came with Solly's part of the Key. I don't think it was a paradise, though, from what I read. It's just another planet, like Clandoi. But it's home.'

Kepler and Aube both leaned forward. She felt she had to explain.

'The people of Earth thought they had discovered a group of genes that only criminals had. They tested the world's worst criminals and their families, and all the ones with the genes were put on a ship called the Queen of the Stars, and sent to Clandoi. They worked out that humans could survive here. Maybe they did succeed in making Earth into a paradise after that, I don't know. But I do know that all you Wayfarers and Pelegians are descended from two brothers: the worst criminals of them all.'

'What had they done that was so awful?' said Aube.

Lalune took a deep breath.

'They had begun the work that they continued here

on Clandoi. They created a farm of cloned human beings, so that they could sell their organs one by one until the clones were dead. Fully harvested. My people – the Appaloosians – we were those clones. That is why we have no souls. That is why we can never truly belong to the Being.'

'My dear child,' said Aube, squeezing Lalune's hand as she wiped away tears. 'Is that what you have been nursing all this time?'

Lalune nodded.

'But don't you know that the Being never turns away anybody who calls on him?'

'I don't have a soul,' whispered Lalune. 'How can the Being ever love me?'

'The very fact that you are able to question this *shows* that you have a soul,' said Aube. 'And as for the other . . . there is nobody alive who has earned the Being's love. But he still gives it.'

Kepler gave a big sigh.

'I don't think there was ever any such thing as a "criminal gene",' he said. 'I suspect that on this planet, this Earth, the people probably thought themselves safe from crime once they had dispatched that ship. They will have discovered their mistake: humans are humans, and they will do wrong.'

'And a great deal of right,' Aube said. 'By their reckoning, we are all criminals of the worst sort. Yet we have not *all* murdered each other and degenerated into some kind of society of terror.'

'You are quite certain that you know nothing of our return to this Earth?' said Kepler.

'Quite certain.'

'Hmm,' said Kepler. 'I was sure you would know. Maybe this other boy, Solly: maybe he knows.'

'He's never mentioned it,' said Lalune. 'Why would we know?'

'Because, with Seachrán and Solly, you are to lead us there.'

51

Lalune's head reeled. It was bad enough that she and the others were supposed to restore Clandoi's climate; now they were supposed to take the people back to Earth?

'I don't even know where it is,' she said. 'All the Book said was that it took three generations to get here. I'm not even sure what that means.'

'The grandparents left Earth, and the grandchildren arrived on Clandoi,' said Aube. 'Most interesting, most.'

'Of course, it might never get that far,' Kepler said. 'The Wanderer has appeared before, and that time the Holders failed.'

'*What?*' said Lalune.

'It's only a story. Maybe it never really happened. Even if it did, this may well be our last chance. It is quite possible that next time, the three celestial bodies won't coincide . . .'

'What do you mean, they failed?' said Lalune. 'What's the story?'

52

Solly had always resorted to action before. Now he had to think his way out, and it was difficult. He wished he had Lalune here to talk to.

This boy who was *snoring* in Solly's body: it made Solly want to punch a hole in the wall, thinking about it. This Imperator had only limited control.

Admittedly, the limits were pretty big. The Imperator could move Solly's body and speak with his mouth. Solly couldn't. The Imperator could, if he wished, harm Solly's body, perhaps even kill him. And Solly didn't think he could stop him.

But the conversation with Dollysheep had shown that some of Solly's own emotions were there, strong enough that the Imperator feared them.

Maybe I can make him do things?

What things?

I need to practise, see what I can make him do.

But what if he starts to resist? He's stronger than me. They might find a way to remove me forever.

Solly clenched his fist. And looked at it in surprise.

But he's asleep.

He punched the wall. Pain throbbed through his hand: exultation throbbed through Solly's mind.

The Imperator murmured and turned Solly's body over, but didn't wake.

I can have control when he's asleep, thought Solly. *I can use my emotions to make him do things when he's awake. It's not much. But it's all I have.*

He thought about what Brise would have said.

A real hunter uses what he has. He doesn't worry about what he doesn't have. A hunter plans, and then is ready to act on instinct. If he starts with his instinct, he's a dead hunter.

There was one other thing that Solly had.

The Being.

53

Kepler looked at her uneasily, and began to recite.

As the three passed, silence fell on the town of Peleg. Inside the simple huts mothers kept their children indoors behind twitching curtains. Fathers stood in their doorways, uneasily aware that armed huissier were stationed on every corner.

The footsteps of the three rang unnaturally loudly in the empty streets. One of them coughed nervously and clutched his staff tighter.

In the tower the Imperator, ruler of the Pelegians, waited, watching for them. He wore a sneer on his lips, though his stomach was churning.

If the Seer's prophecy was correct this was the end for him.

From this window he could see the Ne'Lethe brooding on the northernmost horizon. Over it the returning comet, the Wanderer, burned a greenish streak across the sky. It was close enough for the people to see the swirling patterns on its icy surface: close enough to affect the tides.

The three turned a corner and paused for a moment, staring up at the comet. The Imperator leaned out of the window so that he could see them better. All he knew about them was that they were the same age – exactly the same age – and had been chosen by prophecy. He was eager to see the faces of those who would bring him down.

'You can't be more than sixteen!' he sneered, derisive and afraid. 'You are nothing but underfed maggots.' He stretched out his hand and made as if to squash them between his thumb and forefinger. 'When you have failed, this is what I shall do to you.'

But they carried on walking.

The time was almost here. The fierce Clandoi sunlight was beginning to fade. The sky turned from brittle blue to mauve to orange. An eerie light lit up the western sky, marking where the Blue Moon would soon be rising. The orange moon, the one they knew as the Bane Moon, would follow soon after.

Now that they were closer he could see their faces. There was no certainty there, no arrogance, which was what he had expected. He wondered how they felt. They had not chosen this any more than he had chosen to be his father's heir.

A silver ray of light suddenly pierced the air. The full Blue Moon was rising. The three began to run.

'No, you must not be late,' he murmured.

They disappeared into a doorway. He turned and saw the Seer.

'Now we shall see who is right, Wise One,' he said as mockingly as he knew how.

'It matters not,' said the Seer with an irritating look of complacency on her face. 'If not this time, then next, or the time after that. Every two hundred and eighty years three shall be born for this task, until it is accomplished. Even you cannot alter the dance of the heavens, Imperator.'

He resisted hitting her.

'There are other things I can alter,' he said.

'Haven't you done enough?' she said. 'There is only so much abuse a planet can take. And you can't stop the people from remembering . . .'

She stopped because of the footsteps. The stairs were wooden:

a cruel and incredible decadence on Clandoi. It sounded as if the three had taken their shoes off to tread on them.

The Imperator stared at the Seer as the sound of them passed upwards into the great tower of the Queen of the Stars.

He hadn't wanted to watch. But now that the time had come, he couldn't bear not to.

He followed them up, and after him came the Seer, panting up the steep stairwell. Perhaps she was just as apprehensive as he was.

When they got there the girl turned and saw them.

'You can't stop us.'

He could hear a sweet tone humming: one of the Keys was already in place. It set his teeth on edge. Red light from the setting sun was focused through it in a thin line across the room.

'I don't intend to try,' he said lazily, though his heart was pounding so hard they must hear it, and he couldn't stop his eyes from flicking towards the Seer's staff. He had seen what she could do with that staff: the very real power she claimed came from her God, this 'Being'; and the more subtle authority she would wield over the people, if these three succeeded.

But they won't succeed, he told himself. And when they fail . . .

The girl added her Key. A thin beam of light pierced it, blue this time, from the Blue Moon, converging with the first so that the ceiling was sprayed with magenta light. A small, clear note was added to the sound from the first Key to make a two-note chord: a perfect fifth.

The major third was yet to be added.

The last of them held up his Key.

'Hurry,' said the girl. 'The moon . . .'

He nodded and went to slot it in place.

218

But he fumbled.

'Hurry,' said the girl.

Frantically he twisted it. He had put it in back to front: the green beam of light would not line up. He took it out and repositioned it.

The comet's meagre light whitened and strengthened. The Imperator's stomach twisted.

But the added note was a minor third.

It grew louder second by second.

The boy tried to remove the Key, but it was stuck solid.

The three looked at each other in despair.

The Imperator folded his arms and relaxed his shoulders, though the noise hurt his ears terribly. He walked calmly to the window and gave a sign to the huissier commander, who was waiting below.

The huissier made their move. The notes from the Keys grew louder still, until the Imperator could feel his teeth vibrate. A nearby window shattered from the strain. Screams of despair could be heard from the streets below. The people were beginning to feel the pain of the noise. Or maybe it was the huissier, being less gentle than they should.

The three had their hands over their ears.

The Imperator kept his own hands firmly by his sides, though the pain was almost unbearable.

'I have a prophecy of my own, Wise One,' he said as two huissier entered and roughly took hold of the rebels. He had to shout over the noise of the Keys. 'The people will forget. You and your kind have failed. This will never come to pass again.'

He watched the huissier drag the rebels from the room. He could take his time in deciding their fate. Most of the loyalists would be hoping for a public execution of some sort, and he was never one to deny the wishes of his people.

As for the rest, they would forget. The Seer was wrong. He would imprison them all under a cloud of forgetfulness. It was already planned. He had been angry when the technology hadn't been ready to put into place before the three arrived; but this way was better, so much better. The Rebels would no longer remember where they came from, and how they came to be imprisoned; the world outside its cloudy edges; even the sun, the moons and the stars.

Now that he was alone he removed the Keys. The discordant notes ceased. He could hear the wails of defeat from the houses below more clearly. He laughed out loud as he thought of how he would make the Wayfarer rebels suffer.

'I will issue Edicts restricting everything that makes life bearable,' he declared. 'Food, warmth, shelter, and every kind of luxury. Even children will only be permitted on my approval, for my own purposes.'

He was not going to allow the Three of the Prophecy to be born again, to aggravate his descendants as they had done to him.

54

'And that's what happened,' said Lalune flatly.

'It's only a story,' said Kepler, avoiding her eyes.

'So the chances are we will fail anyway?'

'Not necessarily,' said Aube. 'The Imperator ... the one that was then, anyway: he separated the Keys. No good on their own, you know. Even two of them aren't enough, hmm. By the Being, they have all been found again.'

'Do you have any idea what went wrong?'

Kepler shook his head. A steward was approaching them: it was their turn to file past the coffin.

Halig's body had been laid on the platform in the Telling Place. Later she would be carried to the Burying Place, a forest a little way from the main camp, where she would be buried and a tree planted over her. She would become part of the tree, and the tree would become part of her, Si–Sef had explained to them earlier on.

A flower was clasped in Halig's folded hands, and many more in all colours had been braided into her white hair. Lalune and Aube copied Kepler as he scooped a handful of petals from a basket and sprinkled them over her, murmuring:

'Being, take our dear friend Halig,
and keep her soul from decay.
Halig, travel safe to the Being's arms,
and watch 'til we join you one day.'

He wiped a tear from his eyes, and added, 'Goodbye, my friend.'

They stood for a few quiet moments before moving on to let others have their turn.

The carter, Aytem, joined them as they found a place to site. A tearstained child brought them drinks, and Kepler patted her on the head.

'So,' said Aytem to Lalune. 'One of the Holders of the Key, huh?'

Lalune nodded uncomfortably.

'I hear Halig's young ward is another?'

'Yes.'

'So there's a third somewhere here, too?'

Lalune glanced at Kepler. Could they trust this man?

Kepler seemed to think so.

'He should be. Came out of the Ne'Lethe with the young lady. But he's been kidnapped,'

'Kidnapped?' said the carter in astonishment. 'Who would kidnap one of the Holders of the Key? Unless . . . it's not the Imperator's lot, is it?'

'It seems so,' said Kepler.

'Ah,' said Aytem. 'And you're thinking about rescuing him in time for the Encompassing?'

'We hadn't discussed it,' said Lalune. 'But, yes, of course. That's when we have to use the Keys. He *has* to be free.'

222

'And I thought all that stuff was officially superstition,' said Aytem. 'In the City, mentioning anything to do with the Being, or the Migration, or anything like it, is banned. Punishable by, you know, *freezing*.' He made a mock shiver and eyed the Ne'Lethe. 'Where's he being held?'

'In the Palace,' said Kepler.

'Imperator's keeping a close eye on him, is he?'

'Closer than you can imagine,' said Lalune, her stomach knotting.

'Well, we'd better make a plan, hadn't we?' said Aytem.

'We?' said Aube, wiggling his eyebrows.

'Shouldn't Seachrân be here?' said Lalune.

'I shall fetch him,' said Kepler.

'Of course, we,' said Aytem. 'WASPs may be everywhere in the city, but they've not been put in our houses yet, praise the Being. People still talk, you know. I'd say two-thirds of the city saw that comet and wondered if this would be the time. Soon as they hear that the Keys have been found they'll be packing their bags ready. And I'll bet that as soon as I take them word of Halig's death, bless her soul, they'll be flocking here like snargs in the summer, travel restrictions or no.'

'Travel restrictions?' said Lalune in alarm.

'Why yes, didn't I mention that?' said the carter calmly. 'Nobody's allowed to travel without a special permit, linked to their DNA. I got one, of course, as I've got the Imperator's proclamation. Supposed to go to all the outlying farms around Kloster, I am. But there's WASPs everywhere. If your pendant doesn't *pass*, ha ha, *you* don't. And some of them WASPs have guns, now.'

55

Dear Heavenly Being, I know I haven't always believed.

Um, I never did, not until I found the Key, anyway. But I never believed in the sun or the stars and all that, but just because I didn't believe didn't make it not true.

I suppose I'm trying to say sorry.

And, please help me. You did before, when you told me to build the wall in my mind. I think that if I hadn't built it I would have died, and the Imperator would have had my body to himself.

But now I don't know how to get him out. Or me back in. And when I do get out, I need to find what they've done with the Key. And how to use it.

There's so much I don't know, Being. And all that's important, I know, but more than anything I need Lalune. What have they done with her? Please, what have they done with her? And Ma and Pa. I miss them so much. And Lalune's parents and Etolantie's family. Will we be able to rescue them?

Will everything just fall into place when we use the Keys?

Please, Being, I have to know.

56

Focus on your feelings, the Being told him. *The Imperator has never had to consider others. Make him feel.*

Solly concentrated as hard as he could. He thought that the Imperator's family would be a good place to start: love them or hate them, he was bound to have strong emotions about his parents.

It was harder than it sounded. Solly had no knowledge of what the Imperator's parents had been like, let alone where they were now. Directing pictures of Revas and Brise didn't seem to do anything.

And besides, the Imperator had been ill for so long that all he wanted to do now was to experience life, and as much as he could.

At dawn he ordered a skimmer and raced it through the streets. The kaufers had to be cleared out, losing a whole morning's earnings; and he destroyed the skimmer and part of a building, but he didn't care.

He had the huissier bring him their most powerful weapons, set them to stun, and hunted down some of the lower servants in the Palace, running through the corridors and grounds until he had exhausted the power in the guns. One servant was knocked unconscious, and several others were taken to the hospital wing for their injuries; the

Imperator roared with laughter.

Solly, horrified, tried to transmit remorse to this monster; but either the Imperator ignored it, or his sense of exhilaration was too strong to notice anything else.

He commanded the cook to prepare a huge feast, and gorged himself on all sorts of highly spiced meats, and an enormous pile of sweet mallownuts with cream and toffee sauce. The spices made his throat into a furnace, and the mallownuts, though heavenly, were so rich he was horribly sick afterwards.

His head throbbing, all Solly wanted to do was to lie down in a dark room. But instead the Imperator ordered exactly the same feast immediately, and ate just as much all over again.

Nobody stopped him.

Would your mother ever have allowed you to do this? Solly thought, his head spinning from too much wine. But the Imperator just belched loudly.

After this lunch Solly hoped that things would calm down a little; his stomach was uncomfortably full, and the Imperator's chief adviser had asked that he sit in the Judgement Seat to deal with some criminals. That sounded safe enough.

The Judgement Seat was a black throne set on a platform in a grim courtyard. An archway on one side showed the observatory. On the opposite side was the entrance to the deep dungeon, from which there was no exit.

The 'criminals' arrived from the city jail, barefoot and chained together.

'Prisoner AF 7092836. Repeat offender. Petty theft,' the guard read out from a sheet of etched acetate. 'She was stealing bread from a kaufer, Imperator. Prisoner AF 7398577. Same charge. Prisoners JM 7388884, JF 230846, and JF 230845 are all new offenders. All were caught stealing food, supposedly for their families.'

They were all Appaloosians. Solly was taken aback at the thought of Appaloosians going hungry. But the Imperator wasn't an Appaloosian. Sybilla wasn't and neither was Dr Dollysheep. Maybe out here, things were the other way around.

'There's only one way to deal with these low-lifes,' declared the Imperator. 'Find me a battle skimmer. Do we know where they live?'

'No, Imperator. Somewhere in the eastern part of the city.'

'That's good enough. It's about time we showed this vermin what happens to those who disobey my Edicts.'

Solly felt even more queasy. The image that had come into his mind had been of a huge vehicle, bigger than a house. The Imperator intended to take it out and crush an entire street. Any street.

He wished he could do something to stop it happening, but his own legs marched him to the skimmer, and his own hands operated the killing machine.

Being! he prayed. *Can't you do something?*

Keep concentrating on your emotions, Solly.

People ran out of the houses screaming and scrambling for safety. It didn't appear to concern the Imperator that he might be destroying the houses of innocent people. Or that some people might not have escaped.

Keep thinking, Solly told himself fiercely. *Remember Ma and Pa.*

He saw a heavily pregnant woman, gasping for breath, and supported by two other women, stagger out into the street.

She's in labour, he thought, shocked. A picture of Revas burst into his mind. The sounds that he had tried to forget assaulted him: the sounds of the huissier beating her and dragging her away with the rest of the Wayfarers. A terrible feeling of anguish overwhelmed him.

And at last the Imperator took notice. He started at the woman. Solly fed him more pictures of Revas. Pictures of the Imperator's own mother filtered through to Solly.

Solly worked on this. He dredged up every thought of cosy family life that he could. The Imperator responded with some of his own. His mother had been devoted to him; his father was cruel and distant.

Both of them were dead. Solly felt the Imperator's grief, and though it was so strong he felt as if his heart would burst, he added his own agonized feelings about his ma and pa. He'd managed to rescue Lalune, but they were still in the cyberclinic. Or dead.

The Imperator stopped driving abruptly, and climbed down from the skimmer.

'Take it to the Palace!' he ordered. 'I wish to run.'

Solly's body was fit; at least it had been until lunchtime. He was more than capable of running all the way back to the Palace.

The Imperator barely noticed the servants who scurried ahead to clear the way, and the bodyguards forming barriers in front and behind. He jogged swiftly past the shoddy housing until he came to the river.

There was a single bridge across it, guarded at both ends.

The Imperator loped across, pausing briefly in the middle as an enormous fish swam under it, sharp teeth bared menacingly. Solly wanted to stop and watch. It was a snarg. He'd never seen a live one before.

But the Imperator carried on. Everybody they passed bowed low. The Imperator acknowledged none of them.

He took Solly back into the Palace and towards the observatory tower. Guards sprang to open the door for him. He ignored them. A servant brought a towel and iced water.

Mopping his neck, he went straight to a door inside the observatory. He took a key from around his neck and unlocked it.

Solly recognized what was inside at once.

His bandoleer. Lalune's hair. His mother's necklace. The pouch containing fire dust.

And the Book of the Key of Being.

57

Seachrân brought a plate piled high with food. Etolantie and Sunguide were with him. There was a lot of rice, with roasted vegetables that smelt suspiciously spicy; cheese and biscuits, and fruit.

'Is there a shortage of meat here?' Lalune asked, taking an odd-looking knobbly fruit. 'There are food shortages of all sorts under the Ne'Lethe.'

Seachrân looked surprised.

'The W . . . Wayfarers didn't eat meat,' he said, 'so we d . . . don't either.'

Etolantie giggled at this.

'Wayfarers eat meat all the time. Sometimes in winter there ain't anything *but* meat to eat.'

Seachrân looked sheepish.

'I s . . . suppose we were just g . . . guessing,' he said.

'I had to give up eating meat when I came here,' said Kepler crossly. 'Halig insisted.'

'This fruit is certainly new to me,' Aube said. 'Only tiny berries under the Ne'Lethe, hmm.'

'We were discussing what to do about your Keys, Seachrân, and this other Holder, Solly,' said Kepler. 'The three of you have a job to do: it's not fair to make plans without you. The other thing we need to talk about is how we are supposed to leave Clandoi. Where do we go?'

'N . . . neither of us knows,' Seachrân said, nodding at Lalune.

'Maybe Solly knows,' Etolantie said with her mouth full. 'Maybe that's why he was kidnapped.'

'I d . . . don't think the Imperator w . . . wants him for anything ex . . . except a new b . . . body,' said Seachrân. 'He's n . . . not a New Wayfarer like us.'

'Rescuing him would seem to be the place to start, however, hmm,' said Aube.

'You said he was in the Palace,' said Aytem. 'Do you know *exactly* where? We'll need to know that, if we're to rescue him.'

'His is the body now inhabited by the Imperator,' said Lalune quietly. 'Where *he* is, I don't know.'

Or if he's still alive, she thought miserably.

Aytem's eyebrows shot up into his hair.

'That does explain the Imperator's sudden recovery,' he said. 'But the Imperator is heavily guarded. Even more so now. And there are these WASPs on all the roads.'

'The Imperator is a cruel boy,' said Kepler. 'Things have been calm for a while, but I well remember how things were before his illness.'

'I thought he had announced some sort of amnesty?' Aube said.

'It won't be a real one. Only for those he's already decided to show mercy to.'

'Is there no other way for us to reach the Palace without passes?' said Lalune.

'You could go through the forest,' said the carter doubtfully. 'But I don't think you'd survive two minutes.

231

Let me tell you, there are a hundred stories of people who've gone into the forest and never been seen again. This tree sickness is only the beginning. You'd have no chance.'

'They could cut through to the river before they get to the deep forest, and go by way of the water,' said Kepler. 'It's the snarg swarming season. Dangerous beasts, snargs. But perhaps that is the only way.'

'Do we go alone?' said Lalune. 'I mean, will it be dangerous? Should we have somebody with us in case there's trouble?'

She couldn't help thinking of all the wild animals they'd had to face on their journey here. Solly had been with them then. Seachrân didn't look as if he knew how to hold a crossbow or a gun.

'You'll be less noticeable on your own,' said Aytem, but his voice sounded uncertain. 'And children might be less likely to be suspected. If I took you it'd have to be along the roads, and there are WASPs everywhere.'

'I wouldn't know the way, hmm,' said Aube. 'And there's my leg. Not too steady yet.'

'I think Aytem's right,' said Kepler. 'If I go somebody is bound to ask questions. Children might get away with it. But I don't like the thought of you going completely on your own.'

'Not a prrroblem,' said Sunguide. 'I will not be a suspect anywhere. I will go as their prrrotector.'

'Etolantie must c . . . come t . . . too,' said Seachrân firmly.

'No,' said Lalune. 'She's not necessary for the Keys, and we can't put her in danger.'

'I been in danger loads of times.'

'I've been having v . . . visions about her for m . . . months, Lalune,' Seachrân said. 'I d . . . don't know why she has to be there, b . . . but she does. Sh . . . she is important.'

'Besides, I'm best at pretending,' Etolantie added, looking extremely smug. 'You'd never of got away from Sybilla that first time if I hadn't pretended.'

'Then that is settled,' said Aytem, to Lalune's annoyance.

58

The Imperator took out the Book and strode to the door.

'Send Sybilla Geenpool and Belenus Dollysheep immediately,' the Imperator commanded through Solly's mouth.

A servant bowed and spoke into a small WASP. The Imperator didn't watch to check that he had been obeyed. He opened the Book and began to read. He appeared to understand it, though the words were meaningless to Solly.

A servant brought a drink, and two others came with a reading desk and chair. Ignoring them, he skimmed through the rest of the Book.

Suddenly he gave a start.

'How ironic that of all the human components on Clandoi, I should be given this one.'

Solly heard footsteps running to the door. There was a pause, a murmur of voices, and Sybilla came in. When she saw the book she looked startled.

'What do you know about this book?' asked the Imperator, after a long pause.

'Begging your benefaction, sir; I found it in the house at Latrium,' she said. 'It wasn't as ugly as the rest of the things I found there, so I kept it. I thought it might be interesting. How did it get—'

'Did you read it?'

'No, Imperator. I wasn't trained in the languages of the first settlers; I needed somebody to translate. My discipline was in—'

'You were not told that you could keep anything from that house for yourself. You should have sent it here immediately for examination.'

'Please pardon my ignorance, Imperator,' Sybilla said falteringly, staring at the Book as if trying to read it from across the room.

The Imperator said nothing, but read the last page again.

Dr Dollysheep arrived, looking anxious.

'Dollysheep. Your experiment has failed,' said the Imperator.

Dollysheep went pale.

'Failed, Imperator?'

'You assured me that the residual personality of the person who provided this body would diminish. It has not.'

'I am sure that given time . . . I could give you another injection . . .'

'This afternoon I spent some time in judgment over my people,' said the Imperator. 'Theirs were lesser crimes than withholding information, or of harming me, but I destroyed an entire street of their hovels personally.'

He said it with such relish that Solly realized that he hadn't been able to make him feel the slightest remorse. With growing dread he wondered what he was up to.

Dr Dollysheep gaped.

'Do you know the legend of the Wanderer?' asked the Imperator.

'No . . . I mean yes, Imperator,' whispered Sybilla.

'It is tale told to us all as children,' said Dollysheep, making an effort to keep his voice level.

'Every time the comet – the Wanderer – returns the people are supposed to rise against my house. This does actually happen, you know. It was documented by my ancestors, though all public records were ordered to be destroyed. There are always stories, of course, but even the truth, without evidence, soon becomes myth. The comet has been sighted. You know this already. It is one of those events that calls for festivities. I have ordered the people to celebrate.'

'An admirable Edict, Imperator,' said Dr Dollysheep.

'I had thought that there was no sign of an uprising. Just a myth. But then *this* . . .'

He slammed the Book of the Key down on to the desk. Sybilla jumped. Dr Dollysheep eyed the book.

'The Ne'Lethe is the foundation of society. Without it, my family's years of rule will terminate. It can only be controlled by three Keys, used simultaneously at the occurrence of this astronomical event. A natural time delay, if you like.

'My great-grandfather's grandfather tried to destroy them, but he didn't have the technology. So he had the Keys separated and sent to the furthest parts of Clandoi. The rebels who had tried to use them last time were imprisoned under the Ne'Lethe. My ancestor did all that he could to ensure that when the comet returned, the Keys would be nowhere to be found.

'Yet here is one of them. And the event is two days off. If one has been found, so will the others.

'Your punishment, Sybilla Geenpool and Belenus

236

Dollysheep, is to prevent the three Keys from coming together. Prevent the Holders from entering the city. Fail in this, and you will not even be deemed worthy enough to be used as human components.'

Sybilla looked as if she might faint.

'I am indebted by your clemency, Imperator,' she said falteringly.

Dr Dollysheep echoed her words, and they both backed out.

The Imperator turned to a large mirror that was hanging on the wall. Approaching it, he looked piercingly into his eyes – Solly's eyes.

'I know that you're in there,' he said softly. 'I know who you are, sun-boy. And now I know that you have a mother.'

59

Early the next morning Aytem drove them as far as he could get his cart, to where the road came to an end at the edge of the forest.

'What if we can't rescue Solly?' Lalune said, as they watched Aytem disappear in a cloud of red dust. Her forehead wore a worried wrinkle. 'What if he doesn't know the way to Earth?'

'The Being will make sure he does,' said Seachrân.

'You have so much confidence in the Being,' Lalune said.

'I've never known him to fail,' Seachrân said simply.

His eyes filled with tears as he said it. Halig had taught him to trust the Being. And now she was dead.

He shook himself impatiently. Halig wouldn't want him to cry forever. She would want him to do what he had to do, and laugh as if she were still there for him to tell her about it at the end of the day.

'Th . . . this way,' he said.

The gently sloping path started out fairly wide, with a leafy canopy overhead. The wind was strong, but the trees sheltered them. Birds whistled cheerfully, and sometimes darted out in front of them.

'What was that?' said Lalune, startled.

'A y . . . yellow dandan.'

'Yellow?' Lalune said, seeming surprised for a moment. Then she laughed, and waved her staff. 'Of course: it only looks purple to me. This sight the Being has given me reverses the colours.'

'I never *seen* trees so big,' said Etolantie, putting her hand in Seachrán's. 'These are ten times as big as the ones at home. Ain't they, Sunguide? *Twenty* times as big.'

'All trrrees under the Ne'Lethe are tiny indeed,' agreed Sunguide. 'Not enough light.'

'Why's the forest dangerous?' said Etolantie, who seemed to have recovered from her subdued mood.

'Many trees c . . . can hurt you,' Seachrán said.

A branch whipped him in the face, knocking the queggel from his shoulder. He held his hand out for it to climb back up. Etolantie giggled.

'Like that one?'

Seachrán laughed. 'I d . . . don't think that was on purpose. S . . . sometimes things just happen.'

'Like your legs, and your talking?'

Seachrán looked at her, amused.

'Y . . . yes. My mother had a h . . . hard time when I w . . . was born. Nobody did it on purpose. It j . . . just happened.'

'But don't you ever wish it hadn't?' said Lalune.

She was fingering her scarf wistfully. She hadn't been *born* without eyes.

'Of c . . . course,' he said. 'I g . . . get tired too easily. And I d . . . don't like it when p . . . people think I'm stupid because I c . . . c . . . can't speak well. B . . . but some wouldn't like me anyway, b . . . because I'm a half-skin.'

'What's a half-skin?'

'Half Appaloosian, half P . . . Pelegian. The Pelegians think Appaloosians are b . . . bad enough; p . . . people like me are far t . . . too unnatural.'

'When they first made Appaloosians, they said they had no souls,' Lalune said almost to herself.

'Only b . . . because they were afraid,' said Seachrân, ducking under a low branch. 'How can s . . . somebody without a soul l . . . love or hate? Or b . . . be happy or sad? Or c . . . care for anybody or anything other th . . . than themselves?'

At about lunchtime they came to a sunny clearing where somebody had placed logs in a large circle.

'We come here with p . . . picnics, s . . . sometimes,' Seachrân said.

'Can we have one now?' said Etolantie. 'I'm too hungry to walk any more.'

Seachrân nodded. His legs were aching anyway.

'Please, g . . . go and get some w . . . water from that stream,' he said.

'Why? We got water in our bottles.'

'You should have d . . . drunk it all by n . . . now,' he said severely. 'B . . . besides, when it's as hot as this, y . . . you always have to f . . . fill your b . . . bottle when you have the opportunity.'

She pouted, but went anyway.

Sunguide flew up into the trees and roosted there with a happy little sigh. Seachrân took fresh fruit from his bag, and bread and cheese, and they ate, brushing the crumbs on to the ground for the birds. Several came down to eat, and he was proud that he knew all their names.

What he didn't know was the way from now on. Not properly, anyway. But he did know it was going to be more dangerous.

The path was less travelled, and narrow, and they had to walk in single file, with Sunguide fluttering over their heads. It was also very much steeper, and Seachrân's legs still hadn't recovered from the morning's walk.

Though it wasn't time for the sun to set yet it was getting dark. A storm was coming. He'd never known so many bad storms.

'That's a Janus tree, isn't it?' said Lalune as they passed a tree with a great crack down the middle.

'Yes,' Seachrân said. 'Whatever y . . . you do, don't go inside it. It's c . . . carnivorous.'

'Prpr. We found that out alrrready,' Sunguide said with a little shiver.

'Are there lots of carnival-ous trees?' said Etolantie.

Seachrân stopped, partly to rest his legs. He pointed to a tree with white flowers as big as bath tubs.

'That's a f . . . forlornhope tree,' he said. 'The flowers fill with water, b . . . but it's poisonous. Anything th . . . that goes for a drink falls asleep in it and d . . . drowns. Only mubbles c . . . can live in there, but they're always d . . . diseased. There are other trees that b . . . build traps with their roots, and trees with exploding fruit.'

'Exploding fruit!' said Etolantie. 'Can you show me some?'

'If I s . . . see some.'

They couldn't see much sky from here in the forest, but what they could see was fast filling with angry clouds. They had to hurry.

241

'Is it going to be a storm?' said Etolantie. 'Like when we found Lalune?'

Seachrân nodded.

'If there's lightning it c . . . could kill us,' he said. 'If it hits a tree. We need t . . . to get down to the r . . . river.'

Huge raindrops began to burst on the path in front of them.

Somewhere there was a jagged rock. Seachrân hadn't been this way often, and was afraid that he might have missed it. When they came to a fork in the path he stopped. He didn't remember this fork.

'Why's there so much rain, but it's so hot?' said Etolantie. 'Ow, this rain *stings*!'

Seachrân looked up. The tree they were standing beneath had tubular red leaves that caught the rain and dripped it down on to whatever was below, scorching it with acid.

Quickly he pulled, the girls out of the way.

'What is?' said Sunguide.

'Caustic t . . . tree,' said Seachrân. 'We need to find a p . . . plant with blue leaves shaped like a hand.'

'Why?' said Etolantie.

'L . . . look at your arm.'

A ring of blisters had appeared where the acid drop had landed.

'*Ow!*' squealed Etolantie.

'Think I saw such a plant back there,' Sunguide said.

He and Seachrân left the girls and went back the way they had come. They found the plant and brought a leaf back to Etolantie. Seachrân grasped his necklace and prayed. Then he split the leaf open, spilling thick clear jelly over Etolantie's arm.

'That will stop the acid d . . . drop burning you more.'

'Do you know everything about *everything*?' said Etolantie.

'Everybody who l . . . lives near the f . . . forest knows about them. If you didn't, you'd . . . die. People in the c . . . city won't go into the f . . . forest. They think the t . . . trees will k . . . kill them.'

'Perhaps they're right,' said Lalune, rubbing the Janus tree perforations still visible on her arm, and wincing. 'Why did you hold your necklace like that?'

'It helps m . . . my prayers to the B . . . Being to be stronger,' he told her, and she looked at her staff thoughtfully.

'Doesn't it try and take over your will?' she said. 'Solly said his did. I've only held mine once: I was too afraid.'

'You have to l . . . learn to be stronger than your Key,' Seachrân said. 'I've had mine since b . . . birth, so I've learnt how.'

He started off down the path again, choosing the right fork, as it would be at least the right direction.

Lightning lit up the sky, and a few moments later thunder rumbled. The path twisted, disappeared under vines and reappeared again in unexpected places. Seachrân stopped.

'I think th . . . this is wrong.'

'*I* think we're going in circles,' said Etolantie.

'So do I,' said Lalune. 'I'm sure we passed that rock a while ago.'

She pointed into a thick clump of trees, to where a tall rock was sticking out of the ground like a tooth.

'Th . . . that's the rock I was looking for,' Seachrân said, grinning in relief. 'Sorry. I t . . . took us on the wrong path.'

Rather than go back down the path he headed directly through the trees. It was difficult, but now that he had the rock in sight he didn't want to lose it again. He scrambled over a heavily vine-covered log.

But he somehow missed his footing. His leg braces got caught in the vines, and he fell. For an age it seemed that he stayed still while the world tumbled around him.

60

Solly wanted to shut his eyes, but the Imperator wouldn't let him. He had opened up a bubblescreen and tapped in two words: 'Revas' and 'Brise'.

Image after image poured on to the screen. Wuneem striking Brise so hard that he had to be half carried out of their home, blood seeping out of an ugly wound. The huissier smashing Revas' guitar over the head of one of the hunters. Revas angrily shaking off the hands of the huissier so that she could leave her home in dignity. A huissier hitting her in the eye. Brise being forced into one of the pods in the cyberclinic. Revas trying to help a woman with a broken leg, but being rammed against the wall. Revas being beaten. One of the WASPs going berserk and attacking the huissier.

That was Lalune, controlling the WASP. Solly felt proud of her.

And desperately afraid for his parents.

They beat Ma.

He saw Dr Dollysheep and Wuneem discussing cutting Revas open to give her kidneys to Wuneem's wife. He saw a pod being wheeled into an operating theatre, its occupant to be harvested. Was it one of his parents? He couldn't tell.

When the Bubblenet had been exhausted of its footage of Brise and Revas, the Imperator idly swung a pendant key from one finger.

'I have power of life or death over them, sun-boy,' he said softly. 'All I have to do is drop this key into the bubblescreen and give the order, and the cyberclinic will switch off. Unless I order them properly resuscitated, your family and friends will drown inside their pods without ever taking another breath.'

He leaned forward and began the footage of Brise and Revas again.

He didn't need to. Solly didn't think he would ever be able to get the horrifying images out of his head.

They beat Ma.

Solly couldn't bear it. He tried to retreat further behind the wall in his head. But he couldn't.

He watched as the Imperator's hand – his hand – crept towards his mother's necklace. Solly had found it outside the cyberclinic on the night his parents had been taken. It was the only thing he had to remind him of his ma.

What was the Imperator going to do with it?

His fist closed over the purple stones, and pulled them up towards his face.

Only then did Solly realize that he was crying.

61

'Seachrân?' called Lalune. 'Are you all right?'

He started to laugh. Halig would have been laughing, had she been there.

'I w . . . was worried about *y* . . . *you* not knowing the f . . . forest!'

'An' you got caught!' said Etolantie, giggling in delight. 'Is it one of them tree traps?'

'It's c . . . called an ambush tree,' he said, somewhat indistinctly.

He's laughing? thought Lalune. *Solly's body's being used by the Imperator, we've got less than a day to rescue him and use the Keys, then we've got to find our way off the planet, and he's laughing?*

'How can we get you out?' she said, trying not to sound impatient.

Sunguide flew down into the hole, and he too started to laugh.

'Prpr. Hruman boy is upside-down.'

'C . . . can you lower a vine down?' Seachrân said. 'I'll hold on to it. I d . . . don't think I'm s . . . strong enough to p . . . pull myself up, though. S . . . Sunguide, can you t . . . take the queggel?'

The vines were hanging down from the trees above

them. They hardly looked sturdy enough to carry Seachrân's weight. Lalune tugged at the thickest of them until there was enough free to reach him.

'I've g . . . got it.'

Lalune was reluctant to put her staff down. Without it, she was unable to see, even in negative, but she needed both hands to pull the vine. Etolantie held on to her waist and hauled away too, though she didn't seem to achieve anything.

'Pull harder, moon-girrrl,' said Sunguide.

'We're pulling as hard as we can,' Lalune said crossly. 'Etolantie, you're getting in my way. I might be able to do it on my own.'

'I bet you won't,' said Etolantie, sounding annoyed. She stood up and dusted her hands.

'Carrreful, Etolantie,' warned Sunguide. 'Foot is rrright on . . .'

Etolantie screamed as the earth at the edge of the hole gave way. Lalune felt the vine jerk and slide through her hands. She grasped it tighter.

Suddenly it snapped above her. She heard it whip through the air, felt it whack across her shoulders, felt herself tumbling forward into the hole . . .

62

The Imperator flung the necklace across the room. Purple gemstones flashed and bounced in all directions.

'It won't work, sun-boy!' he snarled. 'You may be in my head still, but I'm the one in charge. I'm in charge, do you hear? *Do you hear me?*'

A terrified servant ran into the room.

'Imperator! I heard shouting . . .'

'I am the Imperator, menial!' bellowed the Imperator. 'I am permitted to shout! Clear up these stones and throw them into the river! They are swag dung! And the rest of this damny sewage I want burned. Build a pyre for them. Out there, where I can see it. We'll make it part of the celebrations tomorrow. Cut down trees if you have to.'

The servant paled and made a superstitious gesture.

'C . . . c . . . cut down trees, Imperator?' he said, his voice cracking.

'Are you deaf, or do you want to be put on the fire as well?' screamed the Imperator.

He picked up the Book of the Key and threw it at the servant, who bowed low to the ground and backed out of the room.

The Imperator stood still for a few minutes, breathing hard.

'Now, I will show you that I am still in charge,' he whispered. He stalked after the servant into the sunlight.

'I wish to sit in judgment!' he announced. 'Bring me prisoners.'

63

Lalune just had enough time to grab her staff. She hit the opposite wall of the hole with a thump that left her winded. Below her she could hear the others crashing down and down and down.

The chasm seemed to go on forever. It plunged down at a steep angle, so that it was more of a slide than a fall: even so, she scraped against the walls so much that she wondered if she would have any skin left – or any bones unbroken – by the time they got down. They were going to hit the ground pretty hard. Sunguide knew something about healing, but he was only one Pruppras, and they were three humans. And Aube's leg was still not properly right, and he'd broken it ages ago . . .

SPLASH!

SPLASH! SPLASH!

It wasn't ground at the bottom. It was the tumbling, bubbling, boiling river. Lalune had time for one small breath before she dropped right down into the depths.

Which way's up? Where are the others?

She glimpsed an arm thrashing inside a whirl of silver bubbles. Etolantie's, she thought.

Her chest was hurting.

I need air.

She didn't know how to swim. She felt the riverbed beneath her feet: weeds wrapped around her legs.

She kicked against the bottom.

But the more she kicked, the more entangled she became. The last of her breath burst from her lungs. She watched it leave her for the surface, taking all hope with it. She tasted river water . . .

64

The Imperator sat in the Judgment Seat, a glass of chilled mead wine at his side.

Solly dreaded what he might do in his current mood.

The first prisoner shuffled into the courtyard. She was a girl, nearly as young as Etolantie, and so thin that her collarbones jutted out like tree roots.

'Prisoner JF 230847,' said the guard. 'Charge: pickpocketing. She claimed it was to buy bread, but she resisted arrest as well.'

'Does she have family?'

The guard consulted an etched acetate.

'A mother and four younger siblings.'

'Have them flogged in front of her,' said the Imperator lazily. 'Then send her mother to the freezer, and set the girl free.'

The girl's eyes filled with tears.

'Please, sir, don't punish my family,' she begged. 'They din't do anything wrong! Flog me! Freeze me!'

'Put an iron ring around her neck so that everybody knows she is a thief,' said the Imperator. 'Next prisoner?'

The girl was dragged away, sobbing, 'How'm I going to feed them now?'

'Prisoner AM 49857230. Selling unlawful items.'

The 'unlawful items' were scattered from a basket into the dust. They were books, just like the ones Aube had collected. Solly glanced, startled, at Prisoner AM 49857230. He was an elderly man. Round his neck was a bit of string, from which hung a stone. Solly was sure it was a Seer's stone.

The man looked quite calm.

'Books containing lies about the . . . um . . . the old ways, Imperator,' the guard said hesitantly, as if afraid that he would be punished just for mentioning the old ways.

The Imperator got out of his seat, walked up to Prisoner AM 49857230, and spat in his face.

Prisoner AM 49857230 didn't even flinch.

'Execute him, slowly, for spreading deception. Make sure there's a big crowd.'

The man gave a single nod, and followed the guard serenely into the deep dungeon. His composure made the Imperator angrier than ever, and he hurled his wineglass after the prisoner.

'Add those . . . things to the pyre. And bring more wine.'

He climbed back into the Judgment Seat, and the next prisoner was brought in.

'Prisoner AF 7092836. Repeat offender. Petty theft.'

Solly recognized the woman. She had been accused at the last Judgment Seat, of stealing to feed her family.

That time the Imperator had razed a street full of houses because of her crimes. Solly wondered what desperation had driven her to steal again. Surely her own people must turn against her soon.

The woman's eyes were unnaturally bright, and had a wild look in them that hadn't been there previously.

'I've seen you before, haven't I?' said the Imperator. 'Really, it's becoming very boring thinking up new ways to punish you.'

'You think you punish us,' said the woman, 'but it is you who will be punished soon.'

'Does she have family?'

'Unknown, Imperator. We think they may have been executed at a previous Judgment. She did take in some orphans, children of other prisoners, but they are believed to have died.'

'As you will soon die,' said the woman.

Don't, thought Solly. *You know it'll only make things worse. How much worse can it be?*

The voice in his head wasn't the Being's, nor was it his own. It was the woman's. She stared at him, piercing through the wall in his head, right through to Solly himself.

'Have her chained in the torture room for a month,' said the Imperator. 'Then have her executed.'

You see, I will die soon anyway. My children are dead, even those I adopted. But you: you can change everything.

'Take her away,' said the Imperator.

'You can torture me and kill me,' said the woman in a shrill voice, 'but there will always be those like me who live, spreading the words of hope.'

'Take her away,' repeated the Imperator, annoyed.

'Cut a Janus tree down, and it will root again,' cried the woman. 'Its last strength will be used to cast seeds into the darkness: even through the dimensions, to other planets.'

The guard seemed rooted to the spot.

'I said, *take her away*!' screamed the Imperator.

Remember this, Solly. Remember me.
I will remember, he promised. *I will remember.*

65

Seachrân was head downwards when he reached the bottom of the shaft, so he saw the water and had a chance to take a breath before he hit it. He dived down deep, righted himself and swam up to the surface. Quickly he undid his leg braces and kicked off his shoes. He shed the bag of food too: they would find some more somehow.

Where were the others? He could see the disturbances in the surface of the water where they had fallen in. He dived and swam towards where he was sure one of them would be.

He was right. It was Etolantie. She was thrashing about with no idea where up was. He seized her with one arm, and used the other to swim to the surface.

She heaved and spluttered.

'C . . . can you swim?' he said.

'N . . . n . . . no,' she coughed.

An orange shape fluttered to them anxiously.

'Prpr. Is rrraft caught in the rrreeds over this way.'

Seachrân swam, one-armed, towards the raft. It was made of orange moulded plastic, and looked solid enough, though it was dented as if it had been in an accident. As soon as they were close enough Etolantie grabbed it.

'Lalune,' she choked.

Seachrân nodded, left her with Sunguide, and dived back down.

He thought he knew which direction to look in, but he and Etolantie had stirred up a fair bit of muck in the water. He couldn't see more than an arm's length ahead. He had to trust to his instincts and swim as far down as he could.

When he had reached the bottom he scanned all around, hoping to catch a glimpse of Lalune.

Nothing.

Where was she?

Being? I need you now, he prayed, grasping his necklace.

Something floating in the water caught his eye. It was a golden feather, twirling against the flow of the river.

Seachrân didn't know any birds with golden feathers. He swam towards it, and another appeared a little way ahead. When that disappeared, another replaced it. Then another.

And a hand, floating aimlessly.

Was he too late?

He urged himself forward.

Lalune's bitonal face came into view. Her legs were caught in the weed at the bottom of the river; her hands were stretched towards the surface. Her right hand still doggedly clenched her staff.

Her mouth was open; her face was blank.

Seachrân thrust forward apprehensively. He pulled a knife from his belt and hacked at the weeds. When they eventually gave way Lalune began to float upwards. He yanked at the last of the weeds and lugged her up.

When they broke the surface she wasn't breathing.

Etolantie was sitting on the raft, holding the queggel. He

pulled Lalune to it, and Etolantie helped haul her up.

The raft pulled free, and started to float downriver. Seachrân hardly noticed as he dragged himself out of the churning water, trying to ignore his tired limbs.

'Will she be all right?' said Etolantie.

Seachrân didn't answer. He didn't know.

'Check her mouth forrr blockage,' advised Sunguide.

Seachrân tipped Lalune's head back, and poked in her mouth. Nothing was blocking her throat.

But she still wasn't breathing.

He put his mouth over hers, and blew.

And pummelled her chest.

And blew again, and pumped he didn't know how many times, before she vomited and gasped.

'*Solly*,' she sighed.

She was alive.

67

Lalune could only see Seachrân's face hovering over her anxiously, and the cliffs speeding by. She tasted sick in her mouth, and wiped it shakily on her arm.

'I'm all right,' she said. 'Honestly. I am.'

He searched her face, concerned, but was soon satisfied enough to turn his attention to the river.

'Do you know where we are?' asked Lalune, elbowing herself upright. Her chest was bruised where Seachrân had pounded her, and she felt dizzy.

Seachrân wrinkled his forehead.

'I don't th . . . think we're on the m . . . main river. It's too narrow.'

'Prpr. We trrravel towards it,' said Sunguide. 'You sure you are all rrright, moon-girrrl?'

'I just need to rinse my mouth,' said Lalune. 'I don't suppose anybody's still got their water bottle?'

'I lost all my stuff when we fell in,' Etolantie said cheerfully. 'Use water out of the river. I would.'

Lalune made a face, and tried spitting to clear her mouth instead.

'What are you doing?' said Etolantie, as Seachrân lay down and leaned over the side of the raft as far as he could. The raft dipped as he lunged for a branch that was bobbing nearby. He missed.

'We need s . . . something to steer with,' he explained over his shoulder.

'What about them trees? We can catch the branches to slow, an' get a branch then.'

'We can't pull a branch off a live tree!' Lalune said, shocked.

'I din't *mean* a live one,' Etolantie said indignantly. 'There's millions of branches in the water already. I jus' think it'd be easier to get one if we're a bit slower.'

She stood up to demonstrate how to grab a tree, wobbled, and fell on to Lalune. The raft bounced about so much that they couldn't do anything but cling to the edges for a few minutes, and the trees shot past them.

Suddenly the raft jolted, jarring Lalune's bones.

'Ow, I bit my tongue!' said Etolantie. 'What was that?'

'R . . . rocks in the water,' gasped Seachrân.

The raft hit another rock The water around them began to churn white, the raft sliding over the rocks faster and faster, smashing into them, its sides beginning to splinter.

'Hold on!' cried Sunguide.

But there wasn't anything to hold on to, unless they risked breaking their fingers on the edges.

'Whee!' Etolantie screamed in delight. 'This is fun!'

It was anything but fun in Lalune's opinion. She didn't dare put her staff down in case she lost it, but that meant she saw everything. She had no eyes to shut.

She thought it was all over at least ten times, as they were battered against the rocks time and time again. Just as she thought she couldn't take any more, the river narrowed abruptly, and with one final *whoosh* they shot up into the air and out into the main river.

They smacked down and Lalune nearly slithered off the raft as it skimmed under the surface. But the water out here was a lot gentler, and they soon slowed down, circling round, Sunguide hovering around them to make sure they were all intact.

'I really thought we wouldn't make it,' shivered Lalune.

'Why're we going in circles?' said Etolantie.

'B . . . because there's nothing to g . . . give the raft direction,' said Seachrân. 'W . . . we still need a branch.'

'There's a branch over there,' said Etolantie. 'Near the bank.'

Seachrân shaded his eyes from the afternoon sun to see it, nodded, and to Lalune's horror, dived into the water.

'He'll drown!' she squealed.

'No he won't, he can swim. I wish I could swim.'

Seachrân's blond head soon popped out of the water near the branch, and he towed it back to them. It was a good one, long and sturdy. He plonked it down on the raft and hauled himself out again. When the raft had settled, he stood up gingerly, poked the branch down until it found the bottom, and used it to push them into a straighter path.

'Shouldn't we get back to the bank?' Lalune said.

Seachrân shook his head.

'Th . . . the river goes right into P . . . Peleg City,' he explained. 'We'll be quicker th . . . this way.'

He sounded terribly tired. Lalune knew that she and Etolantie should really offer to take turns with the branch, but if she put her staff down she'd be blind, and Etolantie probably wasn't strong enough. She clasped her knees to her chest, wishing she had a blanket. Though the air was hot, the stiff breeze was making her cold. She was hungry too. Lunch was a long time ago.

The cliffs on either side of the river gradually dropped away. They began to see signs of people: first fields, then farm houses, and finally streets. They had reached the city.

Etolantie pointed downriver, and said, 'What's that?'

Sunguide buzzed ahead of them, and Seachrân peered at what looked like a small wave growing in the river.

He went very pale. Sunguide darted back to them at full speed.

'*SNARRRG!*'

68

The Imperator spun his plate of food at Ninurtus Worldweb as if it were a Frisbee. It hit the cook in the chest and fell to the floor, shattering the plate and splattering the food everywhere.

Ninurtus Worldweb was shaking so hard that little ripples ran over his prominent belly.

'I sent for this an hour ago,' the Imperator bellowed. 'When you finally produce it, it's cold.'

The cook's eyes bulged with terror.

'I have no kitchen help, master. Since the boy left nobody wants to—'

'Did I give you permission to speak?' thundered the Imperator. 'Hire another boy! Hire twenty! Just make sure my food is properly prepared.'

Ninurtus spread his hands wordlessly.

'Speak!' ordered the Imperator.

'They're all leaving, master,' the cook whispered. 'There is nobody left to hire.'

'How dare they leave my service!' the Imperator screamed. 'Menials do not leave. I demand that they stay. Why are they leaving? Answer me!'

'They say the end is coming, master. This comet . . .'

Solly watched with interest.

Ninurtus stopped, licking his lips nervously, as the Imperator slowly got to his feet, his face a fury.

'I gave orders that nobody was to mention that, on pain of being frozen,' he whispered.

Ninurtus's face turned pale lavender.

'Please, master,' he squeaked, his chins wobbling. 'I'm only repeating what I have heard.'

The Imperator stared at him for a long moment.

'Continue,' he said at last.

'They say that the comet heralds the end of humanity on Clandoi . . . that three will arise who will bring an end to tyranny . . . I am only repeating what I have heard, master . . . the three will lead the faithful to the land of the ancestors, by means of a tree . . . a tree that exists both here and there, master . . . it is nonsense, I know, how could a tree exist in two places at once . . .'

His babbling petered out.

Solly wanted to laugh.

His body did laugh, great guffaws that burst out of his body hysterically. The Imperator struggled to regain control, but Solly's laughter won.

Solly was in control.

The cook gaped, and fled before the Imperator's madness could infect him too.

69

The bristly spine of an immense snarg was cutting through the water. It lifted its tail up and smacked it down, shattering the surface of the river into thousands of diamond droplets.

And then another appeared.

And another.

They roared, waving fins and tails, and brushing against the raft so that it was almost lifted out of the water.

Seachrân, Etolantie and Lalune clutched each other in the centre of the raft.

'There's millions of them!' said Etolantie, her eyes huge. 'What are they doing?'

'They th . . . think the raft's a f . . . female snarg!' Seachrân said. 'It's th . . . the spawning season.'

'Eew!' cried Etolantie.

Seachrân was sweating. Male snargs would fight to the death over a female.

He knew it would have been even worse for them if they thought the raft was a male.

It seemed that every ripple of the water was turning into a snarg. It wasn't long before there was a spurt of blood. With a howl one of the huge fish turned on its neighbour. The river became a whirlpool of darkness around them.

The raft was raised out of the water on the back of a snarg, tilting and swivelling so that they had to grab the edge. Seachrân dropped his branch. He tried to grab it, but it slid into the water.

'No!' Seachrân panted in despair. 'We n . . . need it to g . . . get to the bank.'

The raft slithered over the backs of the heaving snargs, plopped down into the water, and rose up again.

'Use my staff!' screamed Lalune.

It was the only thing they had.

She plunged it down into the water. It was too short to give enough leverage.

Seachrân wriggled to help.

'Etolantie, t . . . tell us if a s . . . snarg gets too close.'

Again and again they thrust the staff down and pushed the raft forward. They worked away for what seemed like hours, twisting and turning in the river, until they were utterly exhausted.

'Go away, snargs!' shouted Etolantie, splashing at the fish. '*Ow!* It cut me!'

The viciously sharp scales had sliced her hand. She squealed in pain. Then, to Seachrân's horror, she stood up and kicked the snarg as its great head reared over the side of the raft.

'*Etolantie! No!*'

Stunned, the snarg bellowed with fury, and clamped its huge jaws together on the raft, a finger away from Etolantie's toes. She screamed and fell backwards.

There was a tearing, crunching noise, and the snarg bit a piece off the raft. It spat it out, opened its jaw again, and Seachrân jabbed it in the eye with the staff.

267

'Get it, Seachrân!' yelled Etolantie in a rage.

'Over here!' shouted a voice.

Two boats had joined them on the river. The men in them didn't look too pleased. But they did have guns, Seachrân saw thankfully.

'Go through the gate!' yelled one of them, aiming at the snarg with his gun.

A long stone wall had replaced the mud banks of the river. The gate was wide enough, if you were used to handling boats. Seachrân didn't have time to notice more than that. They were definitely *not* used to it.

He and Lalune pushed as hard as they could.

The snarg's face crumpled inwards, and a moment later the sound of gunshot almost deafened him. He saw Etolantie shout something at the dead snarg, and wave her little fist. All the other snargs leaped on their comrade, tearing it to pieces.

The raft jolted around, then slid out of the boiling mass of fish. Lalune and Seachrân propelled it towards the gate. They hit the side with some force, but at least they were inside. The men swiftly glided though after them and somebody unseen closed the gate.

Seachrân held his hands over his ringing ears. Everything sounded slightly muffled.

'How many times do we have to tell you kids?' growled one of the boatmen. 'River's out of bounds!'

They could still hear the snargs thrashing away outside. Seachrân turned to the men to say thank you, and his heart froze.

Up on the bank two armed huissier were standing.

Waiting for them.

70

'This them?' said one of the boatmen.

The huissier looked at each other uncertainly.

'Anything or anyone unusual, she said,' said one of them. 'You ever seen these three before?'

Who is 'she'? Sybilla? Forcyet? Lalune thought. Somebody worse?

'Nope,' grunted the boatman, poling his boat closer.

'They're w . . . wedging us in,' Seachrân whispered.

'They're only kids,' said another boatman. 'Are you sure, Ten-em?'

'She didn't say *not* kids,' said the huissier.

'What do we do?' whispered Lalune, clutching her staff.

'Pleathe, thir, we only wanted to thee the Imperator,' Etolantie said suddenly, making her eyes as big as she could, and twisting her tunic in her fingers. 'We din't mean to do anything wrong. But they thaid he'th not got the tree thickness any more, and our ma'th ill, an' we jutht wanted to . . . to . . . to thee if he could make *her* better too . . .'

Lalune very nearly let her jaw drop wide open, but stopped herself just in time and nodded frantically. Real tears were rolling down Etolantie's cheeks. Lalune didn't dare look at Seachrân.

'What's wrong with her eyes?' the huissier called Ten-em, nodding in Lalune's direction.

'She's g . . . got it too,' said Seachrân. His voice sounded strangled. Lalune wasn't positive whether it was from fear or laughter.

Etolantie sobbed. 'Our big thithter. If our ma dieth, and she dieth . . . we'll have *nobody* left . . .'

The huissier looked uneasy. They withdrew and had a muttered conversation that Lalune could only just hear.

'He did say that the cure would be available to whoever needed it, Sentiem.'

'You think he *meant* it? More likely it's for whoever can pay. Besides, it's not *his* orders we're following.'

'Shouldn't we take them to the Palace anyway? He might think it good propaganda, to be seen helping half-skins.'

'*She* don't look like a half-skin.'

'The boy does, and the little one might be. Do they come out freckled?'

'No idea. And I'm not sure he's too bothered about propaganda.'

'Mmm. Did you hear what he did to that street?'

'No telling what he might do to these kids. *I* say we follow orders and take them straight to the city jail.'

Lalune and Seachrân looked at each other in horror. How could they use the Keys if they were in jail?

The huissier came back to the riverside.

'Out you get.'

Seachrân bumped the boat against some steps, and they climbed out awkwardly. The huissier stood well back: they didn't want to be infected with the tree sickness.

Ten-em said, 'Leave the staff.'

270

'Please,' said Lalune, 'I need it.'

I don't want to be blind, she thought desperately. *And it's a Key. If I ever get the chance to use it.*

'Her legth hurt,' Etolantie said. 'The tree thickneth. She can't walk without it.'

'*I'm* not helping her walk,' said Ten-em. 'Might be contagious. D'you know how you catch this thing? I don't suppose there's much harm in a blind girl having a staff, anyway.'

'Uh-huh. Looks like the boy's not too well either,' said Sentiem.

Etolantie immediately started to howl, and Seachrân patted her arm.

'Don't you w . . . worry about me, *sister*,' he said with a credible wheeze.

The huissier tied them together. They tried to avoid touching them, still wary of catching the tree sickness. They led them along streets that were strangely empty for a city.

'Funny accent you've got,' said Ten-em conversationally.

'We come from the North,' said Lalune. Her clothes were uncomfortably damp, and she had a headache. It was getting dark, and a hot wind full of sand began to whip little spirals of litter up from the street. The sand stung her face and made her cough.

'I thought there wasn't any tree sickness in the North yet,' said Sentiem. 'Still now, they've found this cure, hey? You'll be all right, hey?'

'Remarkable cure,' said Ten-em. 'The Imperator.'

Seachrân stumbled and Lalune caught his hand. He was trembling.

271

'I was guarding him not three weeks ago,' said Sentiem, 'and he looked like he didn't have the strength to take a breath for himself. Thin as, well as a stick, you know?'

'To see him now, you'd ha' thought he'd never had a day's illness in his life! In just a few days!'

'Could be a different boy.'

'Bit pale, mind.'

'You on duty tomorrow?'

'Nope. Whole family's coming down for the party. The comet, you know?'

'My aunt used to say it marks the end of the world. Fancied herself as a, what do those Wayfarer folk call them, a Seer.'

'End of the world?'

'She once told me she'd seen a vision of the Ne'Lethe disappearing, and all of humankind streaming North, and all of them vanishing too. She's gone up to Kloster Hallow, to see if it'll really happen. Whole load of them have gone.'

'I'd rather party, myself. How'd she get through? We were told to arrest anybody caught trying to leave the city.'

'Word is, so many huissier have left most people get through.'

The city jail was a grim, windowless building that had not been cleaned for some time. The cell they were taken to had six iron beds hanging from the walls on chains, but every one of them already had three or four gaunt-faced prisoners sitting on them. A short wall almost concealed a bucket. Lalune could guess what that was for.

'How long will we be kept here?' Lalune asked, her heart sinking.

Ten-em shrugged.

'That's up to Sybilla Geenpool. Could be a day. Could be a year. Or the Imperator, he might pull you out. Mind you, you're probably better off in here.'

They were each given a smelly blanket crawling with lice. Seachrân crawled into a corner, looking weary enough to fall asleep within minutes. Lalune thought she might not sleep at all.

71

Solly struggled with the Imperator to keep command of his body. He tried to make his legs walk to the door; he wasn't sure exactly what he was going to do, but he had to get the Key back before it was burned.

The servants had taken all of his things outside, and through the open door he could see a large pile of wood being assembled. The Key had to be there somewhere, but it was night time, and too dark to see.

Each step was harder than the last, and he could feel his control gliding away. Sweat poured from him. He gripped the door frame with both hands, and pulled himself through it.

'Help me,' whispered the Imperator through Solly's gritted teeth.

The huissier standing outside the observatory gave him a startled glance. Solly tried to press his lips together, but the Imperator prized them open.

'Fetch . . . Dolly . . . sheep . . .'

The huissier ran to fetch the doctor, who came hurrying within minutes. When he saw the Imperator standing rigidly in the doorway he immediately took a syringe from his pocket and plunged it into Solly's neck.

Solly's knees crumpled. Dr Dollysheep caught him and

laid him gently on the ground, calling for help.

'Drusian injection, Imperator,' he said. 'Bit stronger than taking it by mouth. We'll get you to your bed, and you should be back to normal tomorrow.'

Solly groaned. Though the Imperator was slipping out of consciousness, the drusian made him unable to order his body to do anything.

72

Throughout the night, huissier brought more people in. Seachrân tried to doze, but each time the door opened he woke with a jerk. As the jail got more crowded, it grew hotter, and stingwings buzzed around the bucket.

Lalune fell asleep eventually with her head on Seachrân's shoulder. Only Etolantie managed to get any decent rest, curled up on her blanket in the corner.

They only knew it was morning when tin cups of water were brought in, and some dry bread. At least there was plenty of that. Seachrân gave some to the queggel, but it was more interested in eating his blanket.

The flow of new prisoners continued.

'Not *more* people,' Etolantie said as the barred door opened for the tenth time. 'Go away! There's no room in here.'

'You'd better give it all back!' yelled a furious voice as a girl fell through the door and nearly landed in Seachrân's lap. He had to throw his arms out to stop her banging her head on the ground.

'Thanks,' she muttered, and then shouted at the closed door, 'I know how much coin was there!'

'Ébha?' said Seachrân.

She was the kaufer who sold jewellery.

'Seachrân! What are you doing here?'

'G . . . got arrested. D . . . don't know why.'

'Were you trying to leave the city? That's why they got me. They took all my jewellery, *and* my coin pouch.'

Seachrân shook his head.

'We were c . . . coming in.'

'Coming in? Nobody's coming in! Haven't you heard? The Wanderer's back, the Holders of the Key have been found, and the Great Migration's going to be any day now. I was going to Kloster. Halig'll be part of it, I know she will.'

Seachrân's eyes filled.

'Éb . . . ha . . .'

He chocked on the words. Lalune put her hand over his and said gently, 'I'm so sorry, Ébha; Halig's dead.'

Ébha's mouth opened, and her face paled.

'Dead?' she said in a cracked voice, 'But she was . . . I *saw* her . . . dead?'

Seachrân nodded, unable to speak. Ébha's eyes crinkled and tears spilled down her face. She and Seachrân sobbed and held each other for comfort.

The door opened again, but this time it was more bread and water. Seachrân took the water, but could only nibble at the bread.

'So, why were you coming in?' Ébha said when she had recovered a little.

Seachrân grasped his necklace, unsure what to say. But Ébha's eyes, following his hand, grew enormous.

'It's you! You're a Holder!'

He nodded, feeling ever such a little bit proud.

'Little Seachrân! I remember when you used to run

around Kloster with no clothes on!'

Etolantie guffawed.

'So, are you another Holder?' Ébha said to Lalune.

'Yes.'

'Where's the third? Don't you have to be at the observatory or something?'

'We was on our way there,' Etolantie explained. 'Only the huissier got us.'

'We honestly don't know how to get there,' Lalune said. 'We have to be there by sunset. If we don't make it there won't *be* a Great Migration.'

Ébha regarded the three of them, her brain working fast.

'There's no way out of this prison unless the Imperator decides to sit in the Judgment Seat,' she said at last. 'Before he was cured he was too ill to do it, and most people would never get out. But now he does it all the time. That's your only hope. You just have to make sure they pick you.'

'H . . . how do we d . . . do that?'

'I know a girl who was in here for pickpocketing. She said she cried all the time, because it was the first time she'd ever done anything like that, and her mother was going to be so upset, and she begged the huissier to let her go, every time they opened the door. She made a real nuisance of herself. I think they took her just to be rid of her.'

'Well, that's easy,' said Etolantie. 'I'm the *queen* of annoying. Solly said so.'

73

Solly's eyes opened blearily.

'Imperator?' said a servant.

'Have Dollysheep arrested,' the Imperator slurred. 'His treatment has failed. When I confronted him he assaulted me! He injected me with one of his poisons without permission.'

The servant started to back out of the door.

'Immediately, Imperator.'

'Not immediately, imbecile!' shouted the Imperator. 'Bring me food first. And dress me.'

He was back in control. Solly was made to watch more footage of his parents as he ate a huge meal. Live footage, the screen said. His ma's foot quivered as a huissier struck the side of her pod. She was still alive, but for how long?

The food arrived promptly this time. The Imperator was sick, and then ate again. Solly could do nothing. It was just as it had been at the beginning.

Only worse.

Solly could see the green streak in the sky. The surface of the comet appeared to be boiling. The time was getting near.

Where was Lalune? And what about this other Holder? His heart was in despair. They were going to fail. They were going to be too late. He would never be able to rescue his parents, even if they were still alive.

He would never see Lalune again.

Being. Please help me.

But there was no reply.

74

They had no way of telling how late it was getting. The door hadn't been opened for a while, and Etolantie complained that she'd have no chance to be annoying unless the huissier came back in.

'*An'* I need to pee, an' *worse* than pee; an' I'm not going in that bucket again,' she added.

'Well there isn't anywhere else,' said Lalune wearily.

Etolantie got up.

'Hey! Huissier!' she bellowed, banging on the door. 'Come an' empty the bucket! It stinks in here!'

'Shut up,' one of the other prisoners said. 'It's bad enough in here without you making all that noise.'

Etolantie stuck her tongue out at him and thumped on the door again.

'It smells worse than a swag's den. Worse than your house, even!'

'You'd better make your sister be quiet,' said an old woman tiredly to Lalune. 'They have ways of making our lives even more miserable if you cause trouble.'

'How long have you been in here?' said Lalune.

The woman sighed and pointed at some scratches on the wall.

'Two years, nearly.'

'Two years! How did you survive?' said Ébha.

'By not being noticed.'

'I'm wa-a-a-a-aiting!' Etolantie sang at the top of her voice. 'Is anybody ou-ou-out the-e-e-ere? I'm wa-a-a-a-a-aiting!'

'I don't want to be in here two years!' said Ébha, getting up to join Etolantie at the door. 'Come on, you two. Let's get annoying!'

75

'Light the fire,' ordered the Imperator. 'Let the celebration begin.'

The sun hung low in the sky. Another hour, and it would be too late. Maybe less: Solly wasn't sure how fast the sun moved.

There were noticeably fewer servants than there had been. They lit the pyre with trembling hands. Burning wood! *They* didn't want to celebrate the comet like this. Others brought out tables and food. Fireworks were made ready.

Sybilla Geenpool was there, and Ninurtus Worldweb, supervising the preparations. Both kept throwing terrified looks in his direction. Musicians began to play.

The Imperator began to throw the 'unlawful items' on to the fire, one by one. First to go were the books, which burned quickly, sending ashes flying in the breeze. The Imperator laughed as he watched the sparks wafting about the courtyard. Where they landed on the roofs, the dry moss growing there caught fire. One of the servants hurriedly climbed a ladder to smother the flames; but the ladder toppled and the servant fell screaming to the ground.

The Imperator laughed with glee.

Solly wanted to clench his fists. He could almost see the wall he had built in his mind. It was so solid. How would he ever be able to break out?

I'll have to watch this sacry devil ill-treating these people for the rest of my life.

'Come on, have fun!' the Imperator ordered. 'Dance! Gorge yourselves! I want to see people enjoying themselves!'

Hired dancers began to move stiffly, smiled fixed to their mouths, fear in their eyes.

Above them the moon hovered, full and blue.

How much longer?

The Imperator picked up Solly's bandoleer. His ma and pa had given it to him for his birthday. He tossed it on to the fire, where the smell of the burning leather made tears roll down his cheeks.

'*Stop it!*' hissed the Imperator. 'I'm in charge. I *am* in control!'

The nearest dancer heard this, and tripped over his own feet. His partner hauled him up again, and they carried on. The music accelerated; the dancers whirled, their faces ashen.

The Imperator picked up the strand of Lalune's hair, and savagely hurled it into the flames. It caught before it landed, flickering once and then it was gone.

A sob burst out of Solly's mouth. The Imperator scrubbed it away.

'This is not enough celebration for me,' he snarled. 'Bring the Judgment Seat out here.'

76

The door opened and Seachrân looked up eagerly. But it wasn't a huissier come to fetch them.

Next to him Lalune shivered, and whispered, 'It's Dollysheep.'

He was wearing an iron ring around his neck. He looked around the room at them, and his eyes landed on Lalune.

He looked . . . ashamed.

'Lalune, my dear.'

Seachrân actually heard Lalune's teeth grind. But her voice was quite steady, if icy cold.

'Dr Dollysheep.'

'I didn't think that we would meet quite like this,' he said.

'Where's Solly?' demanded Etolantie.

'Did you not see the proclamation?' said Dollysheep in surprise.

'W . . . we saw it,' Seachrân said quietly, seeing that Lalune was unable to speak. 'L . . . Lalune says that y . . . you've d . . . done something to her f . . . friend.'

Dollysheep sighed.

'Ah, yes.'

'How did you make him say those things?' whispered

285

Lalune.

'His body has been used to transplant the personality of the Imperator,' said Dollysheep. 'It's the Imperator speaking through him.'

'Is h . . . he dead?' said Seachrân. If he was, would they be able to use the Keys?

'All the signs are, no,' said Dollysheep carefully, and Lalune gave a little gasp of hope. 'I did my research, you know. Sometimes the host is lost completely. But I hoped that the drugs I gave him were not quite strong enough for that. And it seems that he is fighting it.'

Heavy footsteps approached the door. Etolantie banged on it again.

'I'm wa-a-a-a-aiting! Smelly hu-u-u-uissier!'

'Quiet in there!' shouted the huissier, rapping on the door. But he didn't open it.

'*Please* be quiet,' said the woman prisoner. 'They'll take it out on all of us.'

'Why are you w . . . wearing the thief ring?' Seachrân said, touching the iron ring around Dollysheep's neck.

'What's a thief ring?' said Etolantie.

'They put 'em on thieves for life,' said Ébha, 'so everybody knows what they did.'

'I *didn't* steal anything,' protested Dollysheep. 'The Imperator ordered it. He thinks the treatment is failing. He'll think up some other way to punish me; this is just the beginning.'

'But you *are* a thief,' Lalune said, touching her empty eyes deliberately. 'You stole my eyes, and countless body parts from hundreds of others too.'

Dollysheep looked taken aback.

'Maybe you're right,' he murmured. 'Maybe I do deserve it. But you have to believe me: I was only trying to do what was right. I took a part to save the whole. You could have died.'

Lalune didn't look convinced.

Dollysheep took her hand.

'Lalune, I swear that if we ever get out of here – if this Great Migration actually happens – I will do whatever is in my power to put it right. I'll find a way to give you back your eyes. I'll spend the rest of my life, however long the Being chooses to give me, rebuilding and replacing what I took. I'll even promise to wear this thief ring forever, if you like.'

'I'm wa-a-a-a-a-a-aiting!' sang Etolantie as the huissier approached once again. Ébha joined her and they battered the door and shouted.

It opened so suddenly that Etolantie was thrown to the floor.

She shrieked furiously. Seachrân grabbed her before she could get up and kick the nearest huissier, who stared at her impassively.

'The Imperator sits in the Judgment Seat,' he said. 'He has expressly asked for Dollysheep.'

Dr Dollysheep paled.

The huissier pointed at Etolantie.

'We'll take you too, and your half-skin friend. The rest of you, take note. *We* get to choose who gets judged.'

'No!' screamed Lalune and Ébha at the same time, scrambling in front of Seachrân and Etolantie.

'You can't take them,' Lalune said. 'They're just children.'

Seachrân felt a warm glow of friendship for both of

them. Everybody else in the cell looked studiously at their feet.

'Do you think he cares?' said the huissier nastily. 'You can go with them. Two extra won't bother him.'

77

It took ten men to haul the Judgment Seat out, even though it was on wheels. Solly felt sick. Every time he'd been made to sit in it, his mouth had called for terrible punishments on the prisoners.

All hope of being able to use the Keys had now gone. The sun was touching the horizon.

The prisoners shuffled in, prodded into a line by an angry huissier.

Solly didn't want to look into the faces of those he was about to condemn. But the Imperator seemed more concerned with burning the last two illegal items from the pile. He picked up the pouch of fire dust and swung it in an arc; it caught on a long branch, suspended above the fire.

'Prisoner AM 53926690, formally known as Belenus Dollysheep,' announced the huissier, pushing Dollysheep forward.

'Ah, Dollysheep,' said the Imperator, pitching the Book of the Key high into the air and catching it again. 'As you can see, I am fully in command of this body. Still, you *assaulted* me, with a needle. I have been thinking long and hard about your punishment.'

He threw the Book again; caught it again.

Solly's eyes followed it.

'I grow weary of executing justice, Dollysheep. I wondered how you would feel if I made *you* do it in my place. Then *I* could have the fun of judging *your* judgments.'

Threw it. Caught it.

Dollysheep cleared his throat.

'Imperator?' he said, very quietly.

Throw. Catch.

'If you are too harsh, or too lenient, the punishment is doubled, and you can join them in it,' the Imperator said with a manic laugh. 'Perfect plan, yes?'

'I could refuse, Imperator,' said Dollysheep.

Solly felt the shock of surprise from the Imperator.

For once he shared the emotion.

The Imperator cast the Key into the heart of the flames, and slowly turned his head.

'Nobody refuses the Imperator,' he said in a voice of steel.

Solly's eyes opened wide, and his heart suddenly flip-flopped.

Lalune was standing behind Dollysheep, looking afraid but defiant. She held a staff set with a blue stone.

The Key.

'What is it?' muttered the Imperator. 'What have you seen? I know you've seen something.'

'Imperator?' said Sybilla, stepping forward. 'Are you . . . do you feel . . . ?'

'Silence!' bellowed the Imperator.

He stalked over to the row of prisoners. Solly's heart was racing.

He'd never thought he'd feel so glad to see Etolantie, who stared at him insolently.

'Stop it!' seethed the Imperator. '*Stop these feelings!*'

There were two others as well. A girl, slightly older than him, and a thin boy, who wore a necklace that drew Solly's eyes. And far above them hovered an orange blur: Sunguide.

Be ready, Solly, said the Being.

Joy filled Solly: drenched him like rain from heaven.

There was a fizzing, popping sound from behind. The prisoners flinched as light flared. Several of the servants screamed, and one fled out of the gate.

A note sounded, pure and clean.

Laughter bubbled up inside Solly.

'I command you to stop!' roared the Imperator, hands slamming to his ears.

'*Ah, intensity of light and sound!*' breathed Dollysheep, looking almost excited.

Something in the fire exploded.

The Imperator screamed.

Now, said the Being.

78

Lalune almost couldn't bear to look at this stranger who was Solly, tossing the Key up in the air as if it were a toy. But she drank him in thirstily, watched him throw the Key into the fire.

Being, she prayed. *How can we get the Key back? How can we get Solly back?*

Be ready, Lalune.

Now Solly was coming towards them. It was as if two people were looking out of his eyes.

'Stop it!' he seethed. '*Stop these feelings!*'

Something fell into the fire. Solly's pouch, full of fire dust. For a moment it glowed, red, blue, green.

A note rang out.

The Key!

Then the fire exploded.

Now, said the Being.

79

Seachrân kept his eyes on the book the Imperator had thrown into the fire. He could hear the note the key sounded: a little higher than his own. The queggel clawed him in fear, and he stroked it soothingly.

He glanced at the sky. The clouds above were gradually turning pink and gold, touched by blue from the Blue Moon. It must be close to sunset.

How much time do we have?

Enough, Seachrân. Be ready.

He hadn't heard the voice before, but he recognized it. The Being.

I trust you, Being.

The fire exploded: light splintered the air.

Seachrân shielded his eyes.

The Imperator screamed, and screamed, and screamed.

Now, said the Being.

Seachrân opended his eyes to find servants and huissier running everywhere, scattered by Sunguide, who was zipping around them, hissing viciously.

Dollysheep said something, but Seachrân heard only the note of the Key, growing louder and louder.

The terrified queggel leaped from his shoulder. He tried to catch it, but it streaked across the garden and shot up the nearest tall thing it could find.

'Get it off me!' screamed Sybilla hysterically. *'Get it off me!'*

And she flew out of the garden, taking what remained of the servants and huissier with her.

80

The wall in Solly's mind shattered. Shards of it seared through him, slicing away at the presence that had possessed him for too long.

'*No-o-o-o!*' cried the Imperator: the cry of a young man who had never been defied.

'*No-o-o-o!*' wailed the Imperator: the entreaty of a child who just wanted the loneliness to end.

'*Please, no,*' whimpered the Imperator.

And then he was gone.

Solly opened his eyes, and found that he was lying curled up into a tight little ball. Lalune's face was hovering over him, concerned.

'It's all right,' he said. 'It's me.'

He reached up and touched her scarf

'H . . . hurry!' said the thin boy urgently. 'The sun is s . . . setting.'

Solly looked at him questioningly, and he held out his hand and added, 'M . . . my name's Seachrân. The one who has always H . . . holder been.'

Solly looked at his hand.

'You have to shake it,' said Etolantie helpfully.

'Prpr. No time!' buzzed Sunguide zooming down to join them.

'My Key,' said Solly.

He struggled to his feet and ran to the fire. Small eruptions of fire dust were still spewing out of it, and the heat was intense. The Book of the Key was turned to blackstone, but the Key itself was still there.

'My staff,' said Lalune, holding it out to him. Solly took it, stuck it into the fire, and with a quick flick the Key spun through the air. He automatically held out his hand to catch it.

'You'll burn yourself,' said Lalune.

But it was as cold as if he'd found it lying on a glacier. And as soon as it touched him it began to vibrate.

He was barely aware of Lalune next to him, slipping the stone from the end of her staff. Cool flames flickered up his arm and down his body, enveloping him. Nothing else mattered.

'It's t . . . time,' said Seachrân. He too was holding his Key. 'L . . . let it bend your w . . . will to its own.'

How could I stop it? thought Solly. *Why would I want to?*

They glided across the room and ascended the stairs into the upper chamber of the Queen of the Stars. Etolantie, Ebha, Sunguide and Dollysheep followed them closely.

Once the upper chamber had been the control room of the spaceship that had brought humans to Clandoi. It didn't look like it any more. The pointed nose was hinged, so that it could be bent back out of the way for an enormous telescope twice the size of Kepler's. Any controls had been removed and replaced with carpets and gilded chairs.

Three huge windows looked out on the city. Through the first they could see the setting sun strewing its amber

296

light over the clouds. Through the second the Blue Moon hovered. Through the third the penetrating light of the comet shone.

Instinctively Solly knew which window required which Key. He walked straight to the window of the setting sun. He held his Key in the light of the dying sun. There was a click as he slotted it carefully into an opening in the centre of the window.

Immediately the note sounded louder, pure and clear. Red sunlight focused into a single beam.

Lalune was next. As if in a dream she approached the window of the Blue Moon. Carefully she slotted her staff into the opening made to fit it, in the low sill.

Her Key's note sang with his: a perfect fifth. Blue light centred on the red from Solly's Key; the room turned magenta.

Keeping hold of the staff so that she didn't lose her eyesight she turned. Seachrân was at the window of the Wanderer. He removed his necklace and carefully slid it into place. He had to twist it straight, until a shaft of green light shot out, converging at the exact spot where the red and green met.

His note sounded.

But the note was all wrong. Instead of a major triad, the three tones together produced a minor chord.

81

Seachrân looked at Lalune. She had let her hand fall from the staff so that she couldn't see. Solly was staring at her. He too had given up hope.

'What's wrong?' said Etolantie.

'Th . . . the notes are wrong,' said Seachrân. '*M . . . my* note is wrong. T . . . too low.'

'Oh, *that,*' said Etolantie.

Seachrân stared at her. She was fiddling with something on her wrist. She hadn't understood.

'We have f . . . failed,' he tried to explain.

'Not us,' said Lalune, dully. 'The Keys.'

'Prpr. How can the Keys fail?' said Sunguide, bewildered. 'All this, for nothing, prpr.'

'What do you do now?' said Dollysheep.

'You've done everything we were supposed to do,' said Ébha.

'There will be another time,' said Seachrân drearily. 'When the comet returns.'

'Not us, though,' said Lalune. 'Some other children. All born on the same day, like we were.'

'You are all so *gloomy*!' said Etolantie. 'The Being won't let all this be for nothing.'

'B . . . but there's n . . . nothing else we *can* do,' said

Seachrân.

Etolantie suddenly held up her hand. Something was dangling from it, sparkling in the dying rays of the sun.

Solly seemed to recognize it.

'Quick, Etolantie,' he said urgently, glancing out of the sun window.

The sun was only two thirds visible. Soon the Bane Moon would take its place.

'What?' said Lalune.

'I got the missing bit,' said Etolantie triumphantly. 'Seachrân's necklace was broken. Remember what Aube told me? Two from one root an' all that stuff? I s'pose we're from the same family, an' he got one bit an' I got another.'

As she spoke she walked to the Wanderer window. Now Seachrân could see that she was holding her bracelet. It was a teardrop of clear crystal, *and it was exactly the same shape as the hole in his necklace.*

She slotted it into place.

The chord changed. A major triad sang into the air, becoming louder and louder. The three beams of light rebounded upwards, and the chord amplified until they had to hold their hands over their ears.

299

82

Up and up and up shot the light, past startled birds, past wispy clouds fired red and purple and orange; up it went, higher and higher, into air too thin for any creature to breathe; and higher still, to the indefinable place where the air suddenly wasn't . . .

. . . and higher and higher and higher, a thin ray of light pouring its power out into the blackness of infinity . . .

. . . where suddenly its path was interrupted, and it bounced down and down and down again, back through the skin of the atmosphere, back down to breathable air, back through the thin clouds until it hit . . .

. . . something thick and warm and timeless, that absorbed the light into itself, sucking it in and in and in, absorbing all that power, spreading it through the curve of the Ne'Lethe, right down until it reached the ground . . .

. . . and the edges began to lift.

83

They held their hands over their ears, trying to stop the unbearably sweet pain of the sound.

Lalune was worst off, as she could only cover one ear if she wanted to see. She saw Seachrân shouting something, and gesturing towards the door. Solly shook his head, mouthing, 'Not yet.'

Her blood thudded in her ears. She was afraid her head might explode. Etolantie and Ébha were both on the floor. Even Sunguide was affected.

What was Solly doing?

She watched as he took a pendant from around his neck. A bubblescreen sprang up, and a startled face appeared. She wasn't sure, but thought it might be Administrator Forcyef, the head of the cyberclinic. Solly leaned as close as he could to the screen, and shouted three words.

Then he turned, and his mouth formed the words, 'Let's go.'

Lalune turned to take her staff; but Seachrân put his hand on her arm. He shook his head, pointing to the light formed by the three Keys.

Remember what I said, Lalune, said the Being's voice in her head. His voice wasn't loud, but she heard it clearly over the noise of the Keys.

What had he said?

Because you are the only one who will be able to see the world of angels. My world. Though evil happens, there is good to be found in everything, Lalune. Even in losing your sight. Nobody else can do what you will do.

She understood.

She had to let go.

She let herself have one last longing look at Solly, and then accepted her blindness.

84

As the edges of the Ne'Lethe lifted, the winds rose. The Sandblaster led the way, tearing sand from the desert and galloping into the forbidden North. Dense cold air over the ice rushed out to replace it. Where the two met they embraced and celebrated with thunderbolts and lightnings: great flashes of electricity that touched the trees with fire. The ocean was sucked up by a great funnel of air, and fell again as hailstones that hit the desert ground steaming, and gushes of rain that extinguished the fires only for the lightning to light them again.

The trees accepted the cleansing fire with outstretched branches. They had already planted their seeds.

Other seeds had watched and waited in the desert sands for centuries for this moment. They exulted in the sudden onrush of water; rooting and shooting until the red desert floor began to turn green again.

A myriad of creatures sought refuge from fire and water in the earth, in the roots of trees that remained after the trees were burned down, in the caves and the secret places; and the trees left untouched by fire also sheltered them.

But not the humans. They didn't belong on Clandoi. They were not welcome.

85

Solly led Lalune down the stairs and out into the open. As they left the room the sound became more bearable, but only just.

'I can't navigate,' she said, her arms outstretched. 'The noise interferes. I'll have to learn, though.'

Solly felt a surge of anger towards Dollysheep, for what he had taken from her.

Rain began to fall, and Solly dragged Lalune to shelter. The others followed: Seachrân, Etolantie, Dollysheep, Sunguide, and a girl. Gradually the pealing in their ears receded, and they could hear just the rain. Though that was heavy enough.

'What were you saying to Forcyef in there?' Lalune asked him.

'I had to start the cyberclinic resuscitating.'

Lalune gasped.

'Then . . . they're alive?'

'What about Ma and Pa, and Ryan?' whispered Etolantie.

'I don't know,' said Solly. 'I'm sorry, I don't know. He kept showing me,' he swallowed, '*my* ma and pa, but I don't even know if they were live pictures. At least I found out how to switch off the whole clinic, and resuscitate them all, and give the order to Forcyef.'

'You resuscitated *all* of them?' said Dollysheep. 'Not all are in a position to, um, *live* without assistance.'

'Do you think they'd survive anyway?' said Solly in a brittle voice. 'After what you did to them? After what Clandoi will do?'

Dollysheep gaped. The rain grew harder. The wind rose, buffeting against them though they were under cover.

'Wh . . . what about us?' said Seachrân. 'What will C . . . Clandoi do to *us*?'

'We have to escape, don't we?' said Lalune. Her voice tightened. 'We're supposed to lead everybody off Clandoi to a different planet. We three. But we don't know how.'

Solly squeezed her hand. Everything *had* fallen into place.

'I do,' he said. 'At least, I think so. There was this woman, a prisoner.'

Cut a Janus tree down, and it will root again, the woman had said. *Its last strength will be used to cast seeds into the darkness: even through the dimensions, to other planets.*

'Aube once told me a legend of a Janus tree that was so strong that it flung one of its seed pods right through the dimensions,' Solly said slowly, feeling his way a little. 'We met a Janus tree, at the North Pole.'

'Met?' said the strange girl.

He looked at her suspiciously.

'Solly, this is Ébha,' said Lalune quickly. 'Seachrân's friend.'

'Yes, met,' he said, trying not to be irritated. It was hard for *him* to understand, after all. 'Janus trees are telepathic. When we got close, it called me and tried to make me go through a door, to the most beautiful place ever. What if

305

that place is this . . . where is it we're supposed to go?'

'Earth,' said Lalune.

'Then we have to go through the Janus tree, back to Earth, where we came from.'

He didn't mention the other part of what Aube had said. Janus trees exchange a passage to heaven for a soul. Obviously, *he'd* have to be that sacrifice. He couldn't ask anybody else to do it. He didn't want to leave Lalune. But at least this way, she'd have a chance to live.

Anyway, there were more immediate problems.

'How do we even *get* to the North Pole?' said Etolantie. 'It must be days an' days walking to get there. An' there's a hundred people living in Kloster Hallow. That's where Seachrân comes from, Solly. Two hundred. Ain't there, Seachrân?'

'M . . . maybe two th . . . thousand?'

Solly's heart sank.

'Prpr. Skyboats will prrrobably help,' said Sunguide. 'Once in their terrritory.'

'We could take the skimmers from here,' said Dollysheep. 'There must be fifty, maybe more, each carrying four or five people. We could squash six in each. And there are more at the cyberclinic, aren't there?'

'Would there be enough?' said Solly. 'How many people are there altogether on Clandoi? Does anybody know?'

Lalune let go of his hand and walked out into the rain.

'Ten thousand in the cyberclinic,' said Dollysheep. 'If they all survive, that is. Twice that number out here.'

'There are s . . . sandcamel carts,' said Seachrân doubtfully.

'How many could the skyboats carry, Sunguide?'

306

'Maybe one orrr two thousand at a time? But could make severrral trrrips.'

'Good,' said Solly, trying to do the sums in his head, though he knew it was hopeless. 'There aren't any snowcamels left at Twilight, I let them free.' Thirty thousand people? It was impossible.

'Look,' said Lalune.

'We're two days from here to the Ne'Lethe, walking,' said Ébha. 'At least, where the Ne'Lethe *was*. How far after that?'

'I don't know,' said Solly. 'We came by skyboat before. They're really quick. I don't see people walking it, and camping. We'll need skimmers or something. It's too cold for people out there.'

'Look,' said Lalune again.

'I've been cold before,' said Ébha dismissively. 'Once, I got locked out of my lodgings, and I had to spend the night in the street, and I only had my coat to cover me. I ached ever such a lot in the morning.'

'It's ten times colder than that,' said Solly.

'A million times colder,' said Etolantie. 'It's so cold, if you lick a window your tongue gets stuck to it, an' they have to pour hot water on it to unstick it again.'

'Look,' said Lalune, and this time they looked.

86

She was pointing to the north. Seachrân strained to see, but there was nothing there but weather: rain and hail stretched all the way to where they were standing.

'What is it, Lalune?' said Solly gently.

'Oh, you can't see them,' Lalune said. 'Of course. The Being said that only I would be able to see them. At least, I think that's what he meant.'

'What, Lalune?'

'The angels,' said Lalune. 'Remember, I could see angels when I first got out of the cyberclinic? They helped me to find my way, then they went. I thought they'd gone forever, but they're back. They're here to show us the way. To carry us.'

'Carry us?' said Ébha sceptically.

'She *said* carry us; she must of *meant* carry us,' said Etolantie, growling at the other girl.

'I was only *ask*ing,' said Ébha, just as fiercely, though there were at least ten years between their ages.

'Are there enough of them?' said Solly. 'I mean, not just for us seven, here: for everybody.'

Seachrân was amused that he included Dollysheep in that 'us'.

'There are enough,' said Lalune. Her face shone.

'Everybody has an angel. Some have two, if there's a need.'

'And they can carry us all?' said Solly in disbelief.

The next moment he was picked up by some invisible force, and turned upside-down.

Lalune laughed.

'Solly, you believe in the Being,' she cried, as she too was picked up. 'Now believe in angels!'

Seachrân felt couldn't feel anything holding him, let alone see; but his feet were swept from the ground.

He could see Lalune and Etolantie laughing as they were borne along on invisible wings. Ébha had her eyes shut tight. Dollysheep, ashen-faced, appeared to be praying. Solly bellowed until he was turned the right way up, then continued to yell as his angel flew him up high into the clouds above.

They flew so fast and so high that the lightning storms were below them. It was noisy up here, with the wind rushing past them. Dark too, now that the sun had set. But there was a glowing outline around them all that must have been from the angels.

It can't have been more than an hour before he saw Kloster Hallow enveloped in the rain. And he could see figures he recognized rising up towards him: Kepler Coriolis, Si-Sef, boys and girls he had grown up with; teachers and mentors; other faces he knew no name for. They all had the angel glow; most looked absolutely terrified. He wondered what they had thought when they started to rise up like that with no cause.

'Don't be afraid,' cried blind Lalune. 'The angels are flying us to safety.'

Etolantie started to shout too, and Solly joined in,

reassuring everybody that this was the Great Migration they had been promised.

Seachrân wished he could see the angels. But it was enough that they were flying at speed to the place where the Ne'Lethe had once been.

The air began to bite. He felt angel feathers encircling him, their warmth spreading through his body. Angel breath heated his toes, his fingers, his face. Fluffy white blobs swirled around them, blurring visibility. Snow, Etolantie had called it. He held out a hand and let a bit fall on to it. It was colder than he'd ever imagined, but it melted soon enough. He sucked up the water it left.

'Don't be afraid,' Lalune kept crying.

Nearby he saw Sunguide in earnest conversation with Etolantie.

'An' it's got to be *me*?' he heard her say. He didn't have time to wonder what they were talking about, though, as somebody shouted, and he saw that they were approaching what used to be the Ne'Lethe.

If he looked up he could just see what remained: a tiny grey disc in the sky. Snow whirled about them, sometimes mixed with hailstones.

He glanced down, eager to have his first sight of land under the Ne'Lethe: but the snow around them made it look as if there was no land. They were in a staticky emptiness. He wasn't sure that he would notice if the angels suddenly turned him upside-down. He laughed. Maybe they had?

Lightning lit up the snow, and several people around him screamed. Seachrân felt perfectly secure. The thunder rolled seven seconds later, which meant that they were quite safe.

When he grew thirsty he caught more snowflakes, and Kepler floated up to him waving a magnifying glass.

'Have a look,' he shouted. 'What do you notice?'

'That y . . . you can't stop t . . . teaching!' Seachrán yelled back with a grin.

But he looked anyway.

'Six sides,' he shouted. 'Th . . . they all have six sides.'

'And all different,' shouted Kepler. 'Every single one is different.'

Suddenly they were out of the snow and into the night. It was harder not to feel dizzy here, as their height above the ground was so great.

But it was decreasing. Seachrán's stomach seemed to lift into his ribcage, and he saw that everybody was being spiralled downwards towards some dark regular shapes that must be buildings.

'Why are we stopping?' yelled Etolantie.

'It's Twilight,' Solly shouted back. 'We're stopping at the cyberclinic.'

87

Solly was so glad to land that he wanted to lie on the ground and never get up. Skyboats were one thing: being in the air with nothing visible to hold you up though . . .

He looked around quickly. Lalune was still reassuring people that this was supposed to be happening, that they had stopped here to rest and to help the patients from the cyberclinic.

Nobody seemed to have remembered the huissier guarding the clinic. They were outside the main gate, and nobody had come running out. If Solly had seen thousands of people landing from the sky, glowing like fiery stingwings, *he* wouldn't have come running.

He wished he had his bandoleer: without it he was weaponless.

'Prpr, should check forrr enemies,' said Sunguide very quietly next to him.

'I hadn't forgotten,' said Solly, a little irritably. He was so damny glad to be on the ground, but his legs were still shaking.

'Arrre some huissier frrrom the city in the crrrowd,' said Sunguide. 'You want I brrring them?'

'Yes,' Solly said, shivering. Whatever had kept them warm in the air wasn't doing it now. And these people weren't used to the cold. They had to get inside quickly.

Five huissier with guns arrived. The angels had brought them too.

'Uh, we were told by, uh, that orange thing that you're in charge,' one said, looking surprised that Solly was so young.

'Only because I used to live here,' Solly said. 'We need to get everyone inside, but it will be guarded.'

'Show us where,' said the huissier.

'Two on the gate, and one outside the main door. Maybe more inside.'

The huissier nodded, and beckoned to his colleagues.

Something snuffled in his ear, and he turned around joyfully.

'Star! Oh, Star, I thought you were left behind.'

He hugged his snowcamel tight. Very soon he would find out it Brise and Revas were still alive. If they weren't – well, he still had Star.

People were still landing in the snowy waste. Nearby he could hear Dollysheep instructing a small group of medical workers about caring for the people from the cyberclinic. Lalune, her face radiant, was encouraging people with the news that the Keys had been used, and the Great Migration had begun. Seachrân was doing the same, with Etolantie sucking her thumb and looking thoughtful.

'All clear, except for this one,' said a huissier, touching him on the arm. 'We found him wetting himself in a corner.'

He was holding Wuneem. Solly scowled at the man who had assaulted and arrested his parents; but Wuneem was too hysterical with fear to notice.

'The end has come!' he babbled. 'The sky! Don't let me see it! We'll all fall off Clandoi!'

'There'll be others, so keep your eyes open,' said Solly. 'Thanks. Let's go in.'

'What should we do with this one?'

They're asking me like I really am in charge! thought Solly. *Beat up his family, and send him alone into the night, and see how he likes it, why not?*

'I suppose we should hold him and anyone else we find, and give them the choice of coming with us as prisoners, or staying here,' he said. He started to walk rapidly towards the door. 'Though I'd rather not take him. We don't know what this place we're going to is like, or what we'll need to survive. We can't afford prisoners. Come on, everybody, let's go in!'

'Where *are* we going to, Solly?' said the huissier, dragging Wuneem along behind him.

'Place called Earth,' Solly said over his shoulder as he broke into a trot. *I'm coming, Ma! I'm coming, Pa!* 'Don't know anything more, except that it's the most wonderful, beautiful place there is, ever!'

He ran through the door and into the cyberclinic. It looked empty, but he could hear the rumble of confused voices. Following the sound he burst through door after door, until he came to the first corridor where the Appaloosians were held.

Had been held. Pod after pod was empty, the patients looking bewildered, still damp from the orbal oil that had been their world for so long.

'What's happened?' someone cried as he raced on. 'I'm blind!'

314

'You're free!' he shouted. 'Saved! We're going home!'

He didn't care if it made no sense. Somebody would tell them soon enough.

I'm coming!

'Where's my daughter?' demanded a sharp voice.

Toayef, Lalune's mother, clamped a hand of iron strength on his arm, and he nearly pulled her to the floor as he fell.

'She's outside!' he said breathlessly. This was no time for anger, even if she had been the one who'd forced Lalune into this place. 'She's fine. Uh, she's blind, but fine. We've come to free you all.'

Toayef dropped his arm, and her beautiful face, so like Lalune's, went grey.

'So it's true,' she whispered, clutching her side. 'The computer helper, Kenet, kept referring to us as human components, and telling us we were to be cut up for body parts, and I didn't want to believe it. But I have scars where they've taken . . . what about Threfem? *What about my husband?*'

'I'm sorry,' Solly said, as gently as he could, though his eyes darted along the corridor. 'I'm sorry, he . . .'

'He's been fully harvested,' Toayef finished faintly, and swayed.

Solly had never thought that she even liked her husband very much, but right now she looked like she was going to faint. He helped her to the ground where she was, next to her pod.

'Somebody will come soon to help,' he said. 'Look, do you know where they might have put my ma and pa? Is there a prison block somewhere?'

'So they took Wayfarers too?' she said numbly. 'Take

315

a lift to the lowest level. I expect they're down there somewhere.'

Solly bolted to the nearest lift and punched buttons.

I'm coming!

He had no way of telling how fast the lift was going. Three seconds would have been too slow. His feet couldn't stay still, and he tapped the door impatiently.

At last he was down. The scene was the same as the one upstairs, but gloomier.

'Ma!' he yelled. 'Pa!'

There were fewer people here. Some pods were drained of orbal oil, but the occupants had not moved. They hadn't survived.

'Ma! Pa!'

'I can't find my baby!' cried a woman, grabbing at him. 'And my little girl, my Etolantie.'

'Etolantie's fine!' he said, not stopping. 'She's great! Upstairs, top level. Ma! Pa!'

And then he saw them.

He skidded to a halt.

They were holding each other and crying. Both of them, crying.

Solly's eyes misted over. *They thought he was dead!*

'Ma!' he shouted hoarsely. 'I'm here! I'm still alive!'

And Revas and Brise turned and saw him, and suddenly they were running towards each other; they were clutching each other and the tears didn't stop.

88

Lalune deliberately woke early. She knew what she had to do. She had to prove that she wasn't a monster: that she had a soul.

She had thought it through over and over again.

Solly wouldn't want her if she had no soul. Nobody would. She would be an outcast.

And what good would she be to him, anyway? She was blind. She had done her bit seeing the angels, but she would just be a burden in this new land.

And Father still hadn't been found. Dollysheep said that there were still corridors to be searched, hidden passages where he had put those he'd pretended to harvest fully; but she knew in her heart that he was dead.

The only way to prove that she had a soul was to sacrifice herself to the Janus tree. If it used her to let the others go through to this other world, she would be dead, presumably, but she would know that she had a soul. And that soul would go to heaven.

If it rejected her, she would *know* that she had no soul.

She hadn't thought through what she would do then.

She dressed, but only because it was so cold. She didn't want to freeze to death before she'd reached the tree. She had deliberately laid out her clothes so that she wouldn't need any help putting them on.

Then she crept out of the cyberclinic.

They had all slept on the floor, wherever there was a space, piling what blankets and coats could be found over them, and huddling together for warmth. She had slept next to her mother. Solly was with his parents.

'Goodbye, Solly,' she whispered when she got to the outer door.

And she stole out.

89

Solly planted a kiss on Revas's cheek, and another on Brise's hand. Neither stirred.

'I'm sorry,' he whispered.

Stepping carefully over the sleeping bodies that lined the corridor, he tiptoed out of the cyberclinic, out of the Great Gate, and into the snowcamel barn.

Star woke blearily and nuzzled him. Seachrân's sandcamel, Modya, was there too, and several others that the angels had lifted from Kloster Hallow. He would need their help, and not just to pull the sledge. Hopefully Star would be willing to stay with them, rather than following him into the Janus tree.

He harnessed four of them quickly, and sped out into the snow.

90

Seachrân woke with a jerk, frozen to the core.

And frozen in his soul.

He was suddenly completely aware of Etolantie, and what she intended to do.

He scrambled and tried to dress in the dark. Everything in him screamed to get to her, not to bother with clothes; but he remembered the awful burns Etolantie had got from not knowing how dangerous the sun was, and knew that the icy coldness could hurt him just as much.

But his fingers were too numb to cope with buttons. He managed his trousers, socks and gloves. He blundered down the corridor, treading on several people on his way.

'S . . . s . . . sorry, s . . . sorry,' he gasped, hopping over the last body and floundering out into the entrance hall. The front door was quivering from the strong wind outside and he pulled his coat close.

The appalling cold froze the breath in his chest and turned his face to ice. He had forgotten to pull his hood up. With trembling hands he did so, and peered into the darkness.

How can anybody survive in this? he wondered. *But they had, for three hundred years.*

And now Etolantie was going to . . .

He could see a pale shape bobbing about in the distance. She'd taken a skyboat. They were the fastest vehicles: if he took a skimmer he wouldn't get there in time.

He stumbled towards where the drowsy skyboats had been moored for the night.

'H . . . how do you fly th . . . these things?' he muttered, tugging the nearest one free.

'I will fly forrr you,' said Sunguide, appearing suddenly in front of him.

'S . . . S . . . Sun . . . g . . . g . . . guide?' Seachrân said, stuttering even worse because his teeth were chattering.

'Is girrrl,' said Sunguide. 'She has gone to Janus trrree. You knew?'

Seachrân nodded.

'I d . . . d . . . dreamed of her.'

'Come,' said Sunguide. 'Not that skyboat. Is slow and prpr-obstinate.'

'H . . . how does sh . . . she kn . . . know now t . . . to fly?'

'Has been watching me. Prpr. I am the best flyer. Win rrraces.'

They hurried to a skyboat nearer to the gate. It was already expanding. Seachrân tumbled in, and Sunguide got it to fly before it had finished inflating.

91

Solly cracked the whip over the animals' heads. They were fast, but not fast enough. He didn't want to think about what he was going to do. He just wanted to do it. Then he wouldn't be afraid.

Star trotted on and on into the dark. Good old Star. He really hoped that his pet would be sensible enough to follow the others away from the Janus tree when he'd . . . when he'd finished what he had to do.

He knew they were getting close when his ears started to feel as if they were being mashed into his head.

He hurried the sledge onwards. Something was glowing ahead of him: the angels had flown somebody here before him.

And Sunguide was here too!

92

Lalune thanked the angels for carrying her. She hadn't thought they would, but they didn't even question her when she'd walked out of the cyberclinic and called them.

Silence filled the world. Not the usual silence. This was thicker, somehow; *more* silent then she'd heard before. Even though the wind was so strong it should have deafened her.

But there was a noise inside the silence.

She heard a jingle, a harness of some sort. Snowcamels pulling a sledge.

Her heart beat rapidly.

'Solly?' she said, and felt stupid. Of course it was Solly. 'What are you doing here?'

'What are you doing here?'

'I was going to . . . um, I thought that if I . . . I mean . . .'

Solly nodded.

'Me too.'

93

Seachrân lay curled in a ball in the bottom of the skyboat, too cold to do anything else. The floor was warm enough to keep him from freezing completely, and his shivers did the rest. He *much* preferred flying with angels.

Once he thought he heard an ugly buzzing, like a skimmer, but he was too cold to look. The skyboat passed it too quickly anyway.

At last he sensed that Sunguide was coaxing the skyboat down in a wide spiral. They must be there. The North Pole.

He looked at the sky to see if it was morning yet, and remembered that here it was always night. There wasn't even the faintest tinge of pink from the dawn that he was sure must have started by now. He couldn't see anything below either. It was the blackest night he had ever known.

'We herrre,' said Sunguide.

Seachrân scrambled out of the skyboat.

'Wh . . . where is sh . . . she?'

'Herre,' said Sunguide, starting to glow orange. 'I help you searrrch.'

Seachrân put his hands on the fungus and found that a little warmth seeped through his gloves. Amber light spread out over the immediate area: not a lot, but enough to see by.

Enough to see a small figure ahead of them.

'Et . . . Et . . . Etolantie!' he called.

She turned back briefly, saw who it was, and carried on walking.

'S . . . stop. P . . . please.'

'I can't stop,' she yelled. 'I have to go. It's in the Prophecy.'

'What do you m . . . mean?'

Etolantie stopped and faced him, the wind dragging her hair across her face.

Seachrân's ears felt strange, as if they needed to pop.

'It's what Aube said. *The known will start the task, the unknown will complete it.* It wasn't jus' about using the Keys. It's about getting back to Earth.' She sounded much older than eight. 'You an' the others, you're the known. Nobody even *knew* about me until we was in the observatory. I'm the unknown. I got to finish it.'

'You d . . . don't have to,' Seachrân shouted, though he knew she was right. 'S . . . somebody else will d . . . do it.'

Though he knew they wouldn't.

'No, they won't,' she yelled. 'Besides, this'll make up for what I did.'

'What d . . . did you do?'

His head felt like bursting.

'I betrayed Lalune an' Solly. I told the kidnappers where they were.'

'Etolantie . . .'

She turned and started walking again.

Seachrân ran to catch up with her. Somehow sound seemed to stop here, as if the air was so full of it that there was no room for any more.

'W . . . what about the rest of the P . . . prophecy?' he said, and he quoted Aube: '*I see t . . . two plants entwined. T . . . two beginnings and one end. The kn . . . known w . . . will start the t . . . task, the unknown will c . . . complete it.*'

She stared at him, tears in her eyes.

'We're entwined, y . . . you and me,' Seachrân said. 'T . . . two beginnings, one end. I c . . . can't let you d . . . do this alone.'

'I din't think you'd understand,' she whispered.

He took her hand in his, and they went to the Janus tree together.

94

Sunguide seemed agitated.

'Prpr. You must go back. The hrumans, they will need you to guide them, prpr.'

'But who's done it?' said Lalune. 'Who went into the Janus tree?'

'You have to go back,' said Sunguide. 'It's the Prrrophecy.'

'It's Etolantie, isn't it,' said Solly. 'Aube Saw something for her. That's it, isn't it?'

Sunguide seemed to slump.

'Yes,' he said. 'It was prrrophesied long ago, by ourrr people. Etolantie, she has prrrovided passage to you all.'

'What Prophecy?' said Solly.

Sunguide fluttered solemnly.

'It was prrrronounce at the same time as the one for you, Solly. *After the thrrree will come a fearrrless soul, a selfless soul, to finish the task and open the doorrr for all humankind.*'

'Why didn't you tell me?'

Sunguide shrugged.

'It was neverrr yourrr prrrophecy.'

'And you *let* her do it?' cried Lalune. 'Somebody else could have done it. I could have done it! I'm blind; I have no soul. I'm no use to anybody. She had a whole life to live . . .'

Her voice cracked.

'Don't you *dare* think you being blind means you're useless,' Solly said, astonished. 'Look at everything you've done since you became blind. And how could you ever think you have no soul?'

'Prpr. Nobody could be willing to self-sacrrrifice if they have no soul.'

'But she's just a little girl.'

Sunguide swayed solemnly.

'Prpr. Not *just* a little girrrl,' he said. 'A brrrave and innocent soul. A child of prrrophecy, as you two werrre childrrren of prrrophecy.'

'You can't argue with these prophecies,' said Solly, as Lalune turned to him for comfort. 'They have a way of getting themselves fulfilled.'

He held her tight as she cried into his shoulder for a few minutes. Then he brushed away the iced tears from her face.

'Come on, Lalune. We still have a job to do.'

95

Administrator Forcyef was discovered cowering under her desk. Many huissier had locked themselves in, too, and it was only the promise of skimmers and the right to stay on Clandoi that made them come out. It seemed that the now unpredictable climate of Clandoi was preferable to the unknown Earth, and punishment.

Solly and Lalune led everybody else to the Janus tree, surrounded by the angel glow. Not all wanted to repeat the eerie flight though: some went by skyboat, some in carts, others in skimmers. Toayef was with them: different, somehow. Subdued. Revas and Brise were hand in hand behind them. The Pruppras arrived by the thousand to see them safely to the Janus tree, lighting the way with their glowing bodies.

'I see you have brought Star, hmm,' said Aube.

'I couldn't leave him again,' said Solly.

'He will pose an interesting puzzle for fossil hunters of the future.'

'Where is Seachrân?' Lalune asked.

'Helping the searchers, I expect, my dear.'

Many people were still missing, so volunteers were continuing to searching for them. Lalune shivered.

'I hope he finds Father while the Janus tree is still open.

And that little girl, Rayon.'

'They'll be found,' Solly said. 'Dollysheep said there's loads of unused corridors.'

'That tree should stay open for years, now,' added Aube.

As they got closer to the Janus tree Solly was expecting the same extreme silence he'd felt the last time. The air still pressed against their ears, but the silence was gone. Instead they could hear singing.

'Etolantie,' whispered Lalune.

'And somebody else. Maybe it's the Janus tree itself, singing.'

'She *is* fearless, isn't she,' said Lalune. 'She tried to kick a snarg in the face.'

'Fearless, or dumb?' said Solly. 'And would you call Etolantie selfless?'

'No. But definitely fearless.'

Solly held his breath as he came within the tree's telepathic range, but it didn't try to capture him. It looked like an ordinary tree. An opening split its trunk in two, and a magnificant Appaloosian woman, her skin leaf-green and creamy-white, was waiting for them. Her hair swayed as if she were under water. She smiled at them in welcome. Two insubstantial figures emerged from behind her, holding out their hands.

'Etolantie,' said Solly. 'And *Seachrân*?'

'He must have gone with her into the tree,' said Lalune, unbelievably. 'Oh, Solly, why didn't we stop them?'

'Because we couldn't have,' said Solly. 'It was prophecy. Both of them.'

'Selfless,' Lalune said with a hiccup. '*He's* the selfless one.'

They came to them and held their hands, murmuring

reassuringly. There was something not quite real about them: when Solly turned around to look at his parents, they too had their hands held by Etolantie and Seachrân. As did Toayef; as did everybody else.

'They're illusions,' Solly said. 'Somebody we recognize, so that we're not afraid.'

'*I* am afraid,' said Revas, looking at Toayef.

But Revas was calm: it was Toayef who was terrified.

Lalune held out her hand to her mother. Solly stood between his parents. The fantasy children pulled them into the tree . . .

96

. . . into an extraordinary meadow. They felt as if they were underwater, but they had no difficulty breathing. Birds sang overhead, fish glided, flutteries danced, and other strange two-winged insects that something inside them recognized, though they had forgotten the name.

Running feet and laughter could be heard ahead. Etolantie and Seachrân were chasing towards them.

'Come on!' they cried. Their voices were contained in bubbles that burst over the humans. 'It's time to go home! Follow us!'

'Come on!' shouted Solly, starting to run.

'Come on!' whispered Lalune, squeezing Toayef's shaking hand. 'We're going home!'

'Come on!'

The words were passed back along the line of people, and soon they were running but never growing tired, skipping and dancing, and they still had enough breath to sing, because they were going home.

They ran for a year or a day, they couldn't say which, until at last they arrived at another opening. Etolantie and Seachrân stood one on each side of the green woman.

'Go on through,' she said. Her voice was beautiful.

Etolantie pushed something into Solly's hand.

'I kept this for Rayon,' she said. 'Can you give it to her?'

It was a rag dolly with the words 'Rayon's Ba...

in wobbly letters.

'If I can,' he said.

Then Etolantie kissed them, and Seachrán gave them a ...
and they stepped out on to Earth.

97

Lalune held on to her mother's arm gently, wishing she would speak to her. Wishing she still had her staff. She wanted to *see*.

She could smell something fruity, and hear a roaring noise. It was warm, but not as hot as Clandoi. A salty breeze cooled her forehead. The ground under her feet was firm, with some kind of springy plant covering it. Insects buzzed, and somewhere nearby an animal was bleating.

The others were moving around, mostly not speaking at all.

I wish I could see.

Lalune gathered as much as she could from her other senses. Next to her, Toayef sounded completely bewildered as she muttered, 'I can't believe it! I can't believe it!' repeatedly.

'You will have to tell me what it's like,' Lalune reminded her in the end. 'I can't see.'

Toayef made a curious gulping noise.

'Mother? Are you all right?'

'I'm sorry, darling,' she said, in a quiet voice completely unlike her normal tone. 'I feel so guilty about you. And . . . and you can't know what it felt like to wake up like that, and the Ne'Lethe had disappeared. I thought I was going to fall off the ground. And then the wind and the rain. We were all terrified.'

'We had the same where we were,' Lalune said. 'And don't forget, *I* was the one who first found out what they were doing to us. To Father. *I* was afraid too. *I* didn't know what to do either.'

'Yes, I know,' Toayef said sharply. Then her voice softened as she said humbly, 'I'm sorry. I *am* very thankful that you found out. And that you escaped and . . . did what you did. I don't think I would have believed you otherwise. And I'm not used to being wrong.'

This last bit was said so faintly that Lalune almost didn't catch it. She hid a smile, and decided to ignore it.

'And then, to have no choice but to follow you and . . . and Solly.' She paused, seeming to struggle with herself a little. 'I'm also not used to . . . to not being in control of things. I had my own department in the cyberclinic. Two hundred people answering to *me*. Relying on *me*. And your father . . . I loved him dearly, but he wasn't a strong-willed man, was he?'

Lalune was astonished. She had never heard her mother admit any feelings for anyone. And now, her voice sounded unexpected grief-stricken.

She was saved from having to say anything as Toayef moved away from her.

'Why, they look just like purple-berry vines,' she said. 'Uncultivated, of course; but then, nothing has been cultivated here yet, has it?'

'Mother?' said Lalune, stumbling towards her.

'I'm sorry, darling,' Toayef said, returning and taking Lalune's arm.

335

'You can still have me to rely on you,' said Lalune hesitantly. 'If you like.'

'Thank you darling,' she said, after a long, surprised pause. 'I'd like that.'

'Tell me about what you can see.'

'We're near the sea,' said Toayef. 'The sky is very blue. And we're in a field. Uncultivated, but these grains look familiar.'

'What about the vines?' said Lalune, thinking that Solly was much better at this, but wanting her mother to do it anyway.

'Do you remember all those lessons I made you do on grain management systems?'

'I remember.'

'I always wanted to have a go at farming. You said that we once came from this planet. I think we may have brought these grains with us. Maybe the vines too. I don't think it would be difficult to cultivate them. We would have to test them to make sure they were edible, of course. But I seem to know how to do that. Funny, I don't remember studying it.'

'It's the mind knowledge,' said Lalune. 'You don't know that you know something, but then it pops into your head.'

'Well, I'm glad that the cyberclinic gave us something,' Toayef said wryly. 'I suppose giving us the mind knowledge was all part of the deception.'

'They couldn't very well have not given it to us,' said Lalune. 'Somebody would have noticed in the years it took to persuade us to enter.'

'*I* certainly would have noticed,' said her mother. 'Now, we shall have to clear some ground of course. But there's

336

plenty of room. And it would take a few years. But there's plenty of sunlight here, and I can see at least three streams for irrigation . . .'

Lalune, slightly bemused, let her chat on enthusiastically. She had never known her mother like this. Except about entering the cyberclinic.

'You do know that you can do all that now?' she said, when Toayef had finally finished. 'We won't need Senior Technicians as much as we need farmers.'

'I suppose I can, can't I?'

'I never knew that was what you wanted to do,' said Lalune. 'Not that you would have been able to, on Clandoi. You were always trying to get me interested in maths.'

'Was I? I hated maths!'

Lalune giggled.

'So did I!'

'All those years I spent becoming a technician, and trying to make you into me. The "me" I thought I was. And now I discover a whole new me that I never knew existed.'

Lalune heard a rustle as Toayef turned towards her.

'That was wrong. You were always going to be you. I promise that I shan't make that mistake on your children.'

Lalune choked.

'*My* children?'

'Well, you and Solly *are* going to marry, aren't you? Oh, look . . . Sorry, darling, um, Solly's on his way over now. When we've built basic shelters I shall hire a few workers and get a farm going. You two can help. Solly knows all about hunting, don't you, Solly?'

Lalune could feel suspicion flowing out of Solly as he took her hand. But Toayef rushed on.

'You can hunt at first. We need meat. But if you can catch pregnant females it will be easier. Those animals there look docile enough to become domesticated. We can farm them for meat. Maybe milk too. And wool. And I can grow grain and vines. This land you've brought us to is so abundant . . .'

She was almost bubbling with ideas. Lalune pulled Solly towards her and kissed him thoughtfully. Sometimes her mother was absolutely right.

Five Years Afterwards

'Do I look all right?' asked Lalune, nervously fingering her bandaged eyes.

'You're fine,' said Solly.

'Are there many here?'

'Everybody's here,' said Solly. 'You know they are.'

Lalune did know. She could hear them all chattering expectantly, finding spaces for their sitting cushions so that they could see clearly. Nobody wanted to miss this.

Behind the noise they made, the wind rustled the leaves of the Janus Tree. People had started to call it the Singing Tree: often Seachrân and Etolantie's voices could be heard singing. The area around it had become the new Telling Place.

Lalune liked to think that Etolantie and Seachrân were part of their lives still. She knew that many people used to come and whisper their secret longings to the tree: to the tree and to them. She'd whispered quite a few of her own.

'Is he here yet?' asked Lalune.

'In a few minutes.'

'You're sure my dress is all right?'

She could hear the laughter in Solly's voice.

'It's perfect. Your mother picked out the colour especially.'

'I bet it's pink.'

'I am sworn to secrecy.'

'I'm still not sure about it,' said Lalune, picking at her bandage again. 'There are so many others who need more help than just eyes. I've got used to being blind . . .'

Solly laughed again. They had had this conversation so many times already.

'They all wanted you to be the first, and you know it.'

'He's here,' somebody cried, and Lalune quaked. Just a little.

'It'll be fine,' said Solly.

Lalune heard the clinking sound of the iron band around Dollysheep's neck.

'Well, Lalune,' said Dollysheep. 'Do you feel ready?'

'Not really. Not with all these people here.'

'Think of it as healing for everybody,' he said, leading Lalune up on to a small platform that had been built especially. 'Psychological. We have done more than just survive: we have progressed medical science. Well, shall we begin?'

He helped her to sit, snapped on some gloves, and carefully started to unwind the bandage.

Lalune could hear the gathered people hush expectantly, and she clasped her hands to stop them from shaking.

Dollysheep pulled off the last layer of bandage and peeled back the dressing.

'Just clean it up a little . . . there. You may open your eyes, Lalune.'

Lalune opened them. Everything was fuzzy. The eyes were glass, not harvested, and would last longer than she would, Dollysheep had told her.

'It's blurry,' she said.

'It will take a few days for you to get used to them,' said Dollysheep anxiously. 'Blink a few times. Look up . . . down. Good. Now left . . . right . . .'

Lalune blinked, and concentrated on focusing on the shape that she knew must be Solly. Gradually his face became clearer, and Lalune had to work hard not to cry from happiness.

'I can see!' she said, and smiled as everybody cheered. And smiled, because she could see their Earth home for the first time. And smiled, because it was more beautiful than she had thought possible. And smiled, because there was Solly: a little heavier, and bearded, but still Solly.

Lalune glanced down at her dress and was relieved to see that it was blue.

'Do you like it?' said Toayef anxiously. 'We thought it would match your eyes.'

'It's lovely, Mother, thank you. How do my new eyes look?' Lalune said.

'Here, look in the mirror,' said Dollysheep.

For the first time in years, she could see her own face. Her eyes were startlingly familiar: deep blue with star pupils. He'd given her the choice, but she was used to stars.

Besides, hers would be the last generation whose pupils were not round.

Lalune looked at her mother and smiled again. Toayef was older, tired, but somehow more relaxed.

'As gorgeous as they always did,' said Solly softly. 'I've missed those eyes.'

Aube joined them on the platform, and cleared his throat.

'This is a wonderful day for us all, hmm?' he said loudly enough for everybody to hear. 'It's not just that Lalune can see again: it marks a new beginning for many. And new hope, of course.'

Lalune let her eyes wander over this new world, amazed at how green it was. Clandoi, the part she had known, had been grey and colourless. Here the colours were like jewels, the only grey bit being the Janus tree. Its leaves stood out, charcoal-grey against the brilliant blue of the sky.

'Dr Dollysheep and Si-Sef assure me that they are ready to repeat this operation immediately. And others too, hmm. Ah, I expect he meant after we have feasted!'

'The Tree looks like it's opening,' she murmured, noticing the vertical shadow that fell down its front. It was probably an optical illusion: it would be a while before she learnt to refocus her eyes quickly.

'And I believe the food is ready,' Aube continued. 'It only remains for us to thank the Being for this day, and then we shall, ah, eat. *Supreme Being, Creator of all . . .*'

'Solly,' whispered Lalune, standing up. 'The Janus tree. It looks like somebody's coming out of it!'

'It'll take a while before you can see properly,' he said.

Lalune squeezed her eyes shut and opened them again. In a few days she would have better eyes than anybody else on the planet, but she still had to get used to them.

The two tall figures were still there.

Who are they? she thought, peering at them. *Who could be coming through this late?*

She was the only one looking at the Janus tree. Everybody else was praying with Aube.

342

Quietly she stepped off the platform and walked towards the tree. The figures had stopped, blinking in the sunlight, probably unnerved by the sight of so many people.

She recognized them. And began to run.

Aube stopped praying mid-sentence and gaped at the two.

'Well, heaven's blessings on us all!' he exclaimed, and then everybody looked.

'Who is it?'

'It can't be!'

Solly ran to catch up with Lalune, and they were the first to reach the tree. They all stopped, uncertainly.

'Etolantie!' breathed Lalune. 'Seachrân!'

Etolantie nodded, grinning. Seachrân smiled shyly, a step behind her.

'It's Etolantie and Seachrân!' shouted somebody. '*Etolantie and Seachrân!* It's really them!'

They had both grown upwards and outwards, and Seachrân's legs no longer looked frail, but as if the Tree had given them strength. There was a motion to them that hadn't been there before: something like the grace of branches moving in the wind.

Lalune staggered forward and hugged them both at the same time.

'How?' said Solly.

'The J . . . Janus tree died;' said Seachrân.

'She was ever so old,' added Etolantie. 'An' two of us was more than she could take. Hello Aube! So she sent us through. We din't know if we'd come through to the right place, she had so many babies all over.'

She hugged Aube and half a dozen other people. There were cries of amazement all around.

'In other worlds? Now there's the thing.'

'Loads an' loads of 'em. She let us see out of 'em.'

'We have to build a f . . . fence around the tree,' Seachrân said.

Etolantie nodded.

'I nearly forgot. This one'll be hungry soon, now we're not there, an' you don't want to lose anybody.' She rubbed her stomach. 'Din't you have a feast planned for today? We've had nothing but tree syrup for five years. I spec that's why we got so big. But I could really do with some proper food. I'm *starving*.'